Run

Ellie

Run

Run

Ellie

Run

by

Dee Shaw

YAV PUBLICATIONS
ASHEVILLE, NORTH CAROLINA

Copyright © 2012 Dee Shaw

Second Edition

ISBN: 978-1-937449-12-4 (soft cover)
ISBN: 978-1-937449-13-1 (eBook)

Published by:

YAV PUBLICATIONS
ASHEVILLE, NORTH CAROLINA

YAV books may be purchased in bulk for
educational, business, or promotional use.
Contact Books@yav.com or phone toll-free 888-693-9365.
Visit our website: www.InterestingWriting.com

3 5 7 9 10 8 6 4

Assembled in the United States of America
Published July 2012

List of Characters

Ellie Wallace – Main Character

Owen Wolf – Drug Dealer

Joe Wallace – Ellie's Father

Caroline Wallace – Ellie's Mother

Kurt McCoy – Owner of Gas Station

Ray Vinson – Employed by Kurt

Maddie Russell – Ellie's Grandmother

Sam Reynolds – Police Officer

Clara – Housekeeper at Wallace Home

Chapter 1

ELEANOR WALLACE'S EYES remained on her science teacher, but her thoughts were on something that had nothing to do with chemistry or what Mr. Henderson was saying. Attempting to appear as though she were interested in the instructions he was giving for the following day's test, she allowed one hand to dangle below her chair. Her nimble fingers began searching for her cell phone deep inside one pocket of her backpack.

This was the last class of the day, and in mere seconds the bell would ring making this school day history. Ellie wanted to call Brennie before they both climbed on separate buses and headed home for the evening. Once again she had changed her plans and was about to disappoint her most loyal friend.

Yesterday Ellie and Brennie agreed to study together for their chemistry test, but those good intentions would need to be postponed. Early that morning before Ellie had left for school, her father agreed he would take her to the mall to look at the gorgeous, but expensive, jacket she asked the accommodating saleslady to put aside for her. Hopefully, after three days that yummy jacket, her latest must have, had not been purchased and was still safely being held at the store.

It was already Tuesday, and if the jacket had not been sold to another lucky kid by now, she was positive her dad would buy it after seeing how great it looked on her. Of course, as always, he would check the price before he gave his final approval for the purchase. Even though it was an expensive jacket, marked down only 15 percent off the original price, Ellie just had to have it in spite of the amount. She was prepared to plead or even beg her dad if that was what it took, and Brennie would definitely understand why she was not able to study with her tonight for tomorrow's chemistry test.

Brenda Siegel's dad recently lost his full-time job, and everyone in her family was making an all-out effort to curb their spending on all unnecessary items. They were determined as a family to financially make ends meet. For months Brennie's father had been working two temporary jobs. One was delivering catered lunch meals for six upscale tech corporations in a busy part of town as a full-time day job, and the other was stocking food on shelves at a nearby grocery store during the night hours. Until he could find something suitable that had better employment opportunities, he decided to work hard at both jobs to support his family.

Somehow, Ellie was not able to relate to cutting corners in her spending habits because she had never experienced anything like that in her entire life. Her father was a prominent attorney in the city, and for years his income had been more than sufficient for his family to live quite comfortably. Although both Joe and Caroline Wallace never considered it wise to waste money on foolish purchases or intentionally spoil any of their three children, they were generous, contributing liberally to needy causes, their church and other worthy organizations. They made sure they placed ten percent of their income into a saving account each month and made a few investments.

In spite of all their careful management of household money, Ellie, their youngest, had learned early there was always enough available money for her latest whims. Especially during the past three years she had mastered the skill of persuading her parents to buy almost anything she wanted. Clever manipulation had come easy for Ellie, and her big-hearted parents were proof. Without being aware of what they had done, Joe and Caroline had overindulged their only child still living at home.

The bell sounded, and every student in the class began to stir. Ellie grasped her phone from her backpack and dropped it on her lap. Out of habit, she quickly glanced down at the lighted buttons and was ready to punch in a few numbers the instant Mr. Henderson made his last remarks and released the class.

Once her teacher ended what he was saying, every student stood and was heading for the hall. At that very moment Ellie looked in the direction of Mr. Henderson and caught him looking straight at her.

"Miss Wallace, please stay a few minutes after class. I wish to speak to you."

"Oh! No!" Ellie muttered under her breath. Attempting to not show disappointment with his request, she slammed her chemistry book shut and looked in the direction of the windows trying not to allow Mr. Henderson to see her bored facial expression or to suspect she was irritated. Hopefully none of the kids thought much about his asking her to stay after class. Gathering her notebook and other items, she jammed them all into her backpack and sullenly walked to the front of the room.

On the way to his desk, she noticed several kids staring at her and became embarrassed. One girl was whispering in another girl's ear as they left making what must have been a snide remark. Ellie could not hear what had been said, but both girls left with a noticeable grin on their faces. Ellie's thoughts were less than charitable toward either of them.

"Mr. Henderson, you wanted to see me?" Ellie faked a smile trying to exhibit calmness and a good attitude.

Once every student left the room Mr. Henderson looked at her for a moment and said, "I'm concerned about the homework you've been handing in lately, Ellie. Your tests indicate you understand chemistry quite well, but we both know you could do much better on what you hand in weekly. I'm convinced you have the ability to be one of the best students in this class if you would apply yourself and spend more time on the assignments and study harder for every quiz and test. Tell me, Ellie, am I off track on this?"

"I'm trying Mr. Henderson. Really I am, and I'll definitely study tonight so I can do better on tomorrow's test."

"I'm sure you will Ellie. You're quite capable and always manage to get a better than acceptable grade, but remember what I said about using your ability and spending quality time working on each assignment. I want you to excel in this subject because I know you're more than capable, and we both are fully aware that your parents want you to do as well as you can in this class."

She had heard it all before from Mr. Henderson, and a few other teachers as well. Sensing her teacher wanted to continue scolding her in a gentle manner, she quickly said, "Okay, Mr. Henderson, you're right about my parents. I promise you I'll spend more time on my homework, and tonight I'll study longer so I can do exceptionally well on tomorrow's test. I know this one is really an important one for my grade."

Uncomfortable and trying to escape from discussing any more of her lazy approach toward her weekly assignments, Ellie attempted to speak politely in a meek manner so she could leave, "Is that all you wished to speak to me about?"

"No, that's not everything I wanted to say, Ellie." Hank Henderson expressed his words with a bit of doubt in his voice. He often wondered if Ellie cared much about what he said. After a moment's delay he continued, hoping to get her full attention. "Doing well in chemistry isn't easy for most of my students, but you have so much potential. All the class work seems to come much easier for you than for others. I wonder if you're experiencing any kind of trouble here at school with any of your other subjects, or could something else be going on that should be corrected?"

"There's no trouble at all, and I'm fine. Really I am. You're absolutely right that I should work harder on my homework. And believe me, I do enjoy your class, and I think you're a great teacher. You make it all seem like such fun. I confess I have been lazy at times and don't always want to do the work."

"I'm here to help all my students, Ellie, but I just wanted to remind you of your above average potential of grasping this subject and to encourage you to do a better job especially on your homework. They're very important too, you know."

"Thanks, Mr. Henderson, and you've got my word. I'll definitely be ready for your test tomorrow. You can count on it." Ellie didn't wish to have him lecture her more, so she gave him a sheepish grin as she stepped back to leave adding, "I'll be more serious about all the homework you assign too. But, Mr. Henderson, please don't talk to my parents about this. I plan to do much better. I promise. Okay?"

Her teacher had said what he wished to say and could only sigh hoping she was serious about her promise.

As Ellie turned and walked away, a satisfied grin crossed her face as she thought about how easily she fooled Mr. Henderson once again when she made that promise. Then for only a brief moment she wondered if he had genuinely bought it because this encounter was almost a repeat of what had happened six weeks ago when she used most of those identical words promising him she would work harder. Certainly nothing had changed since that little talk.

Knowing Mr. Henderson would not be able to hear, she mumbled, "What an absolute dork he is! He seems to believe anything I tell him."

Already walking down the hallway, she quickly headed toward her locker. Ellie considered if it wasn't for Mom and Dad wanting me to take chemistry in the first place, I wouldn't have to make those unintended promises to that lame, dumber than dumb teacher.

Holding her phone, Ellie's face lit up with a huge smile as she reached Brennie. "Hey, it's Ellie. Sorry I'm late, but I had to talk to dear old Mr. H for a few minutes. I'll be at my locker in less than 30 seconds. About tonight, though, my dad agreed to take me to the mall to buy that scrumptious jacket I told you about yesterday. I know this is not what we planned, but my dad always seems to have gobs of work to do every night after he gets home. He usually can't drop it all to take me to the mall, but this morning he said he would."

With disappointment in her voice Brennie answered, "Ellie I was really counting on studying with you tonight for our chemistry test. You understand it so well, and I struggle with it all the time. I'm trying to get a decent grade in the class. English and French may be easy for me, but never chemistry. I can study by myself tonight, but maybe we can go over a few things during lunch time tomorrow. Hey, Ellie, don't feel bad because I understand.

You and I can get together tomorrow sometime before the test, but I seriously need all the help you can give me. Hey, if you don't leave for the mall immediately after you get home from school, please call. We can always meet first thing in the morning too."

"I'll call you when I get home to tell you what I expect will be on the test. We can talk then, Brennie. Gotta run."

Climbing aboard after running to catch her crowded bus, Ellie had the choice of sitting beside either Jim Tankerson or Floyd Decker. Neither spot made her happy, but in less than 20 minutes she would be two blocks from home and jumping off the bus. She sat down beside Floyd, and, as he grinned at her, she returned a little smile. Ellie knew Floyd had always been shy around her, and he quickly turned his blushing face toward the side window so hopefully none of the other guys would notice. For a year he had not been able to hide the crush he had on Ellie. Along with some of the other kids at school, she was aware of the crush, but she was not about to let him know she knew it or was thinking about it now. This evening Ellie's mind was fixed on owning that cool, beautiful jacket. She knew the item had the Juicy label, and was no ordinary jacket, but she had convinced herself she must have it.

After hopping off the bus, she noticed how drastically the weather had changed since early morning, and she pulled her warm coat tighter around her as she felt the chilly wet air. Familiar fluffy white flakes were floating softly down covering especially her hair and nose. After easily walking the short distance of two blocks to her home, Ellie found her house key and unlocked the side door. Hesitating for only a moment, and without hearing any movement inside, she closed and locked the door behind her. She hurried through the kitchen and then up the stairs to her bedroom skipping several steps on her way.

Ellie always seemed to be in a hurry getting ready for school, hurrying to her classes, running to meet friends and almost always running late even after she set definite times to meet someone. Bursting into her room, she tossed her backpack onto the bed and flung her coat down alongside it. Seconds later she was in her bathroom studying her face in the mirror.

She decided to brush on a few layers of eyelash mascara that had faded during her long day at school. Bending forward and looking closely at her bright blue eyes, Ellie frowned slightly. Without taking her eyes off her reflection, she reached into her vanity drawer, and with her fingers, she hunted for the new auburn mascara her mother purchased for her recently. Each time she placed the reddish brown color on her lashes, she could see her brilliant blue eyes and was reminded of the color of her father's eyes because they seemed to be staring back at her now. The blue shade of her eyes was exactly the same shade as his. But she had definitely inherited her mother's strawberry blonde hair color, but the thick strands of her shoulder length hair insisted on curling up on their own, which annoyed her. No one else in her family had any curls, and this peculiarity was something she disliked, but in recent months she had discovered ways to straighten her hair.

"Why do I have to look so much like a Wallace?" She silently asked herself this question with a frown as she continued to glance at her face. This was the same question she often asked as she stood in front of a mirror. "I don't look much like my mom except for this crop of thick, bushy, unmanageable hair, but I sure look like the rest of the family. Ugh!"

With another full brush of makeup, she carefully spread each eyelash till she was satisfied with the coverage. One more gentle lift of the brush on each of her lashes, and she dropped the tube back into the drawer. With one habitual circular movement, Ellie turned her head enough to view herself. Twisting her head for another quick glance, she caught the profile of her youthful face. Never completely content with her appearance, she screwed up her nose with disapproval. Not only was her hair too thick and curly, her forehead was too high, her lips far too skinny, and her eyes did not have the dramatic impact of Claire's dark brown eyes.

"What a dull face you have!" she said almost in a disgusted tone as she stuck out her tongue at her reflection in the glass. Then almost laughing, she began displaying a more cheerful attitude as she glanced again in the mirror to view her complete reflection before leaving the room. "I'll change into my new jeans, and I absolutely love wearing my new cool hoodie."

Springing into her large closet she opened the bottom drawer of her dresser and grabbed her jeans along with the dark gray sweatshirt. Whipping them both out and tossing them high over her shoulder in the direction of her bed, Ellie turned around to change into them as she hummed a few lines of a recent favorite popular tune that lately had been running through her mind.

With one swift movement of her right foot she kicked the jeans she slipped out of toward the side of her bed. "Thanks Grandma for your generous gift. The check you sent me for Christmas paid for these new sweet jeans and my new fantastic sweatshirt. Together they've been my favorites for weeks."

Her sweater and shirt were swiftly taken off and thrown on top of the jeans now making a larger pile to kick aside as she muttered, "Clara will come tomorrow morning to pick up everything and wash whatever's lying around. She never seems to mind picking up after me. After all, that's what she gets paid to do." Thinking for a moment about the woman who was their part-time housekeeper and was so kind to her in particular, she added, "She sure has a strange and funny foreign accent."

Feeling a chill, she climbed into the newer jeans and sweatshirt. Pleasant thoughts ran through her mind of wearing the new jacket to school the following day and seeing the look on the faces of some of her friends. Dad should be ready as soon as he gets home from his office to take me to that store in the mall. I've just got to have that super cool jacket! I'm prepared to beg if it's necessary. When he gets home, he will be starved like always, and I plan to be extra nice by offering to fix him one of his favorite sandwiches.

Glancing at the clock on her bedside table, she guessed her dad would be home in an hour and a half. I'll please him by studying for my chemistry test. An hour of cramming ought to do, and then I can call Brennie when I get back from the mall.

Ellie shook her hair loose from the sweatshirt neckline and ran her fingers through her hair. Feeling the soft, fuzzy nap of the sweatshirt, her thoughts were again about the jacket as she squealed.

Locating her chemistry notebook in her backpack before leaving her bedroom, she hurriedly ran into her bathroom once again to briefly gaze at herself. Smiling with satisfaction, she slipped down the stairs toward the kitchen table to study. Turning on the radio she tried listening to a couple of recent musical tunes, but because she never had been able to concentrate on her studies and listen to music at the same time, she turned it off and opened her chemistry book.

"I'll study until Dad arrives," she chattered to herself, "and then we'll go get that sweet jacket. Oooh, I tried it on twice while I was in the store. It was incredibly beautiful! Everyone at school will think it's awesome, and Angle will be so jealous when she sees it. I'll just die if it's been sold to some other kid! It belongs to me."

Chapter 2

JANUARY DAYS IN MICHIGAN were usually short and dreary, and darkness was quickly arriving in the surrounding suburbs of Detroit making it difficult to see without good lighting. Massive wet snowflakes were rapidly descending, and a moderate collection of the white crystals could be seen covering rooftops of homes, buildings, and even moving objects. Neighborhood lawns had already received a glistening blanket.

Earlier in the day weather stations throughout the city had been forecasting the temperature would continue to drop possibly below the freezing point by evening, and they were expecting several inches of fresh snow to accumulate during the late evening and throughout the early morning hours. By three o'clock meteorologists had changed their predictions as an unexpected wind began forcing the falling flakes into an eastward direction. People knew if the storm continued and the temperature continued to drop, there might be a possible blizzard on its way throughout the huge sprawling metro area. Millions of residents began preparing for a long and bitter cold night ahead. There was bitter coldness lodged in some hearts already.

Owen Wolf had an urgent important matter on his mind, and he had much to think about as he turned his steering wheel guiding his car toward the designated street.

He immediately began looking for a parking spot close to Mike's Pizzeria, but far enough away to not easily be seen.

This small narrow restaurant was set off by itself close to a main interstate highway. During the past two decades the pizzeria had become outdated and slightly run-down. Years ago it had been a popular restaurant and meeting place for the neighborhood, and its fame had spread into parts of the surrounding suburbs about how the owners insisted on preparing their dishes only in the old authentic European method using the same identical recipes favored for centuries by Italian families.

Also clientele who heard about it from friends or somehow happened onto the place soon became loyal. For hungry suburbanites who loved excellent pizza and other old world dishes, and did not mind the décor or driving further, Mike's place continued to draw those patrons as they had for more than 40 years.

During the 1960s and 1970s Mike's Place was mainly visited by people living in the northern sections of the city and by others who wanted a quiet place to relax and talk. It was becoming obvious the Pizzeria's continued success was being hindered as a result of the uninteresting, outdated appearance, but also for the limited parking spaces. Young couples, college students and especially teenagers no longer considered it a place where they wanted to spend their evenings.

By the late 1990s only those who lived nearby or who could not forget how great the pizza had been in previous years continued to frequent the establishment. Today with all the other choices available, only those who craved the old dishes made fresh on the premises ventured into its confining location in the busy suburban community.

Owen Wolf grew up less than a mile from Mike's Place, and he remembered going there often with his three teenage friends to grab some good food before they climbed in a car to cruise the city streets for the rest of the evening. They referred to the restaurant as The Joint back then because they considered it their own meeting place.

Glancing at The Joint as he drove by, he instantly was reminded of the steaming fresh baked dough, the spicy homemade tomato sauce and the generous amounts of various aged cheeses with the great Italian sausage and his favorite topping of ripe olives. Years ago he had forgotten about those three friends and had never made a single attempt to locate them. Tonight he would not allow himself to think about any trivial memories or about tasty food. Those friends and times were in his distant past. They could not serve his purposes today, and tonight he had to keep his mind on business.

He thought about the job that needed to be cleaned up and believed Ray Vinson would need to do the job for him. After all, Ray was the one who had placed both of them in this difficult situation. Less than an hour ago when he spoke to Ray, he made it clear what must happen at the pizzeria tonight to avoid being under the radar of any law enforcement personnel.

As Owen continued to locate a good parking spot that would offer him a clear view of the restaurant's front entrance, yet far enough away to melt into the neighborhood, he glanced around at the homes on both sides of the street. He grinned broadly when he found an ideal spot more than half way down the block, and slowing his expensive shiny black Mercedes, he expertly maneuvered it into the spot alongside the curb and turned off the motor.

Not wanting to raise any suspicions during any of his secret business transactions, he told his auto mechanic last month to darken his windows enough to prevent anyone from being able to view the interior of his car. And tonight with winter darkness descending, absolutely no one would recognize him. Because it was icy cold with huge amounts of heavy snow continuing to fall, no one would be taking time to wonder why a stranger was parked on their street at this hour.

He allowed his gaze to momentarily fall on a middle-aged woman walking on the sidewalk in the direction toward his car, and he watched her as she came closer. "Harmless," he mumbled. Reasoning she must be returning from a long day of work, he was reassured of his conclusion when she turned into a nearby walkway and within seconds was inside her home and out of sight.

Warm and feeling safe inside his car, he pulled up the lambskin collar of his designer coat to encircle his neck and rubbed his leather gloved hands together to loosen his muscles and the tenseness he was experiencing throughout his body. Massaging his forehead because of the slight headache that was now becoming obvious, Owen raised his eyebrows several times as he tried to release the dull pain. He shut his eyes and inhaled a couple deep breaths. A minute later he began methodically going over details in his troubled mind, details that needed to be reviewed before Ray's arrival, so that not even a single part of his plan could go wrong.

Owen enjoyed being in full control of every detail in his schemes, and because he considered himself a master at figuring out procedures, he demanded that everything happen according to his plans and his methods. That way he was assured nothing would be left to chance. He did not like what he considered stupid mistakes and had learned the hard way to always make all his own plans from start to finish so the outcome would end up in his favor.

⊰◈⊱

For 13 years Kurt McCoy had worked extra hard and put in long hours to manage his gas station. He saved as much as he could along the way to care for his growing family and be able to generously help those in need. He was a good family man and sending two of his three kids through college. Money was tight at times, and occasionally his wife, Molly, and he had to make necessary sacrifices, but both of them were now thankful they finally were free and clear of their debts. The mortgage on their modest home had recently been paid off, and in the past year they were able to make adequate plans to protect all their investments.

For years they had waited to buy a larger home, and finally they felt confident to make the move. Molly always had been satisfied with her small compact kitchen, but, with a two-year-old grandchild visiting them regularly and another on the way, her dream of a larger kitchen along with another bedroom for guests and bath close to the kitchen finally seemed possible.

Little Brian, their first and only grandchild, was an active happy toddler who always brought joy and excitement to everyone in the family. Crawling no longer, he was now free to walk everywhere and reach everything. Kurt and Molly were looking forward to the enlargement of the family with the addition of more grandchildren in the future.

Laughter in the McCoy home was always present, and on holidays and plenty of other occasions, the entire family enjoyed spending time together. Before each Sunday Morning Worship Service, Molly would rise early enough to begin preparing a meal for a full Sunday dinner. Their entire family would be able to catch up with what had taken place in each other's lives during the recent week and what was planned for the week ahead. Political items were often hot topics, and everyone was free to present their viewpoint even though all would not agree on every issue. Hashing over subjects of interest and importance was enlightening, but just being together was the lift each wanted and needed.

Both Kurt and Molly made these family gatherings a relaxing time. Often at the last minute some friends and neighbors were invited for the dinners, but Molly then would hurriedly prepare a special dessert for those occasions.

Almost a year ago Kurt had hired Ray Vinson to work at his station and had immediately been impressed with his new employee's attitude toward his customers as well as the man's work ethic. Pleased and thankful for Ray's help at his busy station, that was only becoming busier by the week, Kurt was glad he had hired Ray. Even when the weather was undesirable, he was there with his welcoming smile and willingness to work hard. He instinctively understood how he should serve different types of clients, and Ray often seemed to do the work of two employees.

For months Kurt had been teaching Ray about the business of running a service station, and Ray seemed genuinely interested and was learning rapidly. It was no surprise when one day Ray mentioned he might want to operate a station of his own some day. Kurt told him he would try to help him with an initial start as long as his station was located at least a mile down the road. They both laughed in good humor at that comment but agreed it would be best.

Late in November was when Kurt noticed his gas station had become much busier. There were many new customers, but somehow he was not taking in more money. At first he thought there had to be an easy explanation for this, and he must be missing something.

On closer observation, Kurt noticed a number of these new people were buying small amounts of gas, but, since the price of gasoline was higher than it had been months earlier, many customers seemed to be purchasing only what they needed for a couple of days. Kurt was reluctant to discuss this with Ray, but he became keenly aware that more customers began appearing each week. He reasoned that possibly other stations in the area were charging more or they were coming because Ray was so helpful.

For over a year Kurt had trusted Ray and appreciated the enthusiasm and energy he continually put into every area of his work, but by early December, and almost overnight, Kurt began noticing many new faces at his business. This was extremely unusual. As an attendant he had proven he was an excellent employee, thoroughly interested in being helpful to people, and one who was friendly to anyone who needed assistance when obtaining a fill-up or any other service. Displaying eagerness and a willingness to help his regulars during even the coldest, most disagreeable mornings and evenings, Ray was always available and attentive. He was a great person to have around. There had absolutely been no cause for Kurt to be concerned before, but in spite of all Ray's good qualities, Kurt had recently become wary and concerned.

Then early one evening Kurt simply glanced in Ray's direction when he was helping a man fill his gas tank and noticed Ray as he slipped something inside his pocket. This did not seem right, but he thought perhaps Ray had made change for the man, possibly the man owed Ray money or he was given a tip by the customer for doing a favor. Kurt dismissed the incident that time because he was busy with an urgent repair, but he would talk to Ray when it was convenient and remind him he was not to accept tips for helping any of the patrons.

Kurt was kept busy most of the time with small routine repairs at his station, but years of constantly staying alert and knowing what was going on at his business had become a habit he had acquired along the way. He found no reason to spend valuable time thinking about that one particular incident, but from his good business sense, he would not neglect his inner instincts. Without being overly conscious of what he had first thought, Kurt made a mental note.

Days passed, and Kurt became alarmed that the currency brought in at his station was not rising. He reminded himself again that people were cutting back because of the slow economy, but he reasoned they were definitely driving more in recent weeks because of the approaching Christmas holidays. He noticed that those new customers who seemed to be coming to his station a few times each week were also the same ones who were purchasing only enough gas to top off their tanks. Another reason for his concern was that the newer customers were also the people Ray would frequently be chatting with for less than a minute in inconspicuous, secluded corners always to the side of their cars.

It soon became apparent Ray always stood beside their cars and out of view. Kurt became aware that it was during those private times that transfers of some sort were taking place between Ray and a customer. Troubled by these incidents he had seen for weeks, he decided to face Ray and ask him what was happening. He had to follow through on what he was observing and what he was suspecting.

On an extremely cold morning shortly after the rush hour, Kurt approached Ray to ask him a question. Ray seemed confused and irritated when asked, "What's going on Ray?"

Stumbling over his words, Ray replied, "I was only making change for that man that just left. That's all, Kurt."

Not wishing to answer any more questions Kurt might ask him, Ray quickly stepped away from his boss to wait on another customer who was arriving. For the rest of the day Ray seemed to be rushing around when he was inside the station. Otherwise he would linger outside in the harsh frigid air. For the remainder of the day Ray refused to look in Kurt's direction.

Dismissing his concern because he suspected Ray was embarrassed by that face to face confrontation, Kurt began wondering if he might have made a big mistake by putting his employee on the defensive. It was obvious Ray was avoiding him as much as possible.

One week later without thinking Kurt found himself looking in Ray's direction. He noticed from the far side of a car a tall customer stood smiling at Ray. Unable to see Ray's face or what was taking place, Kurt had clearly seen the man's eyes light up as Ray seemed to be reaching out with his hand with something and then accepting something in return.

Kurt did not have sufficient evidence, but he began putting together his worst suspicion. Within minutes it dawned on him that it was these new customers who preferred paying for their gas purchases with cash only. He knew this was quite an unusual practice in his business even though some of their purchases were never large.

Credit cards were quick and easy for most people, and Kurt was keenly aware that it was especially on these occasions and with those customers paying in cash that Ray began turning his back to the station as he spoke to them. Kurt was unable to clearly see what was happening, but he almost always was able to see the happy expressions on the faces of those car owners. Almost always there was a big satisfied smile. Kurt made up his mind it was time he needed to ask Ray uncomfortable, hard questions.

Thoughts that Ray might be pushing some illegal drug had been creeping through his mind for days, and he had not been able to shake those suspicions. His worst fears were keeping him from getting a good night's sleep, and at times he had awakened in a sweat with dreadful thoughts about the danger of allowing possible drug deals to persist at his place.

The suspicions were nagging at Kurt, and today he would no longer wait and look on without feeling guilty himself. He had seen enough to be alarmed and was now distrustful of Ray. He must bring up the subject because he was determined he would never tolerate that crime to take place on his property, and he would not in any way be caught assisting the sale of narcotics.

Troubled greatly over his urgent concern, he mumbled, "Not at my place! I will absolutely never allow it here! If Ray's involved in any type of drug dealing whatsoever, I'll soon be in a heap of trouble myself if I stand idly by and only observe."

Inside the station during this extremely bitter cold morning, and after Ray made change for someone, Kurt pulled his employee aside and inquired, "What's going on Ray?"

Caught off guard, Ray stopped what he was doing and annoyed he answered Kurt in an ill-tempered mood, "What? Have I done something wrong here? Have I messed up in some way, Kurt? I'm just doing my job."

"Ray, I just want to know what happened between you and that man who just pulled away."

Displaying irritation, Ray hesitated, "Hey, I've been trying to work hard here for you, and you seem to be accusing me of something. Say what's on your mind, Kurt. What're you driving at?"

"I'll be straight with you, Ray. I've got to ask a serious question, and I want you to be entirely honest with me. Have you been selling or only handing out drugs or even doing anything that's considered illegal here at my station?"

"Hey man, you know I'd never think of doing anything like that here. I work for you, Kurt!"

As Kurt looked at Ray, he wanted to make sure he was not being lied to, "Ray, I really like you, and you know that. I want to trust you, and I'm sorry if I'm making a big mistake, but will you answer my question? I need to be sure you're not in any way involved in peddling drugs here. Have you been distributing any kind of illegal substance to customers?"

Ray began to step away as an undisguised ugly smirk began crossing his face, "I'm done pumping gas and running errands for you. In fact, I'm tired of working for you. You pay me such a pittance, and now you don't even trust me. I can get work elsewhere anytime, you know that. I'm quitting! I'm out of here, and I'm leaving all the work for you to do."

"You've given me reason to distrust you. I believe I saw several transactions between you and customers that caused me to doubt your honesty. I've been here far too long to allow you or anyone else to ruin me by doing something that clearly is against the law. I believe you accepted money from people, and at those times you seemed to be doing it secretly so I couldn't see what was happening. Just now, with that man who drove away, did you give him something? I believe he gave you money in return. Am I right about this Ray?"

Kurt's irritation with Ray was building since he did not receive either a yes or no to his question. It was clear to him Ray wanted to end the discussion, quit and leave. Calming himself as much as possible, Kurt said, "You've been an excellent worker, Ray, the best I've ever had or ever hope to have, but you've got to understand how I cannot under any circumstances allow you or anyone else to sell drugs at my place. You've got to understand that, Ray. Please answer my question! I'll be happy to help you if I can."

For a long moment Ray fumed with contempt as he stood staring at Kurt. Then he answered with intense hostility, "I'm gone. It's all yours now, BOSS! You can do ALL the menial work yourself. And for my two days of pay for this week, I might let you keep it. Or maybe I'll send you a big fat bill for what's coming to me. How's that? Maybe that's what I'll do, but I don't intend to be back. You can be sure of that!"

Stepping back as he opened the door and turned to leave, Ray added as he began walking away, "I'm out of here! I QUIT! Yeah, I'm completely done working for you Kurt!"

Without saying another word, Kurt looked at Ray and thought he recognized hurt in his eyes as he left. Or perhaps it was belligerence he saw as Ray climbed into his truck. From the short distance between them, Kurt was almost sure Ray was using profane language directed toward him before he slammed his truck door shut. Then with a sneer, Ray quickly drove away waving his hand out the window as he displayed a coarse gesture.

For the remainder of the day Kurt was kept busy with the full load of handling the business alone. He ran out into the freezing, damp air to help people and handle chores his employee had always gladly done. He was not sure he had done the best thing he could for Ray. Then mid-afternoon as larger snowflakes began gliding downward, a man drove up to one of his gas pumps and asked if Kurt had anything for him. That was the best solid proof he needed that Ray had been pushing drugs or something. Anxious thoughts and future uncertainties hit him. "I've got to do something, and quick!"

Disturbed about how Ray responded, he was certain he had no other option but to get professional help. He must contact someone immediately. Fearful about what he suspected and had observed for weeks, he wondered who might be the best person to talk to and explain his concerns. He would need to mention Ray's responses to his questions and find out what was best to do. He was convinced after the heated conversation with Ray he had probably waited far too long before confronting his employee.

Within a minute, Joe Wallace popped into Kurt's mind. He knew Joe was an attorney, and, although he did not know him well, they both greeted each other every Sunday at church. A good friend at his church had once mentioned that he had received advice from Joe about a legal matter. Now he needed some expert legal advice himself. It was quite late in the day for calling an office if he waited until he returned home, but he could close his station early. He was quite sure he would be able to reach Joe at his office if he called now.

Convinced he needed to act quickly, Kurt reasoned almost silently, "Although Joe might still be working on something important, he might be able to give me a little advice because I desperately need some. Time is of the essence for me, and if I don't get on this crucial matter right away, I might find myself unable to keep the station."

From the bottom drawer of his desk he pulled out an old greasy telephone book and searched in the yellow pages under the long listing of attorneys. Joseph Wallace was easy enough to find, and Kurt hurriedly pushed the numbered buttons to reach the law office.

On the second ring, someone on the other end picked up his call and cheerfully said, "Good afternoon. Gaylord, Wallace and Fines. What can we do for you today?"

When Kurt asked to speak to Joseph Wallace, the well spoken lady told him Mr. Wallace had left the office for the day. Believing his situation needed immediate attention, Kurt mentioned he needed advice on an important matter. He added he was acquainted with Mr. Wallace because both the Wallace family and his attended the same church. He told her the matter should be dealt with that evening if at all possible.

Responding to Kurt the woman said, "Sir, Mr. Wallace can be reached at his home if that is agreeable to you."

"Great! Could you please give me his home number?" Ten numbers were given, and Kurt carefully wrote each down in the margin of the phone book. "Thank you, Miss. You've been very helpful. I'm grateful for this information. Goodbye, and have a good evening."

Hurriedly Kurt punched in the numbers he'd been given, and as he waited for Joe to answer his phone, he faintly heard someone enter through the rear door of the station. He was not surprised to see it was Ray. Kurt noticed immediately that he had been drinking and motioned with a finger to his mouth for him to wait for a moment as he finished the conversation. On the third ring, Kurt received an answer, "Joe Wallace speaking."

Chapter 3

TEN MINUTES EARLIER, Ellie heard her father's car roll into the driveway only minutes before he received Kurt's call. Leaping from the sofa where she had been sitting answering Brennie's questions about what to study and what they could expect to find on their chemistry test the following day, she interrupted their conversation as she heard the garage door open, "Gotta go, Brennie."

Excited about soon being on her way to the mall to purchase the jacket, Ellie hurriedly said, "Hey girl, my dad just arrived, and I've gotta go. See you during lunch tomorrow. Okay? Meet me at our usual table. Tonight write down any additional questions we didn't cover, and we'll go over them then. That way everything will be fresh in your mind. Also be sure to read the first half of both chapters 14 and 15 and review the sample equations. Go over all the symbols and signs on the inside cover of the textbook. Brennie, I'll meet you tomorrow at lunchtime. See ya."

Running into the kitchen Ellie dropped the phone back into its cradle and headed up the stairs as she heard her dad enter the kitchen. Knowing she would have only a brief time before he'd be ready to go, she raced into her bathroom. A slim line of smoky blue eyeliner was meticulously drawn above her lashes, and she applied a pale peach shade of lip gloss to both upper and lower areas of her lips. She could hear her father walking around in the kitchen and probably taking a peek in the refrigerator for an easy quick bite to satisfy his hunger pangs.

These items seemed to help minimize a few of the features that irritated her. Those bright blue eyes and her reddish hair color. The only redeeming feature she was pleased with was her straight healthy teeth. Receiving numerous compliments from especially older women regarding the unusual shade of her hair and the brightness of her eyes, Ellie always smiled pleasantly at them. Even then she was never happy and frequently wondered what they really thought about her hair and eyes. They never seemed to notice or mention her perfect teeth.

She pouted wrinkling up her nose as she stepped forward for another quick view. Deciding to leave an even thicker, more pronounced coat of mascara on her lashes, she picked up the tube. Then bending even closer she patiently applied another final coat, being careful not to mess up what she'd done earlier. With two swift lifts of the brush for each eye, she finished and dropped the tube back into the drawer.

"Mom's always telling me I need to learn to be content with what I have," she silently muttered. Stretching over her vanity to look closer at herself one final time, Ellie smiled with satisfaction. Then for only a split second as she stepped back, she caught a glimpse of a young girl who was quickly becoming a woman. Her body had filled out some in the past couple of years, and her face was not as round as it had been. Seventeen now and a junior in high school, she felt grown up in many ways, but in other ways, she still felt like a kid.

With the boundless energy with which she'd been born, Ellie bounced out into the hallway and shouted, "Hey Dad, I'm upstairs, but I'll be ready to go whenever you are. Call me if you want me to fix one of your favorite sandwiches."

Knowing his daughter was upstairs Joe replied loudly enough for his daughter to hear him, "Let me take care of a few things first before we leave. I need to drop off my briefcase and computer in the office and check our phone for any incoming messages."

Ellie's mind turned again to dreaming about the jacket and how she would look in it. "Hopefully that saleslady remembered to set it aside like she said she would. Since it was on sale, Dad just might consider it a good buy. Oh, I really hope he likes it."

As she stood in the middle of her bedroom looking down at her recently purchased boots, she began considering whether she should talk to her mom when she returns about purchasing another pair of running shoes. Not yet. I wouldn't dare bring up that possibility to Dad tonight because it might hinder his purchasing that heavenly, fabulous jacket for me. With a bit of luck, he'll not even look at the price tag. But I'll cry if I don't get to bring it home. For sure he'll buy it for me. He just has to.

Remembering the promise she'd made to her dad at breakfast about studying hard tonight for her chemistry test when they returned home from the mall, she picked up her coat and shoulder bag. Under her breath Ellie whispered, "Doing well on that crummy test will make both Mom and Dad happy, but owning that sweet jacket will make me happy. Oh, so happy."

She recalled what Mr. Henderson had said to her after school and mumbled, "What a geek. He's so lame. He loves giving tests to us to prove he's smart, and he had the nerve today to tell me he wasn't pleased with my work and said I was able to do better. What does he know? Nobody likes him except those two brains in the class. I'd much rather be liked by my friends than to get a better grade in his class. Besides, kids might think I'm a showoff if I bring my grades up too much. He's so stupid, and his tests are even more stupid."

After putting on her warm coat she grasped her stylish Coach bag and flung it over her shoulder as she considered the amount of time it would take her to do great on the test. "Both Mom and Dad said I must take chemistry this year. What a total waste it is, but I have to admit I actually do like doing the work sometimes. So what, I'd much rather spend precious time at the mall and have fun with my friends. To get that jacket though, I'll study hard even if it takes me the rest of the night. I'll learn enough to get a great grade from stupid Mr. Henderson. I know I can do well, but I'll never use what I learn in that class!"

As she was about to turn off the overhead light and meet her dad, she noticed the new picture of Casey Miller sitting on her bedside table. He sat beside her in French class and had been Angie's boyfriend almost a year. Yesterday Ellie had flirted with Casey and asked him to email a picture of himself to her, and last night he'd sent one along with a short funny joke. Although Ellie didn't wish to have Casey as a boyfriend, she'd been willing to flirt with him in front of Angie to see her reaction. Yes, Angie had been watching from across the room, and yes, she'd seen jealousy in her friend's sad eyes.

"Why did I do that to Angie? I know it was mean. Casey's not even my type, but it was fun at the time to see Angie's expression. She's been mad at me ever since and refuses to speak to me." Somewhat sorry but still amused by the incident, Ellie bit her lip and almost smiled.

Instantly she was reminded of Brad Nelson. Whenever she thought of a boyfriend, Brad came into her mind. He'd been a friend for several years until his family moved to California the previous summer before starting his junior year. It had not been a boyfriend/girlfriend type of friendship, but they were the same age and both attended their church youth group meetings. They always enjoyed being together, and she had many memories of the fun they'd shared. It was sad for both of them when he left, and she missed him terribly at times. He was someone she could rely on because he was not shy about telling her when she was wrong about something. Tonight she would be sure to get an email off to him before she studied for her test.

At the bottom of the stairs her father broke her thoughts as he called up, "Ellie, we only have a few minutes before we'll need to leave if you want me to take a look at that jacket. If we don't get a move on, the mall will be closed. I want to see how it looks on you before I make my decision. By the way, if it only looks cool you probably won't get it. Understand? So hurry! Our phone is ringing. I'll answer it because maybe it's your mom. We've got to leave soon, Ellie. Now hurry!"

⟫◆⟪

Bending over the desk and listening intently, Joe was still holding the phone to his ear when Ellie reached the bottom of the stairs. As she ran into her dad's office she announced, "I'm ready Dad."

Without looking up Joe concentrated as he listened to the caller on the other end. A minute later Ellie heard her father say, "Kurt, I'll meet you at Mike's tonight at six, but I don't know if I can be of much help. It's not my area of expertise, you understand, but we can grab a bite and talk. I'm sure we'll come up with an acceptable solution. At six. At Mike's. Yes, it's a good time and place for us, so we'll see you then.

Once he replaced the phone, Joe looked up at his daughter who was impatiently waiting for him to take her to the mall for her latest 'must have.'

With concern in his eyes Joe said, "Ellie, that was Kurt McCoy on the phone, and we'll meet him tonight for some pizza so we can talk while we eat. He needs counsel about a difficult matter affecting his business. If we leave soon we should have plenty of time to get to the store before we go to Mike's. The mall is only 20 minutes from here, and after we take a peek at that jacket you want, we'll head over to get some of the best Italian pizza in town. You and I will consider this our evening meal, and then I won't have to explain to your mother that we had soup out of a can again for dinner."

"Your mom should be home within a few days, and then we'll return to healthy eating again. I think that sounds like a rather grand idea for both of us. But tonight you'll need to spend the rest of the evening studying for your chemistry test. It's important you study hard and do well. Promise me Ellie."

"Sure Dad. You'll be happy because I've already studied this afternoon for more than an hour, and I promise I'll put in another hour or maybe even more if it's necessary to get a really good grade. It's an important test for my final grade."

Stepping away from his desk chair and reaching for his topcoat, Joe smiled as he gave his full attention to addressing his daughter, "Ellie, you know we're not interested in your only pulling good grades in your classes. We want you to learn what you'll need for your future. You'll go to college in a year and a half, and your mom and I want you to be prepared. We want you to actually enjoy learning your entire life. You'll never, ever be sorry you studied for these classes during your high school years. I want to remind you that God gave you a good mind, and

Mom and I want you to be thankful for the opportunity to learn about many things. Chemistry is only one area of study."

Observing Ellie's respectful reaction to his words, he continued, "You're old enough to think of your future, and it's up to you. That cool, stylish jacket will only be important for a short time compared to the lasting importance of your school studies. Ned can tell you how studying during high school helped him in the tougher classes he's taking now, and he's studying longer than he ever imagined three years ago when he was your age . . . and that reminds me, we need to call your mom and Ned tonight and talk to them. We might find out when your mom is planning to make that drive home. I also want to talk to Ned about his plans for studying law in a couple of years."

Ellie could see her father's face and sensed how much he missed Ned. His son had left early in August for his sophomore year at the University of Pennsylvania, and although he had come home for the Christmas holidays, he wouldn't be home again until mid May.

There were times when Ellie would glance at her dad and see him caught up in thoughts of Ned. He might be looking out the window at the lonely basketball hoop or stopping as he walked by Ned's vacant bedroom. Her brother had been in college for over 18 months, and his absence had left a huge hole in the family. Becoming accustomed to his absence was difficult.

At their Sunday dinner table his spot was noticeably empty, and it was tough sometimes to talk about him. On occasions it was an exceptionally sad reminder when Mom would cook one of Ned's favorite dishes, and he was not there to enjoy the meal with them because he was hundreds of miles away. Someone might idly say, "This is one of Ned's favorites," and no one had to say anything else.

Joe reflected again on Kurt's call, but Ellie did not know what the men had talked about on the phone and thought her dad was continuing to think about Ned. After a few seconds Ellie said, "I miss him too, Dad. Last night when we talked to Mom, she mentioned Ned and told us she was thinking about him a lot lately and praying for him. She did say she'll come home as soon as Grandma is over that miserable flu. She's the healthiest grandma I know at her age, so I'm sure she'll get better soon. Mom said she'd call us when she starts out on that long trip back."

"Mom told Grandma she was welcome to move in with us whenever she decides to leave her home and friends in Tennessee. She was offered Ned's room because it's empty most of the year. Can you imagine Grandma staying in there with all those over-sized posters of hockey players displayed on his wall. It's even possible Mom might bring Grandma with her when she returns, or she might actually come to stay with us for at least a while. She enjoys helping Mom cook, and she can tell some of those funny old stories of hers."

As they stepped into the hallway and walked toward the garage Joe said, "Remind me, Ellie, to call both of them tonight when we get home because I have a lot of papers to look over, and I could easily forget to call them until it's too late. Now we must get our tails out of here and get to that store to look as that extra cool, unbelievably incredible jacket."

"Oh, Dad, you'll like it. It's more than just cool. Honestly, it's beautiful. You'll see. Let's go."

Chapter 4

WHAT HAD BEEN A LIGHT SNOWFALL in this section of the city an hour previously had become heavier by the minute. The weather was definitely icy cold now, and residents coming home from work could feel the uncomfortable frozen air as they wrapped themselves in their warmest winter garments to keep from shivering. The wind, too, had picked up and was forcing the falling snow to whirl around and gather into soft sculptured drifts. A chilly mist could be seen surrounding each lighted object.

Weather reports from local radio stations were covering the air waves continuously, and they cautioned that much stronger winds would be present throughout the evening hours. They were now predicting eight to nine inches of additional snow to fall during the early morning hours. From all appearances this would be the first, and hopefully last, blizzard of the season.

Moving his head toward the windshield to get a clearer view, Kurt said, "For sure we're getting that giant whiteout predicted days ago!" Slowing his speed because the blinding wintry wetness was hindering what he could see, he mumbled as he took a quick glance at his dashboard clock, "It's almost 5:30, but I should have plenty of time to be on time for my appointment with Mr. Wallace."

Joe had mentioned Mike's Place for their meeting since it had been such a great place to get pizza, and it was close enough for both of them to get there within half an hour. Although it usually would take only 20 minutes to reach the restaurant, severe weather, poor visibility and possible traffic snarls might hamper his ability to arrive on time. Seeing the slow traffic ahead, he was glad he left as early as he did. Looking out his foggy window he continued to think about the conversation he had earlier with Ray, and those unreasonable reactions from Ray continued to interrupt his thoughts.

Taking a quick glance to the side of the road, he could see where a huge truck and car had collided. It appeared to be an unavoidable accident that happened only minutes prior to his reaching the spot.

Once beyond the accident, Kurt's thoughts returned to the harsh words exchanged between Ray and him earlier. Kurt was sure he would miss this excellent station attendant who had served him well. Time after time Ray had proven he was eager to help all his customers, but this morning had been so different. Ray lashed out with anger when he was confronted about whether or not he was selling drugs. Kurt sighed with sadness knowing Ray would never work for him again.

He remembered clearly how Ray's attitude had seemed almost menacing an hour ago when he returned for his paycheck. He had been drinking, which was unusual, and he annoyingly displayed impatience and intense animosity. These traits were all out of character for him. If it wasn't drugs, why would his easy going attendant react so differently today? What was all this about? Was Ray actually selling drugs or was something else going on? But if it were drugs, how long had this been going on?

Distressing possible problems disturbed Kurt's normally tranquil thoughts, but he was convinced he had done the right thing to ask Joe to meet with him so he could ask for legal advice. Soon enough Kurt would need to find another employee to replace Ray because there was absolutely no way he could take care of what had become an extremely busy station. He had to serve a large number of customers that came to have repairs done on their cars as well as help those at the pumps. Winter as well as spring, summer and fall had become extremely busy times at his business, and he was determined to keep it that way as long as he was able to do the work. He would need to continue to make sufficient money to provide for his expanding family.

He was fully aware his two sons were not interested in his line of work, and that was fine with Kurt. His oldest son Jim was going to enlist in the Navy as soon as he finished his community college work. Kurt had been helping him financially for more than two years. Warren, his youngest, said he would enjoy studying some type of engineering after his high school graduation. That was less than 16 months away. College and training in some field of study was costly and only becoming more so each year.

It seemed Sandy, their daughter, had always wanted to get married and become a mother for a house full of kids. Somehow she was able to talk her husband into considering having at least four children. As Kurt remembered Sandy's desire for a large family, he said out loud, "Four kids! What are those two thinking? Both Sandy and Hank are bright and ambitious and could tackle anything they set their minds to. Oh, well, we need smart, energetic parents to raise kids these days. Whew! Four kids! That'll be a handful."

Kurt knew his wife, Molly, had been an excellent student throughout school and would be great at encouraging Sandy's children to do their school work. When she was with them she would make sure they did their homework and everything that was expected of them. Molly loved making cookies for everyone and would love being surrounded by a bunch of kids.

Nervously Kurt again looked at his watch. It was 5:40, and he was thankful the traffic was cooperating and moving well. His thoughts returned to his immediate concern and tonight's meeting with Joe Wallace.

Joe and Ellie were heading out to their car in the mall parking lot with a new jacket encased in a plastic bag hanging over Joe's shoulder. Convincing her dad to purchase the one item that would make her the happiest kid ever had once again proven to Ellie that her dad was a big softie.

At times both Joe and Carolyn's love for Ellie overruled their better judgments. Especially Joe was a sucker, but this evening in the store he admitted the jacket his daughter had to have looked great on her. Joe's conclusion often was since Ellie's older sister, Paula, was now living in England with her husband, Rick, they would not be able to spoil their eldest daughter any more.

Since Paula's husband, Rick, had recently been moved overseas by the United States Military and was involved in some secret work that could never be revealed to anyone under any circumstances, Joe and Caroline had made it a habit of keeping in touch with them every weekend even though they were living abroad and sometimes were difficult to contact. They had all struggled to fully accept this undesired separation, but they were assured Rick was taking good care of Paula.

With his right hand Joe quickly wiped the icy snow off the plastic jacket bag and slipped it onto the back seat hanger inside the car. As they both jumped into their seats, Joe turned on the motor to begin warming the cold air that had settled inside while they were in the store.

For the short time it took them to make the purchase, the wind had become stronger, and the predicted blizzard was definitely on its way. A layer of crusty snow had collected over the entire frame of the car, but with the windshield wipers brushing away the large hardened crusty flakes that continued to fall, Joe waited only half a minute before he could see well enough to pull out of the parking lot and onto the street. They would need to travel through windswept snow for the next 15 minutes to reach Mike's Place. In less than two hours, with the wind hurling around, it had become a full-blown storm. Cars that had not been prepared for cold weather could easily stall on a night like this.

Joe thought again about Kurt's request to meet, and he was sure he had made a good choice when he suggested meeting at Mike's to talk because it was close enough for both of them to reach easily. It would also be a private place to discuss Kurt's concerns.

Rethinking the short conversation they had earlier, Joe was sure he heard reluctance on Kurt's part to talk over the phone about the situation at his station. Kurt had not gone into many details. Possibly Kurt wanted to talk privately without any interruptions, but Joe recalled hearing one short delay during the call and sensed that someone else might have been nearby listening during their conversation.

Kurt and he had never spent much time together, but in the church where both families attended regularly, Joe knew Kurt and Molly were always more than willing and often the first to help needy people in the church and others.

An accident ahead caused Joe to stop thinking about Kurt. The occurrence seemed to be causing havoc as he noticed numerous stranded cars lining sections of the road. Once freed from the congestion, they picked up a little speed and continued making their way toward the restaurant. In minutes they would see the familiar side street and turn the corner.

Joe thought a good parking spot might be difficult to locate, but unexpectedly they were able to park a short walk to the entrance. Opening her door and stepping out, Ellie quickly reached in to grab her new jacket, "Hopefully, Dad, I'll get a chance to try it on again in the women's room while you men talk."

After a short walk in the ever deepening snow, they were safely inside where it was warm. The scent of freshly baked bread filled the large room as they noticed Kurt at the far side already removing his coat.

Greeting both with a big smile, Kurt walked toward them and shook Joe's hand, "Thanks for coming on such short notice and on such a miserable night like this."

As they shook hands Joe explained, "My wife's mother has the flu, and since she's away in Tennessee caring for her this week, I brought Ellie, my daughter. Do you think what we'll be talking about will be a problem? If so we can talk at another table about the matter first."

"I really don't think so. She doesn't know the man I'll be talking about. But I will tell you, this problem I want to discuss with you probably involves drugs."

Looking at Ellie for a long second and then back at Kurt, Joe said, "Caroline and I have had many talks with all our children about drugs. They know how and why they are to stay clear of them."

Clearing his throat, Kurt lowered his voice and added in a whisper, "But if at any time you think she shouldn't hear our conversation, we can sit at another table."

"There's absolutely no reason why she cannot be present. Avoiding drugs is something we've expressed openly, and besides, Ellie has been faced with drug problems in her high school. Kids are often the special target for those criminal punks who are all too quick to offer them a sample."

Glancing around the large room, they all noticed at the same time that they were the only customers. Once they were settled at a table close to the back, they decided to order a large pizza with three Cokes. Within seconds the waiter came out from the kitchen to take their order.

"Welcome to Mike's Place. It looks like you may be the only ones here tonight so if you order pizza, it should be ready within 15 minutes flat. Since we didn't expect many customers because of the snowstorm, we didn't put out the usual amount of salad fixings, so our salad bar is free tonight. Please help yourself."

The restaurant's long-standing specialty pizza was ordered, and they walked over to the salad bar to pick up a few items to munch on while they waited for their pizza to be made. Few words were spoken until after the Cokes arrived. Kurt was nervously fidgeting but ready to begin telling Joe what he personally had observed in recent weeks at his station.

Without making wild claims of knowing exactly what had taken place, he began telling Joe the facts as he knew them. Only what he had seen with his own eyes was included. He was sure this would allow Joe to make his own judgments. Kurt did not wish to make the big mistake of misrepresenting his story, but not knowing everything that had taken place at his station, he wanted to know what he needed to do from a legal position.

After relating the pertinent information, Kurt intentionally stopped and waited to hear Joe's opinion. He was convinced Joe would be impartial once all the facts he knew were laid out. Fairness for Ray's sake and a sound solution were his main concerns tonight, but he definitely did not want this type of trouble to continue at his station. He wanted to know Joe's perception on the matter. Remaining silent as Joe spoke, Kurt concentrated on every word offered to him as he wrote down a few notes. He included the two conversations he had with Ray along with the reactions he received. Also mentioned was the short confrontation they had at closing time when Ray returned to pick up his paycheck.

Before Kurt went any further, Joe reminded him that he was not an attorney who mainly handled cases involving illegal drugs or other crimes, but he was happy to counsel him on procedures he should follow and who he should contact first. Tonight Kurt did not care because he was in desperate need of advice on what he must do first. He then told Joe he was not interested in getting Ray in a lot of unnecessary trouble, but he was relieved Ray had left on his own. He added that he had already resolved he could never consider employing the man again.

Chapter 5

AS JOE AND KURT WERE ENGROSSED in what the other was saying, Ellie was listening off and on and was only somewhat aware of the discussion. Restless because she simply wanted to try on her new jacket, she continued thinking about how the kids at school would compliment her on how cool she looked in it. She could not help but hear the words illegal drugs mentioned, and she observed from Mr. McCoy's facial expression that he was disappointed in his employee.

Drugs were an ongoing problem in her high school, and she along with her friends were aware of how some kids discussed drugs in hushed tones and in quiet corners in and around her school. Ellie's parents had given her information about what getting involved in drugs could mean for her. It was an open, well covered subject in their home, and she had been encouraged not to even associate with kids who even talked about drugs casually. Her parents instructed her to always avoid them. Periodically they asked her if any of her friends were involved in taking or passing out any type of drug.

As in many schools, experimenting with drugs had become a constant problem. Because of gossip that was passed around, Ellie was made aware of the unrelenting grip narcotics and even newer designer drugs could have on a kid. Almost every kid she knew at one time or another knew about some student who struggled with drug addiction or had been approached by some sleazy drug pusher. Choices had to be made to either give in and sample a drug or rely on the good judgment of a parent or another authority who knew the lifelong effect that a harmful drug could have on the physical as well as the psychological development of a teen.

Ellie could remember clearly an episode when one kid in one of her classes had offered her a drug. On that occasion she adamantly refused to have anything to do with it or him even when it was offered to her as a free sample. Also one girl she hardly knew asked her to at least try a couple of prescription pills she had stolen from her mother's medicine cabinet. The girl claimed they were only harmless pills and would offer her only a little jolt. It was easy that second time to say no. Ellie's parents had brought up the subject of drugs only last month during the Christmas holidays, and they suggested what she should say and do if she was with friends who were doing drugs of any kind. They said, "Just say no and walk away."

Earlier that year Ellie had heard through the grapevine of one sophomore girl who had attended a party, and on the spur of the moment, tried a drug offered to her. Since it was given to her by her boyfriend, she foolishly thought it must be a mild drug. Continuing to take it for only a few months, she quickly became hooked on it. Plunging into a haunting, near-fatal experience one night, the girl's parents found her lying in a corner of her bedroom and were unable to awaken her. Frantic, they took her to the emergency room of the hospital. Days later they had to take her for treatment at a drug rehabilitation center in another state. Within months she had quit school. Words were passed around the girl occasionally fell into deep, dark episodes of depression and was tormented with nightmarish dreams.

After weeks, when she finally returned to her classes, she seemed to be interested only in parties where drugs were present. She did not care about her appearance, which was obvious to everyone, and she did not give a rip about what her parents or others thought. She had become disrespectful toward everyone and had a willful nasty attitude. Rumors flew around that even her personality seemed to be affected. These drastic changes in her behavior and attitude were noticed by everyone who knew her, and although she had always been liked before, her friends became wary and invented ways to avoid her. A few months later she left losing all her friends.

Finally ending up in yet another rehab facility, the girl's cousin said her parents moved the entire family to avoid all the rumors that were going around. The cousin said they enrolled her in another school, which was strict on behavioral matters because of her poor choices in making friends.

Ellie also recalled Phil, a senior, who had always been a model student in high school. Phil would often make the best grades in his classes. Good looking and with a great sense of humor, many girls considered Phil to be the one guy they would like to date. After an early football game he sampled a new questionable drug along with several classmates and was bad news within a short time. He absolutely was unable to handle this new drug but was unwilling to do without it. Possibly he left to attend another school in the area, but he dropped off the radar screen before he had a chance to graduate. No one knew what happened to Phil. It was scary for many kids throughout the school, and the weirdness about his disappearance was talked about for weeks. Gobs of speculative talk had been passed around, but absolutely no one heard from him again. For the remainder of the year Ellie's circle of friends became much more watchful of the parties they were invited to once the news about Phil was out.

⟝⟞

Joe Wallace continued listening to Kurt as the sizzling, hot pizza was placed in the middle of their table. And, just as they were about to begin eating, the front door of the restaurant opened, and the cold wind entered along with a man. Three heads turned to see Ray Vinson. All eyes were fixed on him as he staggered toward their table. It was obvious to them that Ray had been drinking heavily. The waiter was about to ask if there was anything additional they would like to have with their pizza when he saw the angry look on the man's face. He stepped aside and left the area walking to the other side of the room to clean the salad serving area.

Intoxicated and displaying a disgruntled look in his blood shot eyes, Ray began glaring at Kurt in particular. Joe more than Kurt knew what this drunken state of Ray could imply and how this might become a bad situation in a short time if it were not handled with a great deal of tact. Ellie sat speechless with her mouth open as she stared at the man's wild eyes.

Surprised to see Ray and without hesitation Kurt said to him, "I was telling my friend Joe about our conversation at the station. He's an attorney here in the city, and I wanted his advice to see what I could do to handle this situation, and . . . Ray, you're welcome to sit down and talk with us?"

An uncomfortable silence filled the air as Ray's countenance did not change. His face reddened as he showed hostility and disgust toward Kurt. Without waiting another awkward second, Joe turned his head and firmly said, "Ellie, go into the women's room. We seem to have a definite problem we need to deal with here. Quickly go and stay inside the women's room."

Noticing from the corner of his eye that his daughter had not moved but seemed extremely frightened by the rage she saw in the man, Joe raised his voice a notch and slowly but firmly demanded this time, "Ellie, go into the women's room. I'll let you know when you should come out. GO! Ellie, GO NOW!"

Understanding why her father had given the order, Ellie glanced once again at the man's unyielding face. Feeling mounting tension, but knowing her father was fully in control, she stood without delay and weakly replied, "Okay, Dad."

In the empty seat where Ellie had placed her new jacket, she quickly grabbed it along with her handbag and headed for the restroom. She was thinking this would be her chance to try on the jacket and get a good look at it while she waited for the man to leave.

Taking a quick look behind her before she opened the Women's room door, Ellie saw that the man named Ray was displaying an enraged, violent expression. He began loudly speaking to Kurt with slurred speech, cursing and insulting him because he had involved an attorney about their private conversation at the gas station.

Once inside the room, Ellie was more interested in her new jacket than what was going on in the outer room. Flinging her handbag onto the worn, outdated vanity, she then began pulling her hoodie sweatshirt up and over her head. She hastily tossed it over one of the swinging doors. Now wearing only her turtle neck top, she reached under the plastic cover and slipped the jacket out.

Uttering a little squeal, she gently slid her arms into the soft new jacket sensing with her fingers its lofty softness and the expensive imitation fur trim collar. Because the ancient stained mirror had been placed too high, she was only able to view the top half of the jacket. Rising on her toes, she stretched her body as high as possible.

Disappointed she complained, "I wish I could see it all, but I do love this gorgeous, oh, so sweet jacket! I really do love it! Thanks bunches, Dad, for buying it for me." Reaching for her handbag, Ellie placed it over her shoulder. "They are so smart together! Tomorrow Rita and Bridget will be so envious of me."

Standing again on her tiptoes, Ellie attempted to see as much as she could of herself in the jacket. As she stood there turning from side to side admiring herself in the glass, she now could hear several voices shouting. Unable to either distinguish who was yelling or what was being said, Ellie's body became tense. Without knowing what was taking place in the outer room, but somewhat alarmed, she suddenly forgot about the new garment she was wearing and was unable to restrain her emotions. She became extremely fearful of what might be happening between the three men.

"But Dad said I should stay inside the women's room until he lets me know I can come out," Ellie murmured as more fear overtook her usual blasé attitude. For yet another long moment she heard the men's raised voices. Now keenly aware of the shrill shouting coming through the walls, she stood motionless and silent.

She blinked hard as two distinct shots were fired, and then a second later a third and final shot. Certain it must be gunfire, she winced and braced herself against the vanity. The sound of the three shots rang again in her ears and resounded in her head. Extreme terror gripped her, and she was aware of the pounding of her heart. Someone began running, and a second later a heavy door closed.

Then complete silence filled the entire building. No noise of any kind was audible, but only a strange stillness was evident after all the previous shouting. She was sure something violent had taken place in the restaurant just beyond the restroom door.

Dreading to open it and feeling the dryness now in her mouth, she inhaled deeply in an attempt to control the racing of her pulse. Ellie knew she must open the door because she was positive something awful had taken place.

Fear she had never known before crept over her entire being, and the quiet was terrible. For seconds she stood stunned staring at herself in the mirror. She did not see her face, but felt only fear. Her father had told her to stay inside, but she had to look out to see what all the commotion had meant and what those three shots she heard implied. With her head spinning, she cautiously turned. In a trance, she walked to the door and grabbed the handle.

Pulling it toward her, Ellie was afraid of what she might see. Breathing deeply and with one foot ahead of the other, she stepped out of her hiding place. Stretching her neck around the corner, she saw both Mr. McCoy and her father lying lifeless on the floor.

Terrified and unable to think clearly, Ellie screamed as she ran to her father's side, "Dad?"

Her father had been shot along with Mr. McCoy. Dropping on her knees she reached out for her father's hand and looked at his face. Noticing the heavy redness running down his shirt and sweater, Ellie screamed again, "Dad? What happened?"

Looking closely at her father's face and afraid he might be dead, she began crying. Slowly he opened one eye. Ellie grasped his hand tightly and realized he was still alive. She felt helpless as she uttered, "Dad, what should I do? You've been shot by that madman!"

Joe Wallace closed the eye, but a second later he slowly opened both eyes. In a hushed, weaken tone he spoke to his daughter, "I'll probably make it Ellie . . . Now do exactly as I tell you . . . Reach inside the right pocket of my coat. Take the car keys and my wallet . . ." Struggling to continue, he almost whispered, "Drive to Grandma's where Mom is, and she'll know what to do."

His breathing was becoming heavy now. " Hurry, Ellie . . . to the car and drive to Grandma's. Oh, . . . and Ellie, get my cell phone from inside my suit jacket before you leave so I can call 911 for myself. . . Then run! That man will be after you as well because you saw his face . . . Leave right now. Drive to your grandmother's house! Run, Ellie, Run!"

Her hands were beginning to shake as she reached for the cell phone. Placing it firmly in his hand and closing his fingers firmly around it, Ellie's eyes began filling with large salty tears. Kissing her father on his forehead she cried, "Dad, I love you so much."

Then with tears filling her eyes and running down her face as they blurred her vision, she cried louder, "God . . . Please . . . Please save my dad."

"Before they call I will answer."

—*Isaiah 65:24*

Chapter 6

ELLIE WAS SHAKING ALL OVER, and though she had not prayed in a long time, she begged God to keep her Dad alive until medical rescue personnel were able to reach him. Rising from the floor she reached over to the empty chair for her father's top coat. Inside one pocket she found his wallet and hurriedly placed it securely into the pocket of her new jacket. Then grabbing his car keys from another pocket and grasping them tightly in her left hand, she tenderly stooped to kiss her father's hand. Placing it gently on his chest she prayed, "Please, God, keep him alive."

Ellie turned toward the outer door and began running, "To the car, then drive to Grandma's," she repeated those few words to herself. "Dad told me to run!"

Barely able to see through her tears, she wiped them from her eyes with the sleeve of her new jacket and turned her head to look at her father again, "Dad, I love you."

Just before her hand was on the door handle, she dropped the car keys on the floor. As she bent to pick them up she took one last look in the direction of her father, "Please, God, please don't let him die." Ellie tried to show courage as she spoke, "I'm going to Grandma's house, Dad," It was then she saw that her father was already speaking to someone on his phone. Taking a firm hold of the door handle, she opened it and looked out. Seeing the dark, wintry night as a background for the huge falling snowflakes that blew onto her face, she strained her eyes to see if anyone was standing nearby. No one could be seen.

In another second she was out the door holding tightly onto her father's keys as the sparkling white crystals completely surrounded her. It was good she had at least put on the new jacket along with her handbag in the women's room because she could not return. With the frigid snow sweeping forcefully around her, she instantly felt the chill. She regretted leaving her warm hoodie behind, but was concerned only with reaching her father's car. Ellie breathed heavily as she purposely began trudging through the thick snowfall. With the blizzard moving at full force, she was unable to see more than three feet in front of her.

Attempting to unlock her father's car on the driver's side, Ellie nervously bit her lip as she mumbled, "Of course, Dummy, it's locked." Reaching inside her pocket, her cold fingers found the key, and with a simple click, it opened.

Heavy wet snow coated her hair and shoulders in the seconds it had taken her to reach the car. Wrapping the new jacket even closer around her body, she tossed her bag onto the passenger seat, slid into the driver's seat and closed the door. She fumbled with the ignition key because her hands were beginning to shake, and she could barely control her fingers enough to place the car key in its slot. After another clumsy attempt, it fell into place. As her icy fingers turned the key, the motor started instantly and began humming.

Unfamiliar with her father's car, Ellie almost panicked until she discovered how to turn on the wipers. Flipping on what seemed like the right switch, she was relieved when the windshield cleared her view with one wide swish of the wipers. The cold, cloudy air had left the windows somewhat misty with bits of ice, and fresh descending snow immediately covered the glass after each sweep of the wipers.

Ellie began to cry again when she realized she could barely see two yards in front of the car because of the blizzard. With tears continuing to fill her eyes hindering her view even more, she tried to control her sobbing enough to put the car in drive. With the gear in place she gently pressed down on the gas pedal, and the car slowly moved forward out of the parking spot. Turning into the street, she spoke softly to herself, "Turn on the lights and press the defrost button . . . Oh Dad! . . . I pray you're still alive. Please help my dad, God. Only you can save him."

Moving onto the main road, confusion overcame her, "Did I do the right thing when I left my dad in the restaurant without waiting for help to arrive? I was unscathed, but my father and Mr. McCoy and I think even the waiter were shot by that dreadful madman."

Her thoughts were jumbled as she thought about whether she should have stayed, but in a flash she was reminded of what her father's last instructions were before she ran from the horrendous site. "Run, Ellie, Run."

Driving slowly, she recalled all that her father said. Plainly he had told her the man might possibly be after her because she saw his face. Her throbbing memory also reminded her, "I was told to drive straight to Grandma's house where Mom is staying because she will know what to do."

For only a moment she considered making a dash home first to gather up some items she might need for the trip, but she reasoned that was completely out of the question. "No, Dad clearly said to drive to Grandma's."

She would do exactly what her father had said. Nothing more. Nothing less. Then just as Ellie turned the corner and her mind was settled about what she must do, reality hit her. Her quiet whimpers became a full cry, "Oh, no! Grandma's house is more than 500 miles from here."

Chapter 7

RAY WAS BREATHING HEAVILY when he reached Owen's car. Jumping inside he said, "It's done. They've both been shot along with a waiter. You can be sure my boss will not be passing on any information about those drugs. Possibly he said something to his wife or maybe someone else, but what can anyone do if it's only hearsay and they don't have proof. The proof is dead. It's done. I'm going to get over to my truck now and drive home. This is one bad night to be out on these roads."

Owen had been careful when he parked his Mercedes-Benz earlier so he would be able to see the front of the restaurant and also Ray as he entered and left the place, but at a distance far enough away to not be noticed by anyone in the neighborhood. Listening intently to every word Ray spoke, Owen had continued looking in the direction of the restaurant. Someone had come out of the building and was moving through the snow. It was dark and the white snow was heavier than earlier, but he was sure he saw the figure of a woman getting into a parked car only a short distance away.

Owen's usual handsome face took on the appearance of dark gloom as he watched the car pull out of the parking space and onto the street moving toward the main road. He had seen two cars pull up earlier. One was Kurt McCoy's car, and the other had been occupied by a man and woman. It had confused him at the time because Ray told him an attorney would arrive. He was not sure it was the attorney who had arrived. From a distance it looked to him like a couple had arrived. He had been watching but unable to see everything because of the heavy snowfall. His sharp eyes were now pinned on a car that was about to turn the corner and would soon be out of sight.

Just as Ray was about to open the door to leave, Owen began thinking what the person who had left in that car could possibly suggest, and the thought was not at all pleasant to him. "Ray, was it possible a woman witnessed the shooting? And what if that woman saw everything?" Owen was pointing in the direction of the restaurant.

Ray had already turned and was about to step out of the car as he said, "Later Owen, we'll get together later to talk . . ."

Enraged Owen interrupted him as he grabbed Ray by the sleeve of his coat and turned to stare directly at him. Owen emphasized each word as he asked with a sneer, "Was anyone else in that restaurant, Ray? Anyone at all?"

There was silence as Ray began thinking for an uncomfortable moment. Then staring into fierce eyes, he did not miss any of Owen's threatening words. Knowing the man demanded an answer, Ray hesitated and was unable to respond because of Owen's menacing stare.

Becoming impatient with the delay, Owen asked the same question again in a hateful tone, "Was anyone else inside that restaurant when you were there, Ray? Did you happen to miss someone? A woman maybe?"

Taking another long moment to answer, Ray took a deep breath as he straightened his body and clenched his fists. He looked out the window at the vacant spot where the mystery car had been parked. Then agitated with Owen, he answered in a failing voice, "There was a young kid, only a girl, but her dad told her to leave and go into the bathroom before I shot anyone. She didn't see me shoot anybody, Owen. I'm sure of that. That kid didn't see a thing! Honestly, she didn't see anything!"

Unsure he could trust Ray's explanation, Owen raised his voice as he pressed Ray with the one more obvious question, "But, did she see you, Ray? Did she see your face at all, at any time, once you were inside?"

Managing to get his mind around what Owen was asking, Ray became nervous and confused. He had been drinking and could not unscramble all that had happened in those few minutes he was in the restaurant. He thought, Now after pushing drugs for months and doing exactly what this man told me to do, I'm being hounded by his insistent questions.

Again the question was shouted, but now by a furious man, "Ray, did that girl ever see your face?"

Closing his eyes and under tremendous pressure Ray replied out of fear, "Yes, Owen, she probably did. Hey, I never thought there'd be a kid in that restaurant tonight."

Thinking for a few moments Owen barked an order, "Think, Ray, think! You're telling me that girl saw your face. Go slowly over everything with me, Ray. Tell me everything that happened tonight inside that place. I'm not sure you know all that did take place. I don't believe you fully understand what trouble both you and I could be in if that girl isn't found or lives to tell the police what happened. If she goes to the authorities, we're in one huge heap of trouble."

As Ray continued trying to recall all that had taken place, he dropped his head and said, "I'm sure she was the lawyer's kid. She was told to go into the bathroom, but I told you she left when her dad told her to go into the bathroom. I didn't see her again, and I didn't see her come out."

Dreadful thoughts of being caught by the police were speeding through Owen's head before he shouted in anger, "RAY, that girl you saw inside was probably the same person we saw drive away less than a minute ago in what must have been her dad's car. You're an absolute idiot Ray! You have no idea what a jam you've placed us both in."

Breathing heavily and then allowing a moment to calm down in order to think, Owen silently reasoned, Would the kid go home to her mother? Or is it possible she would know enough to go to the police? Did the lawyer and mother live together? There could be so many other possibilities. I've got to find out and make sure that girl never has an opportunity to be questioned by the police. She's merely a dumb kid after all, and she'll probably be easy to find and take care of. I've got to first of all find out where she lives because she could bring an end to my lucrative drug business if she's somehow able to escape.

Furious with how it all happened, he struck Ray with the back of his hand and swore as he yelled, "I know she's just a kid, but that lawyer's kid could ruin us. You're brainless! We could land in jail for a very long time! JAIL, Ray!"

Taking another deep breath, Owen asked more calmly, "Do you have any idea how these two men would know each other?"

Stumbling over some of his words Ray weakly said, "I think both the McCoy and Wallace families attend the same church. When I was at Kurt's station this evening, the church was mentioned. I happen to know the McCoy family attends Overbrook Community Church." Ray was immediately sorry he had given Owen that bit of information.

For now that was all Owen wanted to deal with, "Let's find out where the attorney lives, Ray, and maybe we'll get some answers. Hang around Ray because we may need each other. I'll be in touch. Stay close. Don't even think about leaving town for any reason. Now go home. Understand?"

Looking out into the hazy darkness of the neighborhood, Owen could see an elderly man open his front door. The man stood at his doorway turning his head in both directions to see where the noise had come from. Uncomfortable with the icy winter chill and snow swirling around in every direction, he then quickly ducked back inside where it was warm. Owen realized they should not spend any more time near the scene to arouse attention. The police would soon arrive, and it definitely would be risky if anyone wondered why an unfamiliar car was parked in the area, especially once they are made aware of a shooting.

With his head down, Ray sullenly slipped out to return to his truck. Owen quickly turned on his motor and quietly pulled out onto the street. He headed in the same direction as the car he was concerned about. He was assured Ray would heed his threatening words while he set his mind to discover a way to locate the girl.

Chapter 8

THE UNMISTAKABLE SOUND of an approaching siren caught Owen's full attention. He realized too late that he had not asked Ray to return his gun because he was already in his truck and was moving in the opposite direction. He knew he would not be able to follow the car he had seen pull away only minutes ago either, but he knew the make and model.

A police car was now moving quickly toward him, but Owen slowly continued driving in the opposite direction. He saw the flashing lights of an ambulance in the distance. He could catch up with Ray tomorrow and retrieve his gun after he collected drug money tonight from a few other dealers. He first needed a little time to gather information about the lawyer Ray had shot. He would have plenty of time within the next few days to have a nice business talk with Ray.

"You'll pay for your careless actions, Ray! I knew you'd been drinking before we met this evening, and now you'll go home and fall asleep in no time forgetting everything you've done. You're an absolute LOSER!"

He needed a brief amount of time to think up a plan to find the girl. The fact that she had been sent to the women's room during the incident complicated things. This unpredictable kid troubled him. He was unable to release her from his mind. He blurted out, "She slipped away far too easily. That woman I saw getting in the car had to be the lawyer's kid just like Ray said. Her dad was smart telling her to hide in the restroom, but she would've definitely seen the dead bodies on her way out of the joint. I'm beginning to think Ray was more than drunk and careless. He's a completely incompetent idiot."

Then as he pounded his dashboard twice with his fist, he contemptuously said, "You're a BLOCKHEAD, RAY! That kid possibly called 911 and ran home to tell Mommy. We're going to get all the facts because I'm not getting caught up in this. I'll wring your neck, Ray, if I have to, but I'll get every fact out of you first. I'll pin you down until I'm satisfied with all your simple answers. I asked you to carry out a simple little job tonight, and you were inept. You'll never work for me again. NEVER! But you'll pay for tonight's sloppy job, Ray! You'll pay dearly!"

After venting his hostility, Owen attempted once again to calm himself, but another irritating thought stirred him, "What would happen if Ray is found by the police. Or worse, what if the guy should go to the police and turn himself in. All that alcohol he drank definitely clouded his mind."

For several minutes Owen was silent as he drove away from the area, but as other graver thoughts entered his mind, he swore voicing his disdain toward Ray, "Yes, my buddy, you and I will talk, but this will not destroy me. Give me a full day, Ray, and the two of us will have a little chat. That is, after I tend to that lawyer's brat."

Chapter 9

"WHY WERE MY FATHER AND MR. MCCOY shot?" Ellie asked after she realized she must turn the headlights to a brighter setting. For a mile she was unable to control either her emotions or her tears enough to release the vivid scene in her mind of her father and Mr. McCoy lying lifeless on the floor. As she moved into heavier traffic, the horrific picture emerged again. The fresh memory of the scene in the restaurant was so intense. The hideous reality of what had taken place only minutes earlier shook her, and knowing she could do nothing, she cried harder than she had ever cried in her life.

No one in the family was home to help her, and she was entirely alone to escape from the evil man. And throughout the night she would need to stay alert in order to cover hundreds of miles. She had to stick to that single task. Her father was counting on her to run from the restaurant because the shooter might return for her. The expression on the man's face had been terrifying, and she could not forget the hatred displayed in his eyes. She wondered if what she saw would leave a permanent imprint on her memory that might take years to forget.

Grasping the steering wheel with her fingers, Ellie tightened her grip. She was hindered from making much progress because of the sluggish city traffic in blinding blizzard conditions. Doubts continued to surface as she wondered if she should have stayed behind and waited. It was unbearable for her to consider she might have slipped out when her dad needed her most. This unrelenting conflict churned inside her, and each mile she drove would place her yet another mile away from her father. "Dad had been concerned about my safety, not his, when he told me to flee."

Remembering what she had witnessed was taking its toll on her ability to concentrate on the road ahead. Ellie was concerned with her dad's condition. "Will he make it?" In turmoil she prayed with her eyes open as she held onto the steering wheel and drove.

During her prayer she wondered about whether Mr. McCoy and the waiter were still alive. Would they live to go home to their families? The uncertainty whether she did the right thing by leaving her father behind, or if she should have remained, collided in her mind. Almost silently she asked God, "Why did this horrible thing happen? The awful look on the man's face when he looked at Mr. McCoy was ugly, and his slurred, offensive yelling was so crude. It was so terrifying! Please, God, be with me through the night, and mainly please save my dad's life." Ellie was aware that her prayers were beginning to give her mind peace, and her prayers were opening her mind to think more clearly.

She shook each of her hands separately for a few seconds to relieve the tension that had been building. Then repulsed again by what her mind would not release, she shook her head. Desperate for freedom from the mental images and intense pain that lingered, she gave into her anguish and sobbed loudly because she began feeling a type of guilt she had never experienced before.

She remembered when she was in the women's room trying on her new jacket, the new jacket that did not even matter to her now. Remembering how absorbed she was with herself and that wretched unnecessary jacket while only steps away her father was about to lose his life, she wept for minutes until her eyes became sore and puffy.

Straining to see the road ahead through the heavy snowfall and the clogged traffic, she prayed for the life of all three men, and especially for her father. She felt her muscles relax only long enough to reason that she must pull herself together and depend on God, so she could continue moving safely down the highway.

Calmly she uttered to herself, "I must recall what happened so I'll not forget any details. I heard three shots fired from a gun . . . and then I left the women's room and saw the three men lying on the floor. That terrible madman entered minutes before and staggered to our table. I was told to leave and go to the women's room. That man must have shot all of them because Mr. McCoy was getting advice from my dad. The reason he needed to talk to my dad had to do with drugs being sold at his station. That's the reason why my Dad told me to run. Could that man be nearby now? Is it somehow possible he could have followed me out of the restaurant?"

Suddenly Ellie got a tremendously scary thought. "What if he's behind me in a car, and he's tailing me?" Becoming fearful now for her own safety, she whispered, "God, please protect me as I try to escape from him . . . and, dear Lord, I'm pleading for my dad's life."

The incessant sobbing stopped for a brief interval when she heard the faint sound of a siren in the distance. "Emergency medical people must be arriving now to rescue my dad and the other men."

In seconds a faint smile appeared on her tear stained face. "Thank you, Lord, for allowing my dad to reach someone for help. And thanks for protecting me so far. I'm sure I'll be talking with you a lot tonight."

Mentally responsive, Ellie looked out the rearview mirror but was unable to see anyone following her as she crept along the snowy road. As she turned another corner and moved onto the wider main street that directed her toward Interstate 75, by instinct she checked the mirror again to see if anyone had made the same turn. No car was present. Applying more pressure on the gas pedal, her father's Chrysler immediately responded, and she began moving steadily down the dark street toward the highway. She glanced into all the surrounding mirrors to see if anyone was trailing behind her.

Reassured no one was following her, she relaxed as the car descended down the ramp and onto the Interstate. Without thinking, Ellie found herself taking one last peek into the rearview mirror. Sensing God was answering her prayers, and with her eyes glued to the road and traffic ahead, she prayed He would continue to be with her all the way to her grandmother's home. She then pleaded once again that her father would be alive and well when she was able to return home.

━━►◆◄━━

Joe Wallace's car was unfamiliar to his daughter. Ellie's body didn't fill the driver's seat. Her mother had always allowed her to use the compact car she drove to make short trips to the store or to go to a friend's home nearby. She was comfortable and familiar handling that car, but even then there were few times she drove further than several miles from home. Barely 17, she had only months ago received her driver's license. Driving her dad's larger car through the night and early morning hours on a 500-mile trip with icy snow falling around her and being such an inexperienced driver, she knew this trip would prove to be a tremendous challenge for her.

She was thankful there was less traffic than usual and that most drivers were already safely tucked away in their homes. Drivers on the road were moving steadily but more cautious than usual. Because of the wet blowing snow and because she was driving in big city traffic, Ellie would be extra cautious. Beginning to relax she attempted to give an impression to other drivers around her that she knew how to handle herself in such a big car. After all, she thought, I should be able to make this trip to Knoxville by myself. I'll be a high school senior in about eight months.

Diverting her attention to figure out how many hours it might take to reach her grandmother's home, she guessed it must be almost 550 miles. Not sure, she estimated she'd need to drive approximately eleven hours. Possibly it would take her more time to cover the miles if she had to drive too long on wet roads or if she had to make many stops. She would need to purchase gas, get a few quick bites and walk a bit to stretch her legs. She was sure that if she followed Interstate 75 all the way, she would always have good roads.

On many occasions through the years she had traveled this route with her parents, but she never had been the driver. During those trips she had never been interested enough to pay attention to the towns along the roadway. Those trips were taken late in the summer, and she usually was engrossed in a book or magazine. Sleeping in the back seat was her usual way of shortening those trips. Occasionally she might glance out a window and notice where they were, but her parents always took care of all the travel details for her. They had also included some fun on the trip. Tonight she would make the trip completely alone without any help. She would need to be alert and observe the speed limits. She would be required to read every important sign along the highway. She knew this would definitely not be a fun trip. In fact this would be an entirely different kind of trip for her. She told herself, I've got to pay close attention and stay awake tonight.

Small patches of black ice were clinging to the pavement beneath the tires, but there was not the slightest twist of her father's heavy car as she drove at a controlled speed. Remembering her driver's education class from the previous year, she knew she had to turn her wheel in either the right or left direction depending on which way a patch of packed, slippery ice might send her. Hopefully she would not hit any large icy spots below the fresh snow or have any tire problems. She would stay in the right lane until she felt safe enough to move into the passing lane if she had to move around a slow driver.

Her father had put the snow tires on only weeks ago, something she thought at the time seemed silly to her, but she was grateful he had taken the precaution of being prepared for slick icy roads. Every time she thought of her father, Ellie was thankful for having such a great dad. Attempting to reassure herself she thankfully said, "Tonight my dad is in God's hands."

She began recalling times when she thought her parents were paranoid about theft prevention by locking their car doors and their house at night. Medical and dental checkups, good nutrition, enough exercise and accident prevention were important measures to them. Maintaining good health was an ongoing subject at the dinner table. Also accepting responsibilities around the house, attending church regularly, helping needy causes, contributing to missionary work around the world, staying alert in school, and getting a good night's sleep were all fair game at mealtime.

Tonight Ellie was beginning to understand better why her parents were concerned about those things. They loved her, and as she remembered some events of her youth, she was conscious of the unconditional love that had often been expressed toward her. With her mother in Knoxville tonight and her father hopefully now being cared for in one of the city hospitals, she would miss being assured of their love. Tonight she would not have the luxury of getting a good night's sleep in her cozy, warm bed either. At the moment, in spite of her unsettling situation and the bitter cold air around her, she wanted most of all to be assured her father was receiving the best possible care.

Once she was out of the heavier traffic and moving into the state of Ohio, she remembered how her father usually kept his fuel tank above the halfway mark and was uneasy if it read less than one-quarter of a tank. Aroused by that memory, her eyes fell immediately down to the gas gauge. Relieved to see it was above the halfway mark, Ellie gratefully thought, Thanks Dad for what you taught me about watching the gas gauge. I'll keep my eyes on it as well as the road even though I never had to think about any of this stuff before.

A temporary plan entered her mind. She would drive south until the gauge read closer to one-quarter of a tank. She would begin looking for an all-night filling station. That would be an excellent time to get out a map showing the major towns she needed to travel through. Having made a tentative plan, she was sure she would not have to worry about stopping to get gas for at least another one hundred miles. She flipped on the radio to listen to news or music to help her stay alert. She smiled as she was beginning to gain confidence in her driving.

Chapter 10

AFTER DRIVING MORE THAN 125 MILES Ellie looked out the right side window into the darkness that engulfed her. Completely beyond the Toledo area and heading south through Ohio with all its massive farms, she was aware that the snowfall had stalled. It had left behind a diffused, frosted appearance, and the moon illuminated the beautiful wintry scene below. Through the misty crispness a fluffy white covering of bright snow could be seen everywhere, and in the distance tall stately trees cast dark shadows over the wide open fields.

Huge farm homes, barns and other buildings came into view. The fields used for growing corn and other crops in the warm seasons were now filled with fresh snow, and unusually high drifts could be seen at the sides of the highway as she sped along. Only hours previously interesting sculptures had been in the process of being formed by the strong prevailing wind.

Now an eerie quietness lay over the land, and it was that time of night when rural families would be in bed. Lights along the road were becoming scarce, and the frosted air cast a somewhat foggy appearance in front of each distant beam of light. The pavement below the car seemed to disappear into the night as Ellie kept her foot on the gas and her eyes glued to the highway.

Hours passed and few cars moved along this major highway. Still in Ohio, a state she would be driving in for many hours, Ellie caught sight of a sign that listed a small town she would approach within 22 miles. It was satisfying to be reassured that a town was nearby as she breathed a sigh of relief. She would not drive into the town but was assured that she was making progress and moving closer to Grandma Russell's home.

As the miles mounted on the odometer, Ellie was aware of how completely alone she would remain in the darkness on her long journey. Feeling the drain on her body both emotionally and physically, she knew those hundreds of miles yet ahead would be an exercise of endurance for her.

Within the next 50 miles the roads became clear of moisture, and there was only a scant amount of snow lying in clumps along the roadway. With the headlights beaming onto the pavement in front of her, she could see that no additional snow was falling. Hopefully it would be clear for the rest of her trip and she would not run into a single problem.

Moving toward her grandmother's house where her mother would be waiting, Ellie whispered as she reminded herself with a smile, "With every mile I drive, I'll be one mile closer to you, Mom."

Ellie turned the temperature down a notch after realizing she had been driving for the last hour too warm to be completely alert. She was so caught up in the terrible scene in the restaurant and then the fear of someone following her that she forgot about setting the temperature cool enough to be safe at the wheel. Within minutes the car began cooling off, and her head felt better.

With her jacket wrapped around her, she thought about her favorite new sweatshirt that had been left behind in the restroom along with her warm coat while she was admiring herself in the new jacket thinking about how she might impress her friends. Briefly glancing down at it, she murmured, "It's a tear stained mess now. This skimpy turtleneck doesn't help much."

Looking in the mirror to check her face, she could see her stained eyelids and cheeks, which had been smeared from the black substance in her mascara that had run down her cheeks while she was crying, "Oh well, I'll fix myself up when I stop for fuel and a tiny snack."

Again reaching for the radio, Ellie began pressing the knobs and various buttons to listen to some music. Anything to stay alert, she thought, but nothing caught her interest so she turned it off. Soon she was hearing only the steady humming of the motor, which was soothing but monotonous. "This will be one long, solitary night."

Ellie took several deep breaths, wiggled her shoulders and neck and soon began feeling some of her tight muscles relaxing. She thought of her mother and reached for her cell phone to place a call. "She's probably in bed and wouldn't hear the buzzing of her cell anyway."

Laying her phone back near her purse she decided not to try to make the call since the frightening news would only cause her mom to worry for hours throughout the night not knowing her husband's condition. "Besides, talking to anyone would be a distraction when I should be paying attention to my driving. If I tell Mom what happened, she'd feel helpless and cry wanting to know even more than I could tell her. Not until morning, Mom," Ellie spoke gently, "I need to keep my eyes on the road, but I'll call you first thing in the morning. I promise, and hopefully I'll hear about Dad by then. Sleep well, Mom. I love you and Dad more than I ever realized."

Her mind again returned to her father. She was sure that siren meant her dad was being cared for by capable people. They would be giving him life-saving emergency care immediately. They would take him straight to the nearest hospital. They will check his cell phone and discover who he is. Aloud she said, "Since I have his wallet, he doesn't have any identification on him, but I know it's stored in his cell phone."

Looking ahead at the road and without closing her eyes, Ellie wanted to be assured her father was alive. She prayed for him as well as Mr. McCoy and the waiter. She prayed for the emergency men and women, the doctors, the nurses who would be on duty and others assigned to do necessary surgery during the late night hours. Mr. McCoy was someone whom she had known her entire life, and she recalled how he and his wife especially had encouraged her to look to God for guidance every day. Sadly she murmured, "Will this truly kind woman hear bad news tonight?"

At this lonely early morning hour Ellie wished she could talk to her mother. "If only Ned had been home and could have taken this trip with me. If either he or Mom had been home, they could have made sure Dad was well cared for." Her eyes were wet again.

Ellie reached inside her pocket to feel for her dad's wallet. After more than 170 miles she decided to pull into a well-lit truck stop. She would ask one of the truckers if he knew how many miles it was to the Tennessee state line. Cautiously she locked the car, dropping the car keys safely into the pocket of her jacket and walked toward the food store.

After getting a can of Coke, she approached a kind looking man who was on his way back to his truck. Without even thinking he said, "Miss, it's just less than 320 miles from here."

After thanking him, Ellie walked back to the store. In a corner she took out her father's wallet and counted his money. She also fingered several of the credit cards along with three $5 bills. Purchasing food with the cards might be somewhat tricky if someone looked at her father's signature or his picture. She knew she would not fool anyone if she tried using one of his cards. At that late hour, she was experiencing a strong aversion just thinking about eating. Ellie was not hungry, and food definitely was not what she wanted as she was reminded of the horrific site she witnessed hours earlier. But she imagined she might be ready to eat anything that was placed in front of her by mid-morning. She was cold but began drinking the Coke anyway as she filled up the gas tank. Returning to the road was all she wanted.

The driver's seat had not been in the correct position to be comfortable for almost 170 miles. Making necessary adjustments now while she was stopped seemed to be a good idea. She would then be able to reach the petals better for the remainder of the trip. Her legs were a few inches shorter than her father's, and her right leg had been straining at times to stay on the gas pedal. The setting for her dad's headrest was placed in an awkward position also. Somehow she had concentrated on keeping her mind on driving safely and not on the nagging ache that was beginning in a central region in the back of her neck.

As Ellie made necessary adjustments, she wondered if she could stay awake to drive all night since she was already feeling drowsy. Driving for an entire night would certainly be a first for her, but the Coke should begin to help. The only time she tried to stay up all night was during a sleep over at a friend's house. Even then she fell asleep sometime after three in the morning while some of the girls were still talking. She would stay awake tonight by reminding herself for each mile she traveled, she would be one mile closer to her destination. She would not be able to do anything about her thoughts drifting off to those horrible twenty minutes or so spent at the restaurant, but she was determined to follow her father's instructions and reach Knoxville by morning. She was aware her father's words, "Run, Ellie, Run" had deeply penetrated her mind and would continue to reenter her thoughts.

⸻

After another 100 miles with her tired eyes glued to the highway, Ellie desperately needed a break. In the darkness she had been moving slightly over to the left lane from time to time as the dividing line began hypnotizing her. Locating an exit where she could fill up the gas tank again, she focused on reading the various signs as she headed up the ramp. She pulled the car into the brightest parking area she could find, turned off the motor and took hold of her handbag. Again she was reminded to place the car keys carefully inside her jacket pocket to make sure she did not lock herself out of the car. That little mistake could be a disaster for her. Making careful mental notes as she stepped out of the car, she pressed the button on the key to lock the doors and then placed the car keys safely back into her pocket.

She walked into the convenience store to purchase a bottle of water and something salty to eat. Deep in the bottom of her handbag she found her wallet and counted out $9.33. Reaching into her pocket, she took out her father's wallet and grabbed two of the five dollar bills and the credit cards she might need for the duration of the trip. She would hold onto the rest of the cash as best she could and use her dad's credit cards for purchasing gas at the pumps. Purchasing even small items of food with one of the cards would be questionable to an attendant. Precautions were important for the remainder of her trip.

Ellie walked into the women's room to use their toilet. Glancing at herself in the mirror, she gasped as she saw someone she hardly recognized. A disheveled young girl with a pale, strained face stared back at her. Her matted hair gave her a slovenly appearance, and the black smears of mascara from crying were messy under her bloodshot eyes. No one could see her so she moistened a rough brown paper towel and cleaned her face as best she could. Without having a comb or hair brush, several strokes of wet fingers were used to smooth her hair. She looked better but was still a sight.

She almost began to cry, but she smiled at her face instead satisfied that basically she had improved her face and hair. Noticing the obvious strain in her face, she thought of what she had been able to accomplish in the past six hours. Crying and driving alone through the darkness with the cold air continuing to whirl around her had given her a stressed appearance. Wondering about her father's condition had left her helpless, and her sobbing had been intermingled with bouts of worry. She had prayed often thanking God for protecting her, and she asked him to continue watching over her.

Ellie presented a big toothy smile to the stranger staring at her from the mirror, "I'll finish this trip no matter how exhausted I become, but I need your help, God. Guide me and please keep me awake."

She paid dearly for a bottle of water, a bag of peanuts and a chocolate candy bar with one of her father's $5 bills and decided to run back to the car for a bit of exercise. In less than ten minutes she swallowed most of the water, ate the entire bag of peanuts and took three bites of the candy bar. She was anxious to get on the road and head south again in the direction of Knoxville.

"I need to move while I'm awake. I'll try to drive all night and during part of the morning if necessary. I'm on my way, Mom, and will see you soon. Talking out loud seems to keep my eyes open and my mind alert."

Ellie left the station in a hurry, but in the rush, she did not realize she had taken a side road, which was headed in the wrong direction. Fifteen minutes later she was aware of her mistake. "Oh, No! Somehow I think I'm traveling north instead of south."

Chapter 11

CAROLINE WALLACE WAS NOT SLEEPING WELL
tonight, so she slipped out of bed, walked into her mother's
bedroom to check on her. Two days ago her mother was
too sick to get out of bed, but since that episode her
mother had made a good turn and seemed to be feeling
much better. She was not experiencing any more nausea or
fever. Only a slight headache remained. Standing at
Maddie's bedside, Caroline could hear the gentle sound of
rhythmic breathing. Without question, her mother was
better and on the mend. "She certainly doesn't seem to
have any trouble sleeping." Caroline would get herself a
drink of water and go back to bed.

They had talked that evening about her leaving for
home in the morning, and since her mother agreed and
appeared to be back on her feet feeling good in every way,
Caroline felt comfortable leaving at an early hour. Maddie
said she was needed more at home with Joe and Ellie than
nursing an old woman. Encouraged Caroline had said with
a smile, "You won't find me around in the morning."

She was excited to be going home. Sure both Joe and
Ellie would be glad to have her home, she would need to
get a good night's sleep if she were to travel the entire
distance from Knoxville to her home in one day.

For almost an hour sleep was impossible, and, since it
was only minutes after eleven, Caroline slipped into the

bathroom to take a sleep inducer before laying her head back on the pillow. Although her body was ready to rest, her mind was stirred by the excitement of going home. Her thoughts were of Joe and Ellie. Thankful to God for giving her such a devoted husband, she knew Joe loved her. He had been the only man she ever truly loved. Although his work was very important to him, it took second place to her and their children. Caroline sighed, "Wow, am I blessed!"

Her father and mother had been praying for her long before Joe and she had met. Before Joe entered her life, she regularly had been dating another young man. Fully aware of how infatuated Caroline was with the man who they considered a poor match for their daughter, her parents cautiously hinted she should go to college first for a couple of years. Time they knew might change her feelings about hurrying into a marriage with the man she was then dating.

After considering this arrangement for a week, Caroline took their advice, and within months she met Joe Wallace when he was a university senior and considering law school. She dated a few other men, but had not been interested in any of them.

Their meeting happened one rainy October evening during Caroline's sophomore year. Joe and she met in the college library. Caroline was gathering information for an English class term paper, and Joe was doing research for an assigned history of law project. As he hurriedly removed his soaked coat and was eager to get to the upper level where the books he needed would be found, he noticed Caroline sitting at his usual table concentrating on her studies. Knowing he had to finish his project within three days, he left for the second floor.

Unable to concentrate because he wanted to meet the girl that had caught his attention, he grabbed four books he might need and returned quickly to the table. Relieved she was still seated across from his usual spot, he sat down and began glancing in her direction. After several obvious stares, Caroline became a bit irritated with him. But after a short time she looked at him and offered a small smile. No words were exchanged, but for days Caroline had a difficult time releasing him from her thoughts. He had invaded her life without her ever knowing it. For days she wondered if she would ever see him again. She realized she would not even recognize his name if she heard it spoken by someone. Because she thought about him, she had a difficult time concentrating in a few of her classes.

One evening when they again caught a glimpse of each other in the library, Joe awkwardly, but intentionally moved from one end of his usual table to sit directly across from her. At the time she thought it might be unintentional, but he hurriedly scrawled out a note on a small corner of a sheet of paper and slipped it over to her side of the table.

The note read, "Would you like to go with me Saturday afternoon to a matinee?" With an amused smile, Caroline answered in a library whisper, "Yes, I need to escape for a couple of hours sometimes." Gathering her bag and materials to leave, Joe caught up with her outside the building and introduced himself.

Her previous male friend was a thing of the past. Within weeks Joe and she were finding small amounts of time to spend with each other. There were phone calls, short walks across the campus and quickly planned meetings. Anything to be together. Although Joe's finances were limited and he needed to watch his expenses in order to attend law school within another year, they managed to set aside times to meet.

Reminding herself of those times was always delightful to her, and especially tonight. Well after midnight she began thinking about Ellie too. Almost asleep she mumbled, "They're both sound asleep by now." As often was the case, Caroline missed her family when she was away from home. At this late hour her desire was to get a sufficient amount of sleep for her long trip home, but pleasant thoughts continued to creep through her mind.

Joe gave more time than most husbands or fathers to his family, and he even expressed to his law partners that his work did not take precedence over the most significant areas of his life. Some evenings he was detained at his law office and would come home weary, and on those occasions he only had enough time to get ready for bed. At times Caroline did wish he could spend more time with her, but she had no reason to complain. Joe had proven to be a loving, thoughtful husband and a great dad.

Caroline had learned years ago she did not own her husband's time or his life, but as a family they would make the most of their limited time together. Extremely responsible at his work, there were times when he ran the entire practice in which he was presently one of the senior partners. He brought in more repeat clients than the others partly because he was genuinely interested in people. His expertise in writing and administering wills was exceptional, and he was known to have a soft heart since it was impossible for him to turn someone down when they truly needed him. Both his patience and hard work were the keys to his success.

Reflecting on his relationship with their three children, Caroline remembered those times when Joe and Ned planned fishing trips together traveling to Northern Michigan at times to see who might catch the largest fish. Their oldest child Shelly had been an easy child in every way. Six years ago, after graduating with a degree in engineering, she married Rick. He was a career military man, and they left within months after their wedding day to live in England where his military career took them. From their frequent emails, they seemed to be making plenty of new friends and loving life together there. The marriage had caught Caroline and Joe off guard and happened all too quickly. They wondered if Shelly and Rick would ever return to live in the States? Would she and Joe be able to see the grandchildren often enough?

Somehow tonight their youngest and most precocious child was Caroline's concern. Recently Ellie's future had overpowered her thoughts because of her consuming desire to be the best dressed kid among her peers. She knew this needed to change for Ellie's good. But how? She and Joe could no longer ignore their daughter's pattern of behavior and her attitude of constantly wanting more than she had. Caroline recently had been reminding herself she must not regard this subject as off limits.

Joe was good at grasping Ellie's moods and looking squarely at her temperament before making rash judgments about what they ought to say to her. Joe was Ellie's hero, though Caroline had never heard that fact put into words by her daughter. Caroline wondered if once Ellie graduated and left home for university, would she possibly meet and marry a good man and move away also. Would that close and secure relationship between Joe and Ellie remain?

From time to time they had made it a point to sit down and talk with Ellie, but Caroline knew they should do it more often. Much was accomplished when Joe and she discussed with Ellie her desire of always wanting more, but they somehow had not made much progress lately.

Caroline turned onto her side, and after taking two deep breaths she was ready to sleep. Her last thoughts were that her mother had improved in the last 24 hours and no longer needed her. "Thank you, Lord. She is much better. I can now return home in the morning to be with

Joe and Ellie, and I'll leave as early as possible," she mumbled. "I'm needed more at home than I am here. Six or even sooner should be a good time to pack the few things I brought with me and leave." Before she drifted off into a deep untroubled sleep, she muttered, "What would I do without my Joe?"

<hr />

Molly McCoy was sitting at her dining room table weeping over the news that her husband had died before reaching the hospital. Distraught and without knowing how it all happened, she asked, "Why him, Lord? He was a wonderful husband, a great father and a friend to so many."

Hours earlier two policemen had knocked on her door to give her the news, and she was still in shock. One officer had offered to stay with her if she wished, but bravely she said she would make a call to her son who lived nearby. She told them she also had a sister who lived less than 60 miles away.

Sitting at the dining room table she remembered how Kurt had called late in the afternoon telling her he would be late and not to wait on him for dinner because he had to take care of some urgent business. From what the police had said, Kurt must have been having a quick bite with someone at the restaurant they mentioned. They said another man was with him, and he was shot along with a waiter from the restaurant.

In tremendous grief, Molly banged her fists on the table and wailed as she gave up trying to control her pain, "Why Kurt? Why would anyone shoot him and those two men? Kurt left this morning early, and that was the last time I'll ever see him alive. Oh Lord, help me, and help me know what to say when I call the kids . . .?"

Molly was unable to make the call for another 20 minutes because of her anguish. Sometime after midnight she recalled her son's number. Reaching him, he said he would be over in ten minutes. She unlocked her front door, returned to the table, dropped her head and collapsed crying again.

When her son arrived, he cried as he comforted his mother. He told her he would call the hospital and find out if they would tell him who the other two men were that were taken in along with his dad. He was told to check with the police. Once he spoke to the policeman who was in charge, he was told that an attorney by the name of Joseph Wallace had also been shot and was found near Kurt's body along with a waiter who worked at the restaurant.

This new information was gently given to Molly. In her grief and fragile state, Molly remembered that Caroline had gone to visit her sick mother who lived in Tennessee. "What if she is still with her mother? Could Ellie be at home alone. What if . . .?"

Molly rose to her feet with the little energy remaining and managed to walk to her phone to place a call to the Wallace home. After listening to numerous rings and receiving no answer, she decided not to leave a message. She would continue trying to make calls throughout the night. She began thinking how Ellie was growing up quickly and then wondered if she would have been with her father. She said, "What a horrible thought! If she were there with the men, would the shooter have kidnapped her? When the police came to my door earlier, they said they were attempting to put the pieces together to find out what happened but said it might take time. Not a word was mentioned about a young girl. If Ellie was there with her father and actually saw what happened, would she have willingly gone with the man? No, but I'm quite sure her mom is not at home."

Frantic, she thought of what could have taken place as she looked at her son who was intently watching and listening. Molly cried, "Protect Ellie, Lord. Protect us all."

Chapter 12

AT 4:22 CAROLINE WALLACE AWAKENED. She dressed and packed the remaining items she had brought with her. Hastily snatching an apple from the refrigerator and grabbing a slice of Maddie's homemade bread, she entered her mother's bedroom to kiss her goodbye. Returning to the kitchen she seized her car keys and tossed them in her purse. A hot cup of coffee could easily be picked up along the road. It was earlier than she had planned to leave, but she was in a hurry to head for home.

In a rush she did not notice that she failed to pick up her cell phone and of course check for incoming calls. Thoughts of getting on the highway and being home by the time Ellie stepped off the school bus were driving her to get to her car. Maddie, her mother, had said only last night, "You need to be home with your lovely family. Remember, I'm always better after a visit from you. Now get on your way early tomorrow because you have a long drive ahead. I love you, dear, and you're completely welcome to come whenever you can. But make sure you bring Joe and Ellie with you on your next visit."

As Caroline reached the main highway directing her to Interstate 75, she was convinced the trip had been worthwhile. Within minutes she began thinking about her youngest daughter and how quickly she was becoming a woman, "She'll awake in about two hours and begin dressing for school." She sighed as she thought about Ellie being on her own. "It will happen all too soon for both Joe and me. Time to enter college will be here before we know it. In less than two years, we will once again face a child leaving home. There's so much I want to talk to Ellie about, and hopefully I can cover those things before she is on her own and making her own decisions. And there's still a slew of things I want to discuss with her."

Caroline was aware of Ellie's need for some good sound advice because she seemed so caught up in herself and purchasing stuff. Though seldom did she seem satisfied for any length of time with what she did buy.

Recently Caroline had regretted how they were pampering and over-indulging her when faced with soon having an empty nest. She knew Ellie tended to be prideful like most girls her age, always wanting another article of clothing, shoes galore, and all sorts of accessories. She thought about how she and Joe had been careless at times, often too tolerant of Ellie's whims.

Having always been a sensible woman who wanted the best for her daughter, Caroline knew things Ellie asked for were not what were best for her. "How can I help her realize that always obtaining the latest faddish item, buying that new thing or having more stuff will never satisfy her."

Caroline wished to look on the brighter side, "Ellie's pretty enough, attractive really, and that's always a bonus for a woman. She's smarter than I was at her age," Caroline confessed, "but she's constantly determined to always want something that may satisfy her. Yes, she's determined to get what she wants and extremely manipulative. In fact she's able to wind both of us around her finger, but we've got to manage her somehow and impress upon her to consider how this constant problem of needing more will in the end harm her."

She sighed as she reached Interstate 75 N. Her thoughts continued, "She's such a good kid but never has been placed in a situation where she needed to share, do without like her friend Brennie or be thoughtful for the sake of others. For her own good, Ellie must be helped, and Joe and I have got to put our heads together and find a solution for what could lead to destructive behavior for Ellie as she enters adulthood. This ability of hers to manipulate others could be her ruin."

Ellie's welfare had become extremely important to Caroline during the last year as she watched her daughter mature. She had been fearful of what the outcome might be if they began withholding things when she asked for more stuff and corrected her when they should. This troubled her, and she prayed quietly, "I'll be home soon, and I need You, Lord, to give Joe and me wisdom in what we must do for Ellie."

A simple prayer asking God for help was Caroline's habit, and now after praying, she was determined more than ever before to spend more time with her daughter. The time she had spent teaching her to drive had been fun as well as a good reminder to her how quickly Ellie was growing up and eager to be on her own. Yes, she would do more things with her, listen more attentively and talk to her about her greed. She and Joe together would talk tonight first and then with Ellie. They would come up with the best solution.

She crossed the Tennessee state line and was heading into the Blue Grass State keenly aware that once again she had left the state where she was born and reared. It had not been her home for approximately 26 years, and now moving through Kentucky, she was retracing the same route she had taken to visit her mother a week earlier. She was anxious to get home to Joe, Ellie and her busy life.

Caroline hoped to get the early news or music as she clicked on the radio, but with the noisy static that was much more prominent in the mountains, she turned it off. Traveling 65 to 70 mph she was leaving miles behind. She desperately needed a cup of coffee. Looking at her watch miles later she wondered if she should check on Ellie when she purchased the coffee. Thinking about the woman who faithfully arrived at her home three times each week to help her clean and cook she muttered, "Clara will make sure Ellie is up and gets to school."

As she reached for her handbag on the passenger seat, she instantly knew what she had forgotten at her mother's home, "Perhaps I placed it in my suitcase, but I don't think so. I hope I didn't leave it behind. What was on my mind?"

Digging deeper inside her purse, she was upset with herself, "Sure enough, in haste I forgot to pick it up. It was sitting right there on the kitchen counter plugged into an outlet. I could make a quick stop and call Ellie from a pay phone, but I'd lose at least 20 minutes or more making the call. Clara is good about waking her if she doesn't hear the clock radio. Driving back hundreds of miles to retrieve my phone is out of the question. Mom can use the phone since she doesn't have a cell phone of her own. I'll pick up a new one for myself. I just want to get home."

Leaving her cell phone had been a huge mistake.

Chapter 13

RAY VINSON SAT ALONE in the only chair he had in his tiny apartment and acknowledged to himself he'd made a total mess of his life. He intentionally did not turn on any lights, but sat in total darkness whimpering and making inarticulate sounds as his mind replayed what had taken place hours previously.

In darkness with guilt riddling his mind, he lifted his head and looked around his quarters and then down at his unsteady hands. Noticing the trembling, Ray knew these short jerky movements were not from the cold, harsh January wind outside his walls.

Desperately he tried to explain to Owen what he remembered taking place in the restaurant, but now he was resigned he must accept what he could not change. Owen would surely come looking for him if not tonight at least by early morning, and Ray was quite certain he would be found by a violent man full of rage. Reliving those few difficult minutes in Owen's luxury car, Ray remembered how the usual handsome face had become stony and threatening.

Owen had been unable to conceal his hateful anger and seemed to look deep into Ray's soul as he demanded answers. Desperately trying to push away the nagging thoughts and the visual image of Owen's furious face, Ray's body shook. He knew it was useless to rid his troubled mind of that loathsome face. He continued to make loud sobbing sounds.

All the happiness Ray had felt learning about running a business and the joy he received working at Kurt's place was forever gone. Tormenting laments crawled through his mind, but he knew regret would never undo the dreadful deed he had done. His head and stomach were beginning to ache as he cried.

Standing up and lifting his body, which seemed heavier than usual, Ray tried to shake off the haunting guilt. In his drunken state he actually had shot three men. He was stupid and did what Owen told him to do.

Walking to his window, he looked out into the stillness of the night. A sorrowful prayer boomed from his mouth, "Please, please God, forgive me for shooting those men."

He finally began thinking more clearly. Ray understood his most urgent need was his own safety. Obviously Owen was now his enemy. He must be freed from the grasp of this hostile foe.

With clarity and determination he spoke, "Owen is an intensely revengeful man! Because I fouled up his order to shoot everyone in the restaurant, I'm sure he'll soon be coming after me and won't have a single qualm about wiping me out. He's outright cruel!"

Torn between the fact that Owen had persuaded him to sell the drugs for extra money and that he was responsible for agreeing to the arrangement, he penitently cried out, "Oh God, please forgive me for what I did. I admit I shot and killed those three innocent men as I tried to hide my drug dealing. Because of my stupidity and the wrong I did, members of their families will suffer for the rest of their lives."

In tremendous fear, Ray asked God to punish him instead of allowing Owen to come after him and harm him. Not attempting to make excuses for himself, but somewhat relieved by confessing his sin, he climbed into his bed to hopefully fall asleep. Soon he found himself sobbing in bed too. He again was faced with his dreadful fear and guilt.

Exhausted from the strain of the day, he tightly closed his eyes trying to stop his heavy sobs. He had made several attempts to forget what had happened. He tried to sleep but found his mind would not allow him to rest or release the horrific event that continued to run through his head. If only for a short time he could forget the misery he caused hours earlier, he might be able to turn off his thoughts and sleep for a couple of hours. The attempts were all futile, and there was no way he could keep his eyes closed without picturing those evil penetrating eyes of Owen.

Time passed slowly, and he could hear late-hour traffic moving on the streets nearby, the regular droning sound of his second-hand clock radio, a dog barking in the distance, the occasional creaking sounds in his room, the whistling wind outside and icy sleet as it fell against the glass of his one window. No sleep came, and he knew he had taken a quick road to destruction. His life had changed, and he did not like his new life. Miserable, he was reminded that this was not a time to feel sorry for himself. He must think of those who lost their lives.

If he only had taken time to think, he possibly would not have killed anyone. He was a fool to listen and follow Owen's orders. Drinking had only blurred his senses. He cried, "I'm a wanted man now. How I wish I could live this day over. Being charged with peddling drugs would have been easier. If only I'd been caught and gone to jail for that."

He came to the final conclusion that Owen might mainly want to find the girl, and knowing he was the only one who could identify her, Ray thought of what he could say and do when Owen showed up at his door to ask about her. He knew Owen was a resourceful guy and thought it was possible the man might find out where she lived. He was sure Owen would stop at nothing to find her. Maybe the girl had gone home. What would Owen do if he found her? Ray shuddered.

Almost falling asleep, Ray found himself sweating even though the temperature in his apartment was only 60 degrees. It was freezing beyond his walls, but he was perspiring. Sleep would not come, and he began mumbling to himself, "I was weak and stupid to shoot my boss, a man who'd given me a good job and taken the time to teach me about the business. Kurt McCoy was one of the only real friends I ever had. Then I shot that lawyer too. He seemed only to be helping Kurt." Now feeling a chill he pulled up both blankets to warm himself.

"The waiter was only trying to make a decent living. Now I'm three times a murderer; I snuffed out all their lives. I did so much damage by killing them all in only a few seconds."

He pleaded for forgiveness again because he was in such mental anguish. He prayed that Owen would not be allowed to find the girl. Most of all Ray was sorry he ever had met Owen Wolf and that he agreed to deal drugs to make extra money. It meant absolutely nothing to him now.

In the darkest corner of his apartment he lay rubbing his arms as he spoke to the ceiling, "The man deserves to be dropped into a greasy, worm infested hole and left there. That's where he belongs. Jail would be too good for his kind. He deserves far worse."

With his trembling and whimpering intermingled, the gun he used popped into his mind. He thought of holding onto it because that was the only thing Owen would try to collect from him. It belonged to Owen. And hiding it might be the one thing that would keep him alive. Thoughts trailed off as he recalled how he was given the gun earlier in the evening in the car at Mike's, "I shouldn't have taken it from him. Hiding it now is the only protection I have. I'm trapped because Owen will look for me until he finds me and then ask where his gun is. I can say, it's safely hidden, and no one will ever find it." Weary, he concluded, "I'll find a good hiding place right away."

Believing he should not wait until early morning to decide, Ray jumped from his bed and hurried to retrieve the gun from the coat he wore to the restaurant, "He's so angry that I believe he'll kill me on the spot if I give it to him. I've got to stash it in a secret place now. But where?"

He was staring at his refrigerator, and the idea instantly came to him, "Neither Owen nor the police will find it there." Holding the gun in his hand, he placed the gun on safe to prevent the firearm from discharging. Reaching behind the refrigerator as far as his arm could stretch, he located the place where he wanted the gun to land. He could feel the tight area against the wall. The old coils in the back hindered his hand from reaching very far, but he was sure he could manage and have barely enough room to hold onto the gun while he dropped it. With great care he aimed it toward the spot on the floor that seemed in line with his hand. The heavy metal object fell with a dull thud. "You'll not be found for years," he said as if he were speaking to the gun. It had fallen in the spot he intended, and Ray sighed confident this was the best he could do.

With his thoughts trailing off to what he must do next, he returned to his bed to think about his predicament. He reasoned how easy it would be for Owen, a calculating killer, to get rid of him here in this apartment. He would have no conscience about ending any life that threatened him. Even without the gun being returned, Owen might not hesitate, but he would find a way to keep him quiet. Ray mumbled a few additional words of comfort to himself as his mind finally gave into the only brief amount of sleep he would have.

After what must have been merely minutes, Ray's eyes opened with a jolt. He thought someone was standing directly over him. He broke out in a cold sweat trying to visualize or hear movement. Then as he lay there hardly breathing, he realized he was alone and that his fear of Owen had entered his mind with such force that it had awakened him. The fixed glare and the look of rage he remembered on Owen's face had brought him to consciousness. The conclusion that he must flee to get out of the man's grasp once again loomed in his mind.

Owen's terrifying demanding glare was something too hard for Ray to shake when he had stammered trying to answer the man's questions about the shooting and whether the girl had seen his face. Ray knew he was not satisfied with the way things had turned out and especially that a mere kid could be on the loose and might be a witness to the crime. "Will he be skillful enough to find her? I'm sure he will be."

He decided to stay in his apartment only until early morning and then leave to find a place where he could feel safe. If he could even go to a homeless shelter, he would be out of Owen's reach until he could think of a way to escape. The dreadful thought of being caught in his apartment was beginning to tear away his hope of holding onto his life. Lingering here was definitely too risky, and almost any place where people were present would be better. Seeing himself as a fugitive, he began thinking like one.

He considered the alternative of turning himself in to the authorities and ratting on Owen. He despised the man and hated himself for being stupid enough to listen to him. Ray realized he was exhausted mainly from fear, from his remorseful thoughts and not knowing what he should do, but he must come up with the best possibility because Owen would definitely come for him. At last still awake in the wee hours of the morning, he decided what he must do.

At the first hint of dawn, Ray slipped into his shoes, pulled his blankets up to cover his bed and reached into his tiny closet for his duffle bag. Placing one change of clothing along with a pair of boots and clean socks inside the bag, he put on his coat and walked to his door. He was about to leave when he thought of the money he had placed under his sink and hurriedly went there to retrieve it. Rapidly counting most of the bills, he rolled up at least $4,500 tightly and stuffed it all into two of his socks. He shoved the socks into the bottom corner of his duffle. In an unforeseen emergency he might need the money to get out of town. If someone should happen to see it, it would become a big temptation to steal it. For now he would deal with his major problem, but he must find a place to stay alive.

⟫◆⟪

Ray would rest in this homeless shelter for the remainder of the day and leave when darkness came. The caretakers at the shelter had only asked him a few insignificant questions that were easy for him to answer and then welcomed him inside as they handed him a towel, washcloth, soap and toothbrush.

Purposely placing his duffle bag under the thin pillow they gave him, Ray stretched out on the flimsy mattress. Even in a comfortable position it was difficult to sleep with all the noisy activity going on around him. With his tired swollen eyes closed, the memory of what he had done crashed back into his mind. He remembered the look of surprise on all three faces of the men he shot, and he recalled the booming sounds as he fired. But Owen's fierce eyes glaring at him when he was told there was a young girl inside the women's room disturbed him most. "Will I ever be able to get any peace again?"

He was sure of one thing. Ultimately Owen was after the girl. Finally he vowed to himself that there would not be another person destroyed because of what he did. Tears flowed, but Ray thought, "In a homeless place like this, where many were lonely and heartbroken, no one notices a newcomer overcome with sadness. After all, it was common to be hopeless here." His future was bleak, and his face displayed that bleakness to everyone around him.

Unable to fall asleep because he had that huge chunk of money hidden under his pillow, Ray sat up and looked around. He considered the only plausible alternative he had. He could run, he could hide as he was doing now, and finally run again, or he could go to the police.

In the end the authorities would hunt him down until they found him, and he would be placed in jail. It would pay to turn himself in now and tell the police everything. That way he would not be hounded by both Owen and the law. At least he could make an effort to save one person who was in danger, that young innocent kid who just happened to be in the wrong place last night with her dad. Unable to think of another solution to his misery, Ray made his decision.

Chapter 14

ELLIE GLANCED in the direction of the digital clock on her father's dashboard. It read 4:18 a.m., and both her body and mind were thoroughly drained after an endless night of steady driving. Wiped out physically and mentally, she had never experienced such weariness or emotional strain in her life. For hours she kept repeating, "I'm so tired but cannot doze off."

At 4:30 a.m. she became confused as she looked out the side window into the darkness surrounding her. Somehow she was driving on a narrow secondary road. "Where am I? I must have taken a wrong turn somewhere. How long have I been on this road?"

With her nerves jumbled, sudden fright overtook her. About to tear up, she let out a weak complaint, "I'm lost and out in the middle of nowhere. Oh Lord, how could this happen to me? Where am I? What have I done?" A slow uneven whimper soon became a full-blown cry.

Disoriented and bewildered about how she made the mistake, she realized somehow her thoughts had wandered after stopping to get that little snack. For minutes she was mystified and unable to think clearly.

Physically spent from the long lonely drive, her weariness had taken its toll. Ellie wiped her eyes with the back of a shaking hand and recognized her inability to stop weeping. This trip had taken her far beyond her limit.

Without the strength to control her emotions, she pulled off to the side of the lonely country road, turned off the motor, covered her face with both hands and wailed. Trembling with loud sobs, she was unable not only to think clearly but now to stop crying. Her sobs sounded louder than any crying she had ever done.

Fear entered her thoughts, but her lips moved, "The LORD is my shepherd, I shall not be in want. He makes me lie down in green pastures. He leads me beside quiet waters. He restores my soul. He guides me in paths of righteousness for His name's sake. Even though I walk through the valley of the shadow of death, I will fear no evil, for You are with me; your rod and your staff they comfort me."

At the side of the road she stopped to consider the words that instantly had popped into her head. She had quoted them without thinking. Then smiling slowly, she finished the last verse of the psalm, "Surely goodness and love will follow me all the days of my life, and I will dwell in the house of the LORD forever."

Although lost and tremendously confused, she was assured God would guide and keep her from any danger and the fear she was feeling. Yes, she was definitely on the wrong road and needed no map to tell her that. "Somehow I'll be led back."

She had driven so far to flee from danger only to find she was lost in the middle of nowhere. Minutes later, feeling sick in the pit of her stomach, she silently prayed, "Oh, Lord, I'm too tired to know what I need to do. It's so terribly dark, and I cannot find the road without you. Take me back to the right road." Then raising her head and stiff shoulders and looking out at the dark stillness of the night around her, she was reminded of those last words she had heard her father speak to her. Then she spoke each word, "Run, Ellie, Run."

Reaching for one of the rough paper napkins she had picked up at the last stop, she wiped the tears from her eyes and face. Those three little words spoken by her father expressed the special confidence he had in her. With God's guidance and her father's confidence in her, she knew she would have the courage to complete the trip and reach her grandmother's home where she would be comforted and completely safe.

Turning on the motor, Ellie made a wide U turn in the road. Within minutes with her emotions under control, she was heading back toward the Interstate. This time she would pay closer attention and make the correct turns. Reading every road sign along the secondary road, Ellie recognized the place where she must have taken the wrong turn. Somehow when she was nibbling on the food, she lost her sense of direction and turned toward a rural road and had headed north. Grateful she was now heading in the right direction, she smiled saying, "It's easier to go in the wrong direction than I ever imagined. I'm much too tired to concentrate on more than one thing at a time. Although I've lost precious time going the wrong way, Thank you, God, for all your help."

Once again on the interstate, out of habit, she reached for her phone and placed it in her lap. She would try to reach her mom and dad in about an hour when the first signs of daylight hit the horizon. "Lord, keep me from making another stupid mistake tonight."

After traveling more than 360 miles and hearing only the relentless beating of tires meeting the pavement beneath her, Ellie was once again at the point of exhaustion. She had driven 45 miles since becoming lost, and her nerves were on edge. Keeping a steady watch on the road ahead shown by the illuminating beam from the bright headlights had taken its toll.

Her eyes were burning, and she began rubbing them softly. Her shoulders as well as her neck muscles ached from sitting in the same position so long, but her strained, sore eyes were hurting the most. The constant driving was mesmerizing, and although she was determined to finish the trip as quickly as possible, she was sure she should somehow get a little rest. Deep inside her abdomen Ellie noticed the slight jittery feeling had reoccurred.

Weary from trying to reason why the man had shot her father and why she somehow had been protected, she was certain she must get relief and sleep. She needed to find a safe well-lit parking lot where she could stretch out and at least get a few winks if she was to finish the trip. Even two hours of rest for her eyes might do the trick, but she knew it was not a smart idea to try to locate a motel at this hour because an attendant might consider her a run-away teen.

Convinced also that no motel owner would allow a kid to use her father's credit card to pay for a room, she was left with no alternative but to sleep a couple hours in her dad's car until daylight arrived. "I have to remember that Dad's credit cards will only be safe to use at gas stations, but not inside a convenience store even if I get hungry. I definitely cannot sign for any purchase. Arriving safe and sound at grandma's place is my goal, and I can forego eating if in any way it jeopardizes my trip."

Thinking the next large town might provide her a place to pull off and sleep until she felt rested, Ellie read every roadside sign for the next nine miles. "Where can I find a place to park and sleep once I get there? At a mall maybe? Absolutely not! Those are places where I've spent gobs of time shopping with my friends for clothes, shoes and other things. The patrolling watchmen keep a specific schedule and drive around the spacious parking lots throughout the night."

"A fast food place? Maybe. A trucker's stop? Probably not a good idea for me at this hour. It might come down to finding anything that appeared to be a safe place to park so I can get a couple hours of rest for my eyes."

Unwilling to wait for the next major town, Ellie pulled off the interstate highway at the next small town and drove down the main street. It appeared deserted, almost abandoned compared to the city she lived in, and she was not sure choosing this town had been a good idea. At this hour, with absolutely no other cars moving on the road through town, she experienced an unusual chill but dismissed it.

"This looks like an old ghost town. Lord, I need help because I don't know if this town is all that safe. Nothing seems to be open but that dimly-lit convenience store, but I'll drive on a little further."

Driving around a curve she spied a busier part of the same town. Thankful she could see some brighter lights, she drove slowly and studied both sides of the road. Seeing a strip mall of several small shops with a moderate-sized grocery store tucked neatly in the middle, Ellie smiled for the first time in hundreds of miles.

Certain this might be her best choice, and because she was so tired, she turned into the large parking lot and found a spot directly under a light. This would have to do. There was only one other car sitting in the entire parking lot, which was evidently unoccupied, so she turned off the motor and listened. The immediate cessation of the motor's vibration came as a shock to her body.

In minutes she began feeling chilly from the outside air creeping into the interior of the car. With only the new jacket wrapped around her, which now seemed skimpy against the cold night air, and her long-sleeved tee, her unpreparedness for this flight to Knoxville became stark reality. In those frantic moments in Mike's, she had left her favorite hoodie along with her warmer coat. Now hugging herself and hugging the new jacket closely around her mid section, she began rubbing her arms and aching shoulders with rapid movements of her hands trying to release the tension.

Pulling the jacket even tighter and knowing she did not have anything else to cover herself and would be chilled to the bone in no time, she began wimpering softly. It would be positively impossible to sleep. Spending a few moments feeling angry at her behavior for how she had acted when she practically begged her father to buy the jacket, she regretted it and other times when she insisted on possessing things that now seemed foolish.

Feeling sorry for often using childish behavior to get what she wanted, she thought, "I'm not a baby, and I shouldn't act like one. I didn't need this jacket. What a sorry mess I am!" She was angry with herself and told herself that she would not complain about her present predicament. She would definitely not be a crybaby.

"But I could really use that fuzzy warm sweatshirt now. So why did I only want to get a chance to try on this dumb jacket so I could admire myself in it when my dad had been concerned mainly about protecting me?" Ellie whispered quietly, "Oh, why was I so stupid? Now I'm freezing and unable to stay warm enough to rest. I wish I was in my warm, cozy bed now, and all this was a bad dream."

Heavy tears fell from her closed eyelids and began dropping onto her new jacket, but she didn't care enough to wipe them away. "I desperately need protection tonight, LORD. I'm sorry I'm such a selfish kid, only thinking of what I want."

Grasping the bottom of her tee, she wiped her eyes as she again felt the tremendous need to stretch her limbs. She could not sit upright in the seat but must lay down to rest well, so she climbed over the front seat and onto the back. Up went her arms and legs as she exercised them for almost a full minute. Then curling her body tightly in a ball, she blinked her eyes several times before closing them.

Ellie's eyes flickered as she softly muttered to herself, "Whew, I'm whipped, but I've got to get some sleep, if only for an hour or so. For approximately twenty two hours I've been awake. How do truckers do this? It's time for me to rest. . . Please help me sleep, Lord . . ." Her mind was a jumbled mess leaping in several directions, but she tried to void the insignificant concerns of keeping warm as well as the writhing emotional pain she had experienced in order to stay awake. Brushing her cheeks with her hand, she knew she was crying again. "Thanks for protecting me on this long trip, and please, please take care of my great dad. Thanks for giving him to me. And for only a couple of hours, help me relax. Please allow me to rest because I need to find my way to grandma's house."

Sleep was on its way when lights from an approaching car suddenly awakened her. Raising her head slowly, she peered out the window and saw a car turning in. It moved only fifty feet or so in her direction and then turned around leaving the parking lot and moving out onto the road again. Realizing the driver had only needed a place to turn around, Ellie lay her head down again and began whimpering.

Tears welled up in her sore eyes, and not able to hold on to her emotions, she gave into a full cry for help. That horrible sight of her father lying helpless on the floor would not leave. Neither would those three words her father spoke, "Run Ellie Run." In the darkness she uttered almost silently, "Did that ambulance reach him in time? I've got to know. I honestly need my dad. We all need him, and I believe only God can save him."

Then a thought flew into her mind, "I'll call Mom now. Oh, but now is not a good idea. I'll wait until first thing in the morning when she wakes up. It's only a couple hours from now. I'll call her at Grandma's as soon as daylight arrives. Mom and Grandma will know what's best to do. Then we can check on Dad's condition."

Her troubled thoughts finally ceased. Ellie was asleep. In only minutes she awakened feeling the chilly air again. Thinking she could fall back asleep, she closed both eyes that were now swollen and painful open or closed. She refused to open them, but again feeling colder night air penetrating into the car, Ellie knew it was pointless to try to sleep. She resigned to the reality she wouldn't get any sleep.

"The big ugly blanket! That ratty old rag my folks keep in the trunk to wrap around items to protect them when they have to take something somewhere. It should be in the trunk."

Ellie lifted her head and looked out the window. Nothing was moving around, and feeling completely safe, she unlocked the car and carefully opened the door. Creeping outside she silently reached the trunk to get the blanket. Thankfully it was lying in the corner bundled up waiting for her. Closing the trunk quietly and slipping back into the backseat, she locked all the doors. Twisting the blanket around her feet, she then wrapped the remainder of it completely around her body.

Now feeling the warming fibers of the blanket, Ellie again closed her eyes. A slight headache had made its way behind her tired eyes, but in spite of this twinge of pain, her mind finally gave way to sleep.

More than two hours later Ellie heard a definite tapping at the car window. She jumped without knowing what had awakened her, and she heard the gentle tapping once again. A young boy was looking in at Ellie as she lay there. He smiled a sheepish grin, then left and caught up with his mother as they walked into the grocery store. It was daylight as she looked around, and the old blanket reminded her where she was and why it was wrapped so tightly around her.

Crawling back into the driver's seat, she felt her strength return and knew what she must do, "What a night!" she grumbled as she stretched her arms and took in a deep breath. Her mouth was dry and stale tasting, but she was thankful her eyes were not as sore. She would get a big orange juice at Micky D's, get on the interstate again and head toward Knoxville. As she pulled away from her parking spot, she noticed why the kid had tapped her window. In the foggy darkness last night, she had pulled into the parking spot and parked the car at a crooked angle. With a weak laugh she yawned twice and filled her lungs with fresh air.

The town where she had her nap in the middle of the night looked quite different now. Lifeless hours ago, it was now busy and very noisy. The yellow arch was easy to find as she headed back toward the interstate. With such a small amount of cash, Ellie decided she might try using her dad's credit card there and see how it worked. They wouldn't ask for her signature. Locking the car and again thoughtfully placing the keys into her jacket pocket, she entered the fast-food place and headed for the women's room.

With a quick glance at herself in the mirror, she gasped as she noticed the redness of her eyes, her unruly hair from sleeping and her overall messy appearance. After using the toilet and washing her hands, she went to work to repair and improve what she could. Freshening her face with cool water and pulling back her uncombed thick mane, she began running her fingers through it. Reaching inside her handbag she found a stretch band, and with simple twisting and gathering of her hair she drew it through the band and into a ponytail. She was amazed at how much better she appeared.

Standing in line she told herself she would not make eye contact with anyone hoping she would blend in with other customers. Hopefully she would not shock anyone or even experience a raised eyebrow. She was sure she must look scary to those around her and also to those taking her order at the counter, but she would order something to drink and eat before she left for the car. Getting something crunchy sounded good.

People in line were polite and no one seemed to notice her, but her impatience was noticeable. She decided to smile at everyone even though she felt and looked like a wreck.

Maybe her facial expression would help her attitude. A few smiles were returned, and when the order of a fried potato cake, a cup of coffee and a tall orange juice was handed to her, she changed her mind the last minute and paid in cash. Not much real money was left now.

It was warmer in Kentucky than in the cold, wet air Ellie had left behind in Michigan. That long trip through Ohio would forever be a bad memory. The snow had been deep in many areas, but thankfully the highway had been quickly cleared. Remembering the heavy blizzard she had to go through when leaving Detroit, she was thankful the storm had lasted only an hour or so for her.

She had been so frightened when she saw the blinding whiteness continually dropping on the windshield. After the storm had ended and hundreds of miles were behind her, she was finally given a safe place to sleep. Grateful the frigid weather had not traveled with her, she could dwell on finishing her trip.

Ellie munched on her breakfast and sipped her orange juice in a corner of the restaurant. Her coffee was too hot to drink yet, so she would take it back to the car with her. She was amazed at how far she was able to travel without having any additional problems. But as she was reminded of her escape from a gruesome, savage scene in the restaurant, and how she was forced to run away from her hometown to find safety, she knew who she needed to thank. God had kept her safe, and He had watched over her for the entire trip. He had brought her down a long, long road, but she was safe. She would continue to trust Him because she was sure He would keep her from harm on the road she must yet travel.

As she returned to the car, somehow she had the calming feeling her father was safe and in good hands, and that he was lying in a hospital bed with people caring for him. Why? She didn't know why, but she needed that reassurance to comfort her. She was confident God was able to spare her dad's life last night, and she would continue to pray for him during the rest of her trip.

"God heard my prayers, I know, and possibly he will keep my dad alive. God you must be giving me this hope."

The car had not given her any trouble for more than 400 miles. No one had followed her from Mike's place. She also was able to get some rest during the night. She smiled reminding herself that each time she checked the dashboard during her wild dash down the interstate highway, the gas gauge consistently read she still had plenty of gas, and there had always been a filling station when fuel was necessary.

The Kentucky, Tennessee line was Ellie's next goal, and as she examined the map from her father's car, she could see she should continue to take Interstate 75 into

Tennessee. When she was near Knoxville, she would watch for signs that would direct her toward the city.

She would take another look at the map at her next quick stop because she knew her Grandma Russell lived west of Knoxville, and the interstate highway would be close to where she needed to exit. Ellie was familiar with many of the roads once she approached the edge of the city, especially the roads that took her to those alluring, addictive shopping centers. She was feeling a bit of shame that she would know the way to her grandmother's home if she could locate her favorite Knoxville shopping center first.

She began talking to herself as she returned to the Interstate, "Dad and Mom were right. I should study my subjects like math and chemistry more. Dad said I might enjoy them if I could concentrate on learning instead of giving into my obsession of thinking about the next piece of clothing or pair of shoes I want."

Ellie thought about her close girlfriends. They were constant shoppers too, and hours of their weekends also were spent in the alluring shops looking at the beautiful clothes with the intent of purchasing something cool. Each Monday they would swap shopping escapades among themselves. Intense envy would always follow. Spiteful actions and reactions then occurred. Envy of what someone else was able to purchase was an ongoing problem for most of them, and for Ellie in particular. "Perhaps I should reconsider my values. My values are what really matter, just like dad said. Oh Dad and Mom, I'm so sorry."

Miles down the highway she again felt her need for sleep, but soon the coffee she purchased was beginning to kick in. In time it would keep her awake because she had consumed the entire cup. Her determination to reach Knoxville as soon as possible was driving her to stay on the highway. She was relieved that she had traveled well over three quarters of her trip. Knoxville definitely should be an easier town to drive through than Rochester Hills and the large towns adjacent to Detroit.

For the next hour Ellie wondered what Knoxville was like when her mom grew up. It was much larger now. She had never been interested in her grandmother's town before, but she would ask questions about her mom's early years after she got some rest. Wanting now to know about her mother's childhood, she would ask her grandmother as well as her mom.

Ellie remembered how often on earlier visits they would talk and usually laugh about what happened during the 50s, through the 70s. Grandma had interesting stories to share about what life was like for her as she was growing up in the 50s, and while sitting in that cozy corner of her bright sun porch, they would recall stories about the good old days. "Maybe I even need to study my family history too."

Neither had her brother Ned been interested when he was her age, but he seemed to be showing much more interest in the past few years. In his first year in college he began asking questions about his childhood and was interested in what had happened to other members of the family during their youth.

The last 22 hours of being alone and thinking had jarred Ellie's memory and was helping her see what was important in life. The difficult trip had changed her viewpoint on so many things, and maybe she was changing her outlook on life and certainly about her family. She was more thankful than ever for her parents and the rest of her relatives. She knew she had always loved her mom, dad, brother and sister, but now as she sat in her father's car, she thought about what a great family she had. She was challenged to finish this trip for their sake. Somehow she was more aware than ever before of her great love for all of them.

Ellie's thoughts again drifted back to her dad. Where was he now? He just had to be alive and in a hospital. She was so anxious to know what had happened after she left him. The memory of that man with the angry look on his face haunted her, and she shivered. Why did he shoot my dad? Why did he shoot Mr. McCoy and the waiter? Why? Why? Surely, it was because he was selling drugs, but that did not mean he had to shoot them. Dad had known immediately the man was a danger to her and everyone in the restaurant. These confusing questions without an answer flowed through her mind. Once again she clearly remembered the last words she heard her father say to her. He loved her so much that he was concerned about her safety at that point too, and she reminded herself once again that her father had always, always loved her.

The clock on the dashboard panel now read 7:29, and Ellie wondered what time it would be when she reached the town of Knoxville. She never had driven mountainous roads like these before, but she was now more comfortable in the driver's seat of her father's car than she thought possible last night when she first climbed in to start the trip. Definitely, she never thought she would ever drive this far before, and never ever for an entire night.

It was an adventure she would not have considered yesterday morning as she was lying in her own bed trying to get the last few winks before Clara would walk up the stairs to make sure she was awake. Ellie smiled as she thought of Clara and how she would kindly need to shake her and say, "Ellie, your breakfast is on the table. It's ready and waiting for you." Today she missed hearing Clara's broken English with that gentle reminder, and right now, she missed her alarm going off at 6:45a.m.

Ellie was again aware that every mile she covered traveling south on the highway was one mile away from her dad but one mile closer to her mom. From time to time she rubbed her strained eyes with the cuff of her new jacket, which she knew was not so new anymore. She cried so often on the trip that her teardrops now left ugly stains and marks on it. This morning there was positively no more moisture left for any tears. Her eyes were dry and very sore.

She began consoling herself, "My irritated, tired eyes with the smudged mascara that's on my face will eventually fade in my memory, but I'll remember how God was with me the entire trip. I know you love me, God, and I know you've always loved me."

At her next stop she decided to call her dad from her phone and possibly someone would answer even if her dad was unable to reach his cell phone. She would know something.

Weak from the turmoil still inside her, Ellie realized she must prepare herself to hear bad news when she made that call, but somehow she must hold onto the hope that the emergency personnel were able to reach him in time. That siren she heard must have meant an ambulance arrived within minutes after she left his side. She did not know where they might take him, but the driver would know the best and closest hospital emergency unit. From the time she left the restaurant, Ellie's concern had changed from satisfying herself to praying for her father's life.

"Oh Dad, we all love you and need you," Ellie exclaimed as she reached for her phone. Her welfare had always been her parents concern, and last night as she bent over her father's body fearing for his life, he displayed his love for her again when he told her to leave quickly and drive to her grandmother's home.

"You're the best dad a girl could have," she said softly as if her father were there to hear. "I might never be able to tell you that because I've been such a selfish kid. I know I was definitely spoiled making sure you purchased this jacket for me. Dad, thank you, but I want you to know what you buy me means so little now. You've done so much for me. You're a super dad."

Somehow she was beginning to voice that she wanted to be the young woman her mom and dad wanted her to be. What had made her happy yesterday and how her friends saw her somehow didn't matter. She had been consumed with constantly wanting more stuff to satisfy her cravings. She had been obsessed with trying to look cool, and now she was sad thinking about the envy she caused with her friends. She knew it was nothing but ugly, crummy pride. Today and in the future she would consider her family first and think about pleasing others for a change.

With sorrow for this knowledge about herself she called out, "Dad, Mom, I love you both. I love you more than all the things you could buy me. Forgive me for acting so childish, so utterly selfish." It had been important for Ellie to voice her thoughts. Then pleading she said, "And God, please keep my dad alive so I can tell him I love him. Mom, I'll see you soon to tell you how much I love you."

She began reminding herself of the many times throughout her life when her parents had expressed their love for her without saying a single word.

"You must keep your mind on the road ahead and concentrate," Ellie muttered. "Don't think too long about anything but driving safely. The worst that could happen would be finding yourself lost and on the wrong road again. Stay alert, girl. Keep your eyes on the road."

Chapter 15

"RAY BOTCHED THE JOB! The guy's a half-witted piece of trash! He screwed up one simple job I gave him. What could've caused him to bungle this job? It was important to me. Seeing that young girl, he should have known what to do. Incompetent! He's an absolutely idiot!"

Owen expressed each word savagely as he kicked his watch dog and swore. Slamming his right fist hard into the side of his closet door, he injured one of his knuckles. Furious from the instant pain his uncontrollable temper spiked, he expressed again and again in rage how much he despised Ray because he failed to carry out his orders. His carefully contrived plan had been ignored, and as a result, Owen now had a far greater problem to deal with today.

Without undressing last night he had fallen onto his bed. He was now tightly closing his eyes hoping desperately to relax and possibly fall back asleep. Restless and in turmoil he realized it would be impossible to sleep. His body was drained, but the lingering reality of the teen out there somewhere had not allowed him to fall asleep. "That unpredictable brat probably got a good look at Ray's face and could tell the police everything she saw and heard. They'll look for Ray and then possibly me. I must, and I will find her first."

It was almost six in the morning, and he now sat on the edge of his bed thinking. Opening the blinds, he looked out a window at the street below. He noticed the blizzard had slackened, and now only a bit of sleet could be seen falling onto the pavement.

He rubbed his temples attempting to get his mind around his problem and to come up with an acceptable solution. "If the law finds Ray, he might easily be tricked into providing them with sufficient information about me, but I do have some time." After trying to devise a solid scheme for evading the authorities, he concluded that he must leave town within three or four hours.

At midnight he became fearful of what he might encounter if he waited too long, but he knew he needed to make a solid plan to find the kid. He hoped to make his usual rounds collecting money from those who sold the drugs he supplied them, but instead he spent hours tossing and turning on his bed as he ran the incident of Ray's failure to follow his orders through his mind. The problem of the kid continued to interrupt his thoughts about Ray.

Every option Owen considered to deal with Ray's bungle was brutal. He knew where the guy lived, but he was quite sure Ray would not be a threat to him for at least a day. He would have time to deal with the man later. He was concerned most about finding where the kid lived and where she had gone after leaving the restaurant. He was almost sure she would go home.

In a rage Owen leaped from his bed and blurted out, "That overindulged spoiled brat wasn't supposed to turn up at Mike's with her dad. She messed up my plan and easily walked away. Right under my nose she got away, but she won't be able to escape from my grasp again. My plan went haywire as soon as she showed up, but foolish Ray should have known what to do when he saw she was there. I'll remind him of that serious blunder and the trouble he's caused me. I'll take care of him in my own time and in my way."

His memory shifted back to the girl. He remembered seeing her walk through the snow storm, entering the nearby car, and in less than a minute, driving away. It was dark, and the dense, wet snowfall partially hindered his view of her, but he was confident of what he did see and could recall what the girl was wearing. Her hair was shoulder length. Not dark, but it was impossible to fully see because of the blinding snow. A purse was hanging over her shoulder, and both her hands were in her pockets. Her head was down to avoid the cold wind. She had to be a school kid because those jeans and jacket gave her away. All the young girls wore clothes like that. He didn't miss getting a good view of the slick black Chrysler either that she drove away in.

The two sleeping pills he took hours previously were slowing down his thoughts, and for a moment Owen felt a wave of sleepiness. His mind was however far too active, and he wouldn't give in to restful slumber. His eyelids popped open. Pulling out a bottle of uppers he kept on his night stand and drinking the cold stale coffee left over from last night, he was fully awake within a few minutes as he focused on what the girl might do. She could have hidden because she was scared or might have decided to go to the police, but he believed she would have gone home. Whatever she did after she left presented a big problem for him. His hatred toward her boiled over. The overpowering thought of this bothersome kid who spoiled his plan terrified him. He was more uneasy about what this girl could do to him than what Ray might do.

"My gun! Ray has my gun!" Owen hissed sharply. Although he would enjoy retrieving his gun this morning and be finished with Ray forever, he must temporarily shove those continual thoughts aside for the time being because he was intensely worried about his one looming problem. Finding the attorney's kid was next.

Walking toward his closet, he began mulling over the whole episode systematically and began making a plan. He was convinced the girl was his immediate problem. He must rid himself of her first. He'd settle with Ray later. Acquiring the attorney's home address was his primary goal this morning. It would be his initial step in locating the kid. It could be smooth sailing after that.

"That miserable, rotten spoiler!" he spurted out hatefully. Cooling down from his outburst, Owen calmed himself enough to ponder a possible way to obtain the girl's address. Only the teenager could bring him down and destroy his lucrative business, a business he had spent years putting together after being forced to serve five dismal years inside a jail cell with all those losers. He hated that memory and quickly turned his thoughts back on the girl.

Thinking about her, he recalled that big black Chrysler she slipped into before driving away. He visualized the scene. "Would the little lady have driven home to tell her mother? More than likely. Hmm, but why wasn't Mom with them?"

He was certain word about the shooting was out and printed in some local newspapers by now. The police would be looking for the killer within hours and trying to pick up clues near the restaurant and in the surrounding neighborhood. They would also scientifically examine the bullets fired from the gun, and if they could put their hands on the gun in which the bullets originated, the trail would end before it ever reached him.

Owen remembered how clever he had been when in such a slick manner he was able to steal the gun. One night while men were fighting in a bar he had cleverly found a way of stealing it. There was a fight between two men, and with so much movement among the bystanders who were watching and with everything happening so quickly, no one had seen him steal the gun from the inside pocket of one of the fighting men and slip it inside his big coat. He was sure the police would not be after him because of the gun. That guy in the fight would be charged.

Relieved about the matter of the gun, he thought again of the girl and said in a cruel manner, "The idiotic police will look for the miserable, rotten kid at her home this morning, so I don't have much time."

Owen began plotting, "How can I find out where home is for that rotten kid? Her dad's dead and can't help her. She left in his car, but did she go directly home? Surely she would go there first, and maybe she stayed at home. I've got to get on it now!"

Anyone at the attorney's office would be instantly suspicious of such an inquiry from a total stranger. Since he knew he would never get beyond the front door of Joe's office to obtain the address for the Wallace residence, he would need to invent a way to get the address. Focusing on several possibilities, Owen fixed his mind on a possible easy way in which he might be successful. Replaying in his memory again what Ray had told him about how Kurt and Joe knew each other, Owen decided to visit the church where both families attended. Hopefully someone would be available there early this morning, and he could get the address he needed from an unsuspecting person.

It was already seven, and he would hurry now that he had a plan.

He would dress as a businessman on his way to work. After taking a quick shower, he chose his best suit to make a good impression at the church. Buttoning up a well-tailored shirt and knotting an expensive conservative silk tie, he put on the suit and stood before his long mirror for a moment admiring his appearance. Then chuckling to himself, he rehearsed the polite questions he decided to ask to obtain the address he wanted. Satisfied, he headed out to find Overbrook Community Church.

———◦•◦———

In a new part of town, the tall red brick church covered more than six acres of land and was presently receiving a face lift. A construction crew was busy working on a new wing. Builders were using their noisy tools as Owen pulled up the wide driveway to park his car. One could see it was a thriving church that reached out to the community and probably added members regularly. Noticing the small office sign as he entered the building, Owen walked swiftly in that direction hoping someone would be busy with the regular duties of the church.

A friendly woman was on her phone talking to someone when he stepped inside the outer room. He smiled as he walked purposely toward her desk. Seeing the man enter, she excused herself to the caller for a moment as she looked up at Owen.

"I'll be with you shortly, Sir. Please be seated," she cheerfully said. Returning to her phone she gave the hours of the worship services for the upcoming Sunday to the caller and enthusiastically said, "We hope to see you this Sunday, and hope you have a great day. Goodbye."

Knowing this kind woman had no idea what his line of work was, Owen carefully chose his words, "Miss, my wife and I have recently moved into the community, and we're looking for a good church to attend. I've noticed your building on numerous occasions on my way to and from work, and I was wondering what the times were for your worship service and what activities you have for young children." He noticed how the woman patiently listened to him so he continued, "Having my two boys in elementary school, they need good Christian friends they do not have in the public school where they attend. Our neighbor has highly recommended this church to us."

The question that really mattered to Owen followed. With much poise, he asked the question, "And . . . Miss, would you be so kind as to give us a membership directory of your church. It would be so helpful to both my wife and me."

"Yes, sir, I can give you the information you request. Our church has two services each Sunday morning. The first service begins at 9:30 and the second at 11. Weekly activities for your boys are listed in last week's bulletin, which I'll give to you. Two young couples in our church plan many lively activities for our children. I'm sure your boys would enjoy being with them and with other young kids. You'll find most activities of our church included in the bulletin. I'll also give you a folder that describes our beliefs as a church."

For a moment the woman stopped and looked into the man's eyes. Believing he was genuinely interested, she added, "Sir, we don't usually give our membership directory to people outside the church, but since we'll be making a new, up-to-date version within weeks and have plenty of extra copies, you can have one today."

As she gathered items and handed them to Owen, she heard her phone ring and gently said, "Hopefully I've been able to answer all your questions, Sir. You'll find our telephone number and email address in the directory and in these other materials."

Another ring sounded, which made her a bit anxious to get to the caller, "If you should have any further questions about our services or activities, you can call us at any time during the day. We hope we'll be seeing you and your family soon."

Owen took the opportunity to quickly respond as he moved toward the door and into the hallway, "Yes, Miss, thank you for your time and consideration. I assure you that you've been quite helpful to me."

Glancing quickly at his watch as he heard the third ring of the church phone, Owen stepped toward the hallway as he finally said, "It looks like I've taken up a good amount of your valuable time this morning. I'd better hurry to work now because my boss doesn't understand if I'm late. A new job demands a lot of time and energy. Goodbye, Miss. Thank you for your help."

Hurrying out to his car, Owen could hardly believe his success as he held tightly onto all the material. Amazed at his brilliance, his facial expression was of triumph once he reached his car. Then behind the wheel, he tossed everything except the directory into the back seat as he arrogantly uttered, "So unaware, you silly woman. You gave me just what I wanted."

Grasping the directory and opening it in haste to the listings beginning with the letter W, he found numerous names with their addresses, telephone numbers, and even email addresses listed alphabetically. He could see photos of members placed in the center of the directory, but he was momentarily interested in finding the Wallace address.

A somber look of disappointment crossed his face. "It's not there. This can't happen after all that hassle." Turning to the last page, he almost tore it from the directory. Then with a satisfied grin, he howled, "There it is. Just what I wanted." Within seconds after turning to the photo section, he was staring at the Wallace family as they smiled back at him. He found himself also smiling back but in an insidious manner.

Four family members were pictured. It seemed an older daughter whose name was listed was not present in the photo. Her address was listed as England. Four people were shown. "Joseph Wallace, Caroline Wallace, Edward

Wallace and Eleanor Wallace. There's Little Miss Wallace, the pesky brat who muddled my plan and gave me a tremendous headache."

Staring at her face, Owen placed his thumb on her image. Twisting with pressure, he said with loathing, "You'll not outsmart me. I'll not allow you to ruin me." In a caustic, sinister manner he angrily added, "I'll hunt you down. I'll find you. I'm not sure what I will do when I capture you, but I can think of something really nasty."

Not hesitating another moment, and with his eyes glued to the street address for the Wallace residence, he read the number out loud twice to himself memorizing it. A satisfied, contemptuous, dark smirk crossed his face. "I've got you now!"

Inside his office, Rev. Stevens was finishing with the counseling session for a couple. Briefly praying with them, they left his office and began walking to their car. Concerned with them he stood at his window watching as they walked to their car in the parking lot. It was then he noticed another car sitting nearby. Stepping out to get his second cup of coffee, he asked his Administrative Assistant, "Was someone here asking questions about the church?"

"Yes, Pastor, a gentleman came in on his way to work. He was inquiring about activities for his two young boys mainly. The family recently moved into this community, and they're looking for a good church. I gave him information about our services, last Sunday's bulletin, the folder describing our beliefs and also a membership directory that he requested."

Surprised she had handed a membership directory to the stranger, the minister questioned, "You did? Remember those directories are reserved for our members, so don't give them out to people who haven't been attending and haven't already shown interest in our church. Many of our members would not wish to have information given to strangers who happen to walk through our doors. It's always possible we would run out of copies before our new directories are available. Did this man mention his name?"

"No, I'm so sorry, Pastor. He seemed quite pleasant, but I guess I should have asked for his name. He was in such a hurry to get to work, I was on the phone with a caller, and the man didn't seem to have much time this morning. He seemed interested in what we might have for his two boys."

"That's odd for someone to ask for a membership directory without first attending, but hopefully he'll return with his family on Sunday. We can meet them then, but do remember what I said about the church directories."

Pastor Stevens walked back into his office with his coffee and looked out into the parking lot again. He thought, "Why is the man who was in such a hurry to get to work sitting in the church parking lot so long?" For a fleeting moment he also wondered, "What if he was up to no good?" He contemplated possibilities of what could happen if the membership directory was placed in the wrong hands, and especially in the hands of someone who might have bad intentions.

Chapter 16

OFFICER SAM REYNOLDS STEPPED around the highly visible yellow tape at Mike's Restaurant, which had been put up hours previously to inform everyone the place was a crime scene. Walking with caution inside toward the space occupied by Alvin Underwood, his superior and the investigator in charge of the case, he looked around at the accumulation of objects the police examiners were using. Sam was aware that Alvin must have been waiting for him because he was motioning with his outstretched arm and beckoning fingers for Sam to come closer so they could talk about what had already been discovered.

Not wanting to miss a single detail, Sam had dressed hurriedly after receiving the early morning call from Alvin. Four professional men from forensics were busy using their well-trained scientific skills as they gathered any possible clues that might help solve the crime. Precautions were taken to protect the entire scene, and even the smallest bit of potential evidence was photographed as they worked alongside one another. One uniformed woman appeared to be taking notes given to her by those examining the evidence.

Near one table, an outline had been clearly drawn where two men were found the previous night. It seemed they had been lying on the floor after being shot by a gunman. On the opposite side of the room, another outline could be seen. The outer door had already been examined thoroughly for recent finger prints, and it appeared the entire place was in the process of heavy scrutiny.

Following close alongside Alvin, Sam observed the highly experienced man and his meticulous method of asking only significant questions as he walked from examiner to examiner. The man's techniques in investigative processes fascinated Sam.

Alvin was told by the first detective who had appeared on the scene that only one of the three men remained alive when the ambulance arrived, and he was taken immediately to the emergency room of St. Francis Hospital. His condition was listed as critical, and he was not considered stable enough to receive visitors or be questioned. From the statements the hospital made he might be the one person capable of explaining what happened.

In a quiet tone a nearby examiner said to both Alvin and Sam, "The two other men didn't make it and were taken directly to the city morgue awaiting identification by relatives." Preliminary evidence indicated all three must have been shot from the same gun and at the same angle. They quickly eliminated the possibility that the shooter was a trained killer. It was likely the shooter could have been a man, a woman or even a bad kid.

At first it appeared it could have been a random robbery, but receiving that information, Alvin pulled Sam aside to speak, "I don't believe this was a random act of a thief looking for easy money wherever he could find it. Only one wallet was taken, which leaves us with too many questions we cannot answer now. The man in the hospital is the only man who was missing his wallet, and he was lying there with a cell phone in his hand. It's possible that man might have had a chunk of money in his possession or that someone was after him for some reason. The lawyer was dressed well."

As Alvin indicated the spot where Joe Wallace was found, he added, "Only a few coins were in his pocket. Also he was missing his car keys. It seems highly unlikely for a man dressed that well to be without his keys. There is a problem though. Possibly the shooter had taken his car because there seems to be one missing. It's definitely possible the two men at that table came together. All the cars within a two-block area are being checked as we speak. One car was easily found parked across the street, and it belonged to McCoy, who was one of the two men here last night. He did have his keys and wallet."

Alvin pulled Sam further away from the others and pointed to the spot marked on the floor where Kurt McCoy was found. As he turned and looked in Sam's direction he said, "McCoy's wife was visited late last night by the police, and she took the news really hard. We'll need to send someone to question her later in the day. I'm sure she'll be willing to cooperate and will give us some information we need."

Because this other man was missing his wallet, we don't know his identity yet, but we should know soon because he did have that cell phone in his hand when he was found. The waiter was Fred Smithfield who lived only blocks away. Late last night his family was questioned at the station once they identified their son. It seems Fred was renting a room from a distant family member and didn't show up at his usual time."

Walking toward the back of the large room near the restrooms, Alvin wanted to view the scene from another area. He added, "We'll need to locate and question anyone who's closely connected to these three men. I believe we have a lot of work cut out for us on this case. We'll go to the hospital first to visit the sole survivor when we leave here."

After spending another five minutes checking to see that all the work was being done thoroughly by the examiners, Alvin swept the scene again with his experienced eyes. Finally satisfied and without saying another word, he motioned for Sam to leave with him to make their trip to one of the largest and busiest hospitals in the city.

Alvin continued speaking to Sam on their way to the car about some thoughts that had entered his mind, "Sam, this could have been a random robbery, but with only one man missing his wallet, I doubt it. If it was a robber, the person was either in a hurry or something went wrong. He may have been distracted for any number of reasons and left without grabbing all the wallets. By killing the waiter it might indicate the gunman didn't want any witnesses left at the scene. Let me say, it's never a good idea for any investigator to jump to conclusions too early. Nine times out of ten there's always at least one surprise that will surface in time, and new evidence means you have to backtrack and possibly start all over. We need some solid evidence in this case that points to a motive, and then we can go from there."

While these ideas were offered, Sam was once again aware that the best investigator on this side of the city was talking to him. He was impressed at how Alvin continued to ponder various scenarios based on what he had learned at the crime scene and what he had seen for himself. He was extremely thorough in his work and was always looking for conclusive evidence, not just surface evidence. Both men left puzzled but wanted to understand what took place at the restaurant at approximately 6:30 the previous evening.

Sam Reynolds was new to this town situated only 20 miles from the center of Detroit, and at 27 years of age, he was the youngest man involved in this case in any capacity. Assigned three months ago to work alongside Alvin, he found himself each day awake before dawn looking forward to learning from the extraordinary investigator. When he first joined the force, several high ranking officers told Sam they considered Alvin to be the most experienced and talented man actively doing detective work in the entire state of Michigan. When Sam was offered the opportunity to work closely with him, he jumped at the chance and was willing to put in extra time, energy or whatever it took to learn from the man.

After excelling in the police academy training, Sam knew there was only one tremendous hurdle he had to overcome. Sam did not know the city and its surrounding suburbs well enough with its many main thoroughfares, highways and the thousands of side streets. Each evening, after working at least eight to ten hours on the job, he diligently spent extra time studying maps, memorizing the major intersections, repeating to himself names of the countless streets running through and around the gigantic metropolitan area.

Born and raised in a small town in Iowa's corn country, he knew more about farming than he did about big city police work, but after dedicating himself at the Academy, learning everything he could, and now under the professional guidance of Alvin Underwood, that was about to change. Left to his own wishes he would have chosen to live the remainder of his life in Cedar Falls, Iowa. For the time being though, he was content on working to achieve experience on hard-core cases with Alvin Underwood. To do that he had to be willing to bring his young family to this heavily-populated urban city, a place where he was sure he would learn valuable knowledge about police work.

Since childhood he had worked on his uncle and aunt's large farm every summer. Uncle Ben, a name many of his friends had fun with, was almost a second father to Sam. His own father worked in one of the factories in town, and since Sam considered that line of work rather dull, he took every opportunity as a boy to spend each summer at the 700-acre farm doing chores and receiving the reward of driving the massive machinery his uncle used for planting and harvesting crops.

During Sam's last year of college, his uncle had an accident while moving some heavy equipment from his barn. He slipped and fell under a piece of machinery and broke his leg. Bones in the leg would not heal properly even after two surgeries were performed. Now a good farmer with a noticeable limp was forever limited in his ability to keep up with all the demanding work of a large farm.

After hiring several men for almost three years to do the heavier work, the decision was made to sell the farm. With one daughter who lived with her husband and two children in Chicago, Sam's uncle and aunt decided to move into Cedar Falls to live close to their relatives. They knew their daughter was uninterested in living on the farm or running it from a distance, so they considered the suggestions given to them by family and friends and put their farm up for sale.

Uncle Ben had offered Sam the farm before they made the final plans to sell the place with the understanding he would share one-third of the profits with them. That way Sam within twenty years or so would be able eventually to own all the land including the house and farm machinery. He would then become one of the largest land owners in the county. The offer had been a tough decision for Sam because great opportunities like that seldom came along, but after considering for weeks his uncle's generous offer, Sam and his wife, Linda, decided they would not be happy farming for the rest of their lives. It had been great fun during his youth, but Sam's mind was set on investigative police work. It was why after high school he had considered studying criminology at the nearby community college.

He and Linda loved the wide open spaces in Iowa, the animals, the culture, the conservative attitudes and values of the people. He was even certain someday he and his family would return to make it their home. That would however be after he learned everything he could about solving crimes. There would be a place for smart criminologists in Iowa too, and Sam's plan was to become the best investigator possible when he finally returned. Iowa would always be considered his home.

Every aspect of criminology interested Sam, and although his dad, uncle and other relatives were disappointed in his decision, they told him they understood completely and would support him in his decision. After a tearful going-away party held for Sam and Linda, everyone sent them off along with their two young children to what they considered the 'big city.'

The farm was eventually sold to a young couple who wanted to live and raise their family on a farm. With moisture running down his cheeks, Ben grabbed Sam, hugged him and laughingly said, "Your Aunt Margaret and I have decided to do some long-deserved travel throughout this big country of ours and in parts of Canada too. You can expect a visit from us when we reach Michigan. You know we all love you, and we'll pray for you. Keep in touch." Both Sam and Linda found it difficult to leave their family and friends, people they had known all their lives, to travel so many miles away and live and work in unfamiliar surroundings. Their two toddlers had to be uprooted leaving their cousins, uncles, aunts and especially their grandparents. They were going to a new state, a new city, and a crowded, noisy city at that.

Linda said she was willing to live in the large, cloudy city for a few years so Sam could fulfill his dream. Sam considered Linda a naturally happy person who had always found it easy to make new friends. His confidence in her outlook on life and her ability to reach out to people would be the key for them to be satisfied in their new home. Linda was overjoyed that Sam's job would allow her plenty of time with the children during their early years. She had spent three years as an elementary school teacher after they were married, and she understood from the unhappy home situations she experienced in teaching that if she did not wish to regret spending too little time with her children while they were at her feet, she would need to stay home and enjoy them at least until they were ready to attend school. Working in her profession could wait.

Little Tom and Cathy took more of her time than she ever imagined, but she was extremely thankful for both of them in spite of the constant attention she had to give them. Together their family would make the most of the time they spent in this bustling, energetic, noisy city.

Chapter 17

ALVIN AND SAM TURNED into a hospital parking slot marked "For Official Use Only" and began walking toward the hospital building and then the information desk. Displaying their badges to the receptionist and asking questions about the man who was brought in about 7:00 the previous night, they were given the name, Joe Wallace. They then asked to visit him. They were told he was in the Intensive Care Unit. Without asking additional questions, the two policemen were given directions to the ICU and handed special passes to enter.

In minutes they were standing looking through a long window into a private room filled with numerous life-saving, state-of-the-art medical devices performing their designated functions. In a raised bed the patient, Joe Wallace, was tethered to two of the machines and was sleeping soundly.

Waiting quietly behind the window until the attending nurse came, Alvin whispered to Sam, "It looks like he's breathing without any medical apparatus. That's good, and he seems to be receiving fluids only. He looks better than I thought we would find him. Can't see any bandages on his head. That's good too. His shoulder and an arm seem to be where he received most of the damage." Catching sight of a nurse coming toward them, Alvin in a hushed tone said to Sam, "We don't want any nurses dismissing us so we'll have to go easy. They're really the ones in charge around here."

Displaying their badges again, the nurse hurriedly glanced at them and said, "Gentlemen, I'll contact the head nurse right away who'll be able to help you. Please wait right here for a moment."

Within less than a minute another nurse appeared and briefly glanced at the badges. Holding notes written on a clipboard, she read to them, "Mr. Joseph Wallace was brought in last night at 7:15 p.m. He lost almost two pints of blood before the rescue squad reached him, but care was administered during the trip to the hospital. The examination revealed that he sustained a shot approximately two inches below his collar bone. The same bullet traveled into the lower portion of his left arm. The bullet missed his heart and main artery and was retrieved in the emergency operating room. After two hours in the Recovery Unit, he was brought up to the Intensive Care Unit at 10:00 last night."

She then added the latest information placed on the patient's log, "If he had not called 911 on his cell phone when he did, they would not have gotten him to the hospital in time to save his life. He definitely would not be with us this morning."

Dropping the log to her side the nurse continued, "He was awake for a few minutes earlier this morning calling for Ellie, but I see he's sleeping now. It may be some time before he'll be awake again to answer any questions. It's absolutely amazing this man is alive! His vital signs are all excellent, and from every indication, we're quite certain he'll make it even though he is quite weak now. It will be at least a week before he'll be able to leave the hospital."

The nurse continued, "Gentlemen, Mr. Wallace did not have a wallet on his person when he arrived in the emergency room, but they did have his cell phone, and we can give it to you when you leave. I can tell you he is a well known attorney in this area. We found his business and home number stored on his cell phone. We called the number of his law firm an hour ago and spoke to one of his partners. He was extremely concerned about Mr. Wallace's condition and wants to be kept informed. Evidently Mr. Wallace has been working with the same firm for the past 16 years. We only received his residence answering machine when we called his home number. You can pick up the bullet that was removed during surgery anytime. That's all I can tell you at this time."

Thanking the nurse, Alvin said they would definitely have questions later and would return. They stressed to her they needed to talk to Mr. Wallace as soon as he awakened and displayed any sign of being alert. The two officers stood gazing at Joe in silence for yet another moment before they left.

Formulating the questions they would possibly wish to ask the attorney on their return, Alvin decided to once again walk to the nurses' station to ask when they thought Mr. Wallace might be able to answer a few quick questions. The standard answer was given, "We're doing all we can for Mr. Wallace gentlemen. When he does awaken we'll know better about his condition, and we will definitely call you. Just leave your number for us."

Alvin offered his personal card and wrote his name and number down on a notepad that was handed to him and returned it to the nurse as he made his last request as clearly and persuasively as he could, "Please, don't fail to call us. It's extremely important we spend time with him. Call us as soon as possible."

They left the same way they entered, and Sam was relieved they retraced their steps because he was so turned around in the huge building's pathways and networks. He was sure if he had come alone, he would have gone in the wrong direction and would have lost his way back to the parking lot. Minutes later they made their way to the car and were about to leave the hospital grounds when Alvin received a call from one of the ICU nurses. "Mr. Wallace is awake now, and we are in the process of moving him out of Intensive Care and into Room 506. We'll allow you to ask him a few brief questions in his new room."

Hearing the good news, Alvin swiftly turned the car around. Sam and he hurried to Room 506. Joe Wallace was awake and staring out into the hallway when they arrived. Entering quietly they stood at the foot of Joe's bed for several seconds waiting for the pale looking patient to notice them.

Alvin spoke in a somewhat restrained and slow manner, "Mr. Wallace, my partner Sam and I are from the Birmingham Police Department, and we understand you sustained a bullet wound last evening at Mike's Restaurant. We're glad to know the rescue squad was able to reach you in time and also that you're definitely on the mend. They've taken excellent care of you here. Your nurse informed us who you are, and we are here to ask you a few questions about what happened last night."

Noticing the look of concentration but slow recollection on Joe's face, Alvin continued cautiously, "We're sorry to come at a time like this, but because time is an issue in whether we catch the man who shot you, and because we believe someone by the name of Ellie was involved, we need to ask you a few questions. Do you feel up to answering questions?"

Feeling numbness in the left side of his weakened body and stabs of pain located beneath his shoulder, Joe grimaced as he stared at the two men standing at the foot of his bed. He was trying desperately to recall details of why he was cooped up in a hospital bed. His memory was cloudy as he tried to remember where he was the night before.

Not receiving a reply, Alvin politely and prudently returned to the reason why they had come, "Mr. Wallace, we know you need to rest after coming out of surgery, so we'll not stay long. Do you feel up to answering any questions?"

Continuing to glare at the two men, Joe's memory of the tremendously unpleasant incident began to stir. He was beginning to recall the shooting and what happened after that. Then fully cognizant, he urgently stammered, "Where's my daughter Ellie? She's . . . she's all alone in my car. Has anyone heard from her? Find out where she is. Please."

Lifting his right arm and reaching over to feel his left side with all the bandages and needles, Joe weakly said, "I told my daughter to drive to her grandmother's home in Knoxville where my wife Caroline is staying. Oh, it was last night when I was shot. Yes, and Ellie must be on the highway driving south in that direction. I want to talk to her. Where did they put my cell phone?"

Questions began entering both Alvin and Sam's minds as Alvin inquired, "Sir, are you saying your daughter was with you at the restaurant last night when you were shot? Is that correct?"

Observing Joe as he tried to move on his bed, Alvin motioned for Sam to find an available nurse and ask her for Wallace's phone. Then walking around to the side of Joe's bed he gently said, "Mr. Wallace, we'll help you get in touch with your daughter as soon as the nurse arrives. Can you give me a bit of information pertaining to what actually happened last night? The sooner we can find the person who shot you and why, we'll be better able to help both you and your daughter."

In his bewildered, confused state Joe finally nodded as he replied, "I'm sure I can help you. Forgive me. I'm disoriented, but I'll try to recall what took place even though I'm somewhat confused. Just give me a moment."

Joe tightly closed his eyes. Seconds later he fully opened them, looked up at the ceiling and slowly said, "Ellie must be contacted!" Turning his head, he saw all the modern medical equipment surrounding him. It was then he caught sight of the needle taped to his arm and stared at it for some time before he suddenly remembered something Kurt had said the previous night. He recalled that drugs were involved.

With all his strength he spoke slowly as he stammered, "My daughter must be called now. I remember giving her my car keys and wallet. I told her to run out of the place and drive to her grandmother's house last night where she'd be safe because I was afraid the man who shot both Kurt and me might soon be looking for her. She'd seen the man before she left for the women's room."

His eyes moved around the room before they fell again on the police detectives. The look on Joe's face told them he was still under the effects of the anesthesia but was struggling to recall details of the incident. These were definitely some of the details about the crime they had not been able to put together.

"Well that answers some questions we had. Since neither the medical personnel nor the policemen who first appeared on the scene could locate your car, your wallet or your car keys, we wondered . . ."

Alvin could not finish his statement because Joe interrupted him saying, "I knew then before Ellie left that she was in danger. Do you know if she got away safely? Have you heard anything from her? Last night I saw her leave the restaurant, but I didn't know anything after I called 911 and spoke to someone." Taking a deep breath and still in a dazed state he added. "The 911 operator asked me a few questions, and I believe I gave them the name of the restaurant and streets nearby. I don't remember a thing after that. I want to know what happened to Ellie and my friend Kurt."

Joe experienced another short pain in his shoulder, and he closed his eyes for only a moment before he hurried on, "I need to call my wife to tell her where I am and what happened. I'm sure she'll probably be wondering why I didn't call her last night. Can I have my cell phone? Where is it?"

After feeling another sudden jabbing pain in his shoulder Joe continued, "Kurt's a friend, and we were meeting to talk about a man who worked for him. He was telling me he was almost sure his employee was using his station to sell drugs to customers. Kurt definitely knew the man who came to our table and shot us. There was so much confusion. Perhaps the two of you can help me put the rest of the pieces together."

Alvin looked up as he saw a nurse enter and hand Joe's phone to Sam. Turning to Joe, Sam said, "Mr. Wallace, we'll need your phone for now if that's okay with you. We'll call your wife from here if you can give us her number."

Sam quickly punched in the number Joe recited to him. In seconds a phone began ringing in Knoxville. On the third ring, a voice answered, "Hello, this is Madeline Russell. You have reached my daughter's phone. Early this morning she somehow forgot to pick it up when she left to return home. Could I help you?"

Surprised he was not talking to Mrs. Wallace, Sam said, "Hello Mrs. Russell, I'm a police officer, and my partner and I are with Joe Wallace. We were hoping to speak to your daughter. Do you know where she might be and how we could contact her? We need to give her some information about her husband . . . We really need to speak to Mrs. Wallace if we can."

Alvin stretched out his hand and asked Sam to give the phone to him when he noticed Sam's reluctance to tell the woman where Joe was, "Mrs. Russell, we don't wish to alarm you, but Mr. Wallace has been involved in an accident. My name is Alvin Underwood, and my partner Sam and I are with the Birmingham, Michigan Police Department. We are visiting with your son-in-law in his hospital room. He was involved in an accident last night, and we briefly needed to talk to his wife."

Startled and deeply concerned Maddie said, "Oh, heavens! Is Joe all right? What happened to him? Caroline will want to know about this if she calls me about her phone. She must have left about five this morning, and in haste she left her cell phone plugged into an outlet in my kitchen."

Trying to avoid giving the woman unnecessary information, Alvin spoke with caution, "Mrs. Russell, Joe Wallace is talking to us now, and I'm sure he does not want to frighten you or have you worry about him. He was having dinner with a friend last night, and then something happened. He's now resting securely in a hospital bed. I'll make a note to get back to you as soon as we know more about what happened, and I'm sure Joe will then want to speak to you himself. We understand you live in Knoxville. We will need your address and phone number?"

Flustered and also agitated Maddie resumed, "I live outside the city limits. My! This is such a sudden shock to me. I'm sure you understand. Sir, I dislike giving my address to anyone over the phone. At the moment, I cannot tell you where Caroline is, but I'm sure she's in her car traveling back to Michigan. I believe she's possibly 200 miles north of here on the main interstate highway. Leave your number, and when my daughter calls here, I'll give her your number. Officer, was Joe in a bad accident or are they just checking him over? Can I do anything at all to help? This is all such a shock! Phooey! I'll give you my address with my phone number if that'll help."

Alvin wrote down the numbers, thanked her and tried to offer her assurance that there was no reason for her to worry. He asked her to remain calm and not to alarm her daughter when she called. Then he said they would definitely keep her informed and would ask Joe to call her later that morning. He then gently said goodbye.

Making another attempt to move his body, Joe experienced a lengthy pain as he uttered his daughter's name, "My Ellie. Now please call and see if you can reach her." Joe gave Sam the number so quickly that Sam had to ask for the number to be repeated.

It took Ellie several seconds to reach for her handbag and to locate her phone. Believing it was one of her school friends calling, she answered with her tired, stressed voice, "Heh."

Sam spoke to the tired voice, "I'm Officer Sam Reynolds with the Birmingham Police Department. Am I speaking to Ellie Wallace?" For a moment there he received no reply, but once Ellie thought the man must be who he said he was to have her number as well as her name, she answered, "Yes . . . yes, I'm Ellie Wallace."

"Miss Wallace, my partner and I are in your father's hospital room talking to him."

Excited and relieved Ellie cried, "My dad really did make it. How is he?"

"Yes, he's sitting up in his bed now and has asked us to call you to find out where you are." When Sam finished stating those words, he heard a young girl choke up and begin to cry. Realizing she could not talk because of her fragile emotions, he waited momentarily listening as the cry of relief turned into a full sob. Once Ellie was able to speak again, she swiftly and eagerly said, "My dad, he made it, didn't he? He's OK. My dad's going to live after what happened to him!"

Walking into the hallway to talk more privately to Ellie, Sam attempted to comfort the young girl as he spoke, "Miss Wallace, your father has sustained a gunshot wound in his shoulder and also in an upper portion of his arm. He lost a lot of blood, but, yes, we're quite certain he'll pull through. But at this time he's quite weak."

As Sam continued listening to the grateful sobs he added, "We came to see your father this morning, and we've been asking him questions about what happened at the pizza restaurant last night. I'm sure it was a terrible ordeal for both of you, but we'll need to talk to you in order to finish our investigation. Your father said you were with him last night. What we need to know is why the shooting took place."

Aware that Ellie was listening to him as she must have been driving on a highway, he heard the uncontrollable intervals of sobs coming from the other end of the line. "Miss Wallace, where are you? Are you in a safe place to talk? And are you alone?"

Tearfully she answered, "Yes, I'm alone and safe in my dad's car near a small town just below the Kentucky state line. I've forgotten the name of the last town I passed, and I had to get a few hours of sleep last night before I drove on to my grandma's home. Thank you for calling me. Tell everyone at the hospital to take good care of my dad. He is the best, most wonderful dad a girl could ever have. You can tell him for me that I love him. Tell him that, please. I'm tired from driving all night. Don't forget to tell him I'm safe and should arrive at Grandma's place in a few hours."

Sam did not know the best thing to say, so he repeated again, "Miss Wallace, your father is not able to talk at the moment, but I'll be glad to tell him what you said. We'll need to ask you additional questions later. You're possibly the only one who has the most accurate recollection of what took place after the shots were fired. Will you call us on your phone when you stop and are calmer? You'll need to tell us what you remember, and please be careful as you drive. We can send someone to meet you when you arrive in Knoxville to make sure you arrive safely. You do know your grandmother's address, don't you?"

Pausing to think, Ellie said, "I don't remember her address, but I know I'll be able to find her place. Be sure to tell my dad where I am and that I'll be there within a few hours. I'm sure he told you I was on my way to Grandma's. Also, please tell him that I'm fine and that I'll stay awake for the rest of the trip. Don't forget to tell him I love him. . . Tell him . . ."

As Ellie continued to talk rapidly, she began noticing that their call was being interrupted. Finally unable to hear a single sound from the other end, she glanced at her silent phone. Sickened to see that her battery was more than likely needing recharging, she shook it and threw it over onto the passenger seat. The connection ended so abruptly, and she was sure her phone was almost dead and would no longer be of any use.

Sam guessed what must have happened to their connection, but wanting to find out all he could from the girl, he would need to wait until he could redial her number. A smidgen of battery power might be left in her phone, or she might find a place to recharge it. Possibly when Ellie was closer to a cell tower near a larger town, she might be able to return his call. He did have her number stored.

Alvin had been keeping a close watch on Joe during the conversation, but with all the drugs in Joe's body, he had fallen into a deep sleep again. For the second time, they left the hospital after giving a few instructions for the nurse on duty throughout the day to call them as soon as the patient awakened.

———⊳◦⊲———

Sam enjoyed this part of the job when people were questioned and new facts were discovered. Lately Alvin had been asking Sam what he thought about the various cases they were working on, and Sam enjoyed the discussions and the interactions with his boss. Compatible, they made a good team, and on this case, they were actually becoming good friends.

Both wanted to get in touch with Joe's wife right away, but it seemed it would not be possible. They were now becoming greatly concerned about a tired, inexperienced, young teenage girl traveling alone on such a long trip through several states. It was the coldest month of the year, and she hadn't slept much. She seemed to be wearier than she admitted to them and was certainly disturbed, but she was happy about her dad's condition. After partially witnessing a dreadful crime with the shooting of her father and experiencing what no kid should have to remember, she must still be experiencing shock. Sam wondered if she was even old enough to drive. She sounded rattled and so very young.

Chapter 18

REVIEWING THE FACTS that seemed to be true on one page and putting together on a separate page that which might have occurred at Mike's Place at approximately 6:30 the previous evening, Sam reminded himself not to overlook any possibilities or misjudge anyone too quickly. Only correct conclusions of what went down at Mike's counted. Pieces were coming together quickly, but what absolutely had taken place was still in question.

In Sam's orderly mind he rehashed what they had gathered at this point of the investigation and carefully wrote down only factual details on the clean page of a legal pad. Statements made by both Joe and Ellie were at the top of his list. Other related thoughts were written down on another sheet. Two men and a teenager were sitting at a table eating a pizza. A waiter was at another table on the other side of the large room picking up after some earlier customers. It was possible customers who were there earlier may have returned and shot the two men and the waiter. But Miss Ellie Wallace had been at the table with the two men, and earlier patrons would have known she was present and would have shot her too. He couldn't rule that likelihood out. This kid was told by her father to go into the women's room. Joe Wallace and the station owner had set up their meeting hours earlier that same day to talk about someone who McCoy thought was selling drugs at his station. Reflecting on these facts and pointing to one in particular, Sam mumbled to himself, "This is the point at which we need more facts. We've got to find the man with the gun."

Another cup of coffee was needed to jar his thinking, and Sam left his desk to refill his empty cup as his mind continued in a probing, exploratory mode. Returning to his desk and picking up his notes, he pondered things as he sipped from his cup, "Yes, I believe Ellie Wallace could still be in danger even now. We were told by Wallace that he told his daughter to take his wallet along with his car keys and drive to her grandmother's home. Wallace must have thought she was in imminent danger to send his young daughter on such a lengthy trip alone, throughout the night, and in this kind of weather. A blizzard no less. Was it possible Ellie or Joe were involved in drug dealing in any way. Even this attorney or his kid could have been the problem."

"Joe might not have had an alternative at the time but to send the girl away. Could he be protecting his daughter, and could she be involved in drugs herself? The mother wasn't home because she was in Knoxville with her mother. We have to believe Joe's story at this time." Sam continued to ponder. What Joe's daughter had told him verified his statements. Several facts have been revealed since early morning. These were small, but all facts could be important in an investigation dealing with illegal drugs.

Pushing his shoulders back into his chair and taking a deep breath, Sam was reminded of one of his distant cousins who played with several drugs during his high school years. He dropped out of school, and life it seemed, during his junior year. His cousin's actions had devastated his parents and the entire extended family. No secrets were kept from anyone, which was good, partly because

Ted was sent to a drug rehabilitation facility as soon as his parents knew.

Sam remembered how family members and friends were asked to pray for Ted. Once he was released, he was tempted on one occasion to return to drugs, but he resisted and stayed clean. From his own reading on illegal drugs, Sam knew they had ruined civilizations in the past. Today it had become an uncontrollable, violent crime that ran rampant in American cities and in many schools. It was often unchecked, and definitely a problem on the rise.

"Ted and Sam were the same age when my cousin first experimented with drugs. Ellie is that age today. She didn't seem to be involved, but she's running. Joe's daughter is a junior in school and left in a mighty big hurry." Sam shook his head certain he was on the wrong track thinking Ellie was involved in any drugs. He went back to his notes and began writing a few more thoughts. Draped over a door in the women's restroom, a sweatshirt and coat were found. These two items probably belonged to Ellie. Was she even wearing a coat when she left the restaurant? She didn't say anything about being cold when he spoke to her. Is it possible Joe's daughter was kidnapped? The thought sent a chill through him. She clearly said she was in a safe place, but was she?

No one in the nearby neighborhood saw the actual shooting. Joe Wallace and the girl were the only living witnesses that experienced the mayhem in that restaurant. Early this morning an elderly neighbor who heard some commotion coming from the location of Mike's last night came over to the crime scene to say he thought he heard shooting and someone running on the street, but added that the blizzard was horrendous.

Pointing into the restaurant, the man said the shooting seemed to be coming from that direction, but with his front door closed and his TV on, he wasn't certain. With a brief look from his doorstep, straining to see beyond the snow storm, he said he did not see anyone, so he thought no more about it until minutes later when he heard the siren and an ambulance coming down the street. He said it was bitter cold, and the snow was thick and blinding. Once the ambulance left the restaurant, he went to bed. Seeing police cars parked at the restaurant this morning with the obvious yellow tape surrounding the entrance, he dropped by to talk.

Reaching for his cup and swallowing more coffee as he reviewed his notes again, Sam heard the phone ring. "Reynolds here."

Alvin spoke quickly, "Notification came in minutes ago that a man turned himself in for shooting three men at Mike's place last night. He's a total wreck, hardly able to speak in his emotional state, but what he tells us fills in many of the details we were trying to put together. He has to be our shooter. He knows more than we could have uncovered if we'd worked on this case for months. He handed over thousands of dollars and said he'd been dealing drugs for a man named Owen Wolf. He's got to be the criminal who recruited the man to do his dirty work at Kurt's station. He said this Wolf guy was a former prisoner in the state pen. The man used Wolf's gun to do the shooting. Oh! And yes, he told us where to find the gun."

Pausing a moment Alvin then continued with more details, "Sam, this man who claims to be the shooter mentioned there had been a young girl with the two men at the table, but he was certain she was told by her father to leave the table. Like I said, the man is incoherent, but he seems concerned about the girl's safety after what he did. He cried. Yes he really cried and said Wolf will go after her. He was fearful for her life and his own life as well."

Not missing a word, Sam merely replied, "This Wolf guy sounds like one mean killer who works behind the scenes, and he possibly wants to get rid of the girl since she is a witness."

Knowing Sam understood the critical situation for the kid, Alvin said, "With Wolf loose, we've got our work cut out for us. Since the shooter gave us this information and told us about the gun, at least there's a crack open to us, and maybe we've even got a breakthrough. At this moment we're looking into police records for what we can dig up on this slimy, corrupt individual. I'm glad the shooter came forward with the name of this man he was working for, but he's scared the guy will come after him.

"If this man who confessed was playing with someone in the drug business, he was working with one nasty, treacherous guy. For that matter, all of them are depraved, filthy leaches and are involved in one filthy, illicit business. But now, we have this much to go on, and we'll possibly be able to catch him. We should have some results soon since he's spent time in prison."

Sam was writing down all he could in his notebook. Standing to his full six-foot height he said, "Sounds to me like this Owen Wolf has become a habitual criminal unable to learn from his mistakes, and he's out there attempting to produce additional havoc. My guess is he'll probably be after the teenager since she's a potential witness to what happened in that restaurant."

After a moment of silence, Sam added, "Should we call the Knoxville Police Department and possibly the Tennessee Highway Patrol to keep a lookout for the kid on Interstate 75 heading south of the Kentucky, Tennessee state line? We need to reach her by phone if possible, but when I spoke to her earlier during our visit with Wallace, it seemed her cell phone was running out of power."

What began as a common shooting in the city was quickly becoming a personal cause for Sam. Both Alvin and he were wondering what was best to do with the new information, Alvin broke the silence, "Sam, you and I know more details about this case than anyone else since we've followed it so closely from the beginning. We were able to talk briefly to both Wallace and his daughter. We need to reach this girl before that depraved drug dealer finds her. If our Mr. Wolf is able to get his hands on the family addresses and phone numbers . . . I don't want to think about that possibility!"

After another moment Alvin concluded, "We definitely should contact the Knoxville Police and warn them to keep a lookout for this piece of crap coming into their city. This animal might drive to the grandmother's home if he's able to obtain her address, and it's always possible he might take an airline flight. First we'll ask the police department to send a couple of good capable men to the grandmother's home and be present when Miss Wallace arrives. We could wait until we know more about this guy, but we absolutely cannot wait too long before deciding what to do. Stay close and ready, Sam, because we may have to move fast on this one. Miss Wallace might be in a great deal of danger without being aware of this menacing creep."

Chapter 19

CLARA'S HABIT WAS TO ARRIVE PROMPTLY at the Wallace's home to do whatever needed to be done for the day. Driving up the side drive, she smiled aware of the heavy layer of glistening new snow that covered everything in sight. Turning off the engine, she stepped out of her car. Exchanging her keys for the house key of the Wallace home, she glanced at the nearby kitchen window noticing there were no lights on, but this was not unusual since she often had been the first to arrive for work at the house.

She had a tiny apartment located only a short distance away, and although it was only one large room with a tiny bath in someone's basement, it was all she wanted or needed since she spent very little time there. Recently she had been able to purchase an older car for herself by bargaining with the salesman. He was glad to get rid of it because of the many dents and scratches and the hand sprayed paint finish, but it faithfully took Clara where she needed to go and seemed to run well for the few short trips she made on errands. She was especially thankful to Mr. Wallace for helping her examine the inner workings of the car before she made the final offer. For over a year both Caroline and Joe Wallace were extremely considerate of her needs.

Within weeks after arriving in the United States, Clara had taken steps toward becoming a citizen of what she now considered her adopted country. She was told by authorities of the United States Government it would be necessary for her to attend weekly meetings to learn historical facts and laws pertaining to her new country. But this had been a relatively easy task for Clara because she had been a serious student throughout her Ukrainian grammar school where she was expected to study the English language along with the Russian lessons.

It had been her solid grasp of English that brought her to the Wallace home because they had specifically requested the employment agency to send them someone who could both speak and read English well enough to answer phone calls and communicate with them. They also mentioned to the agency they would need someone who was gentle and compassionate toward a teenage girl.

There were several times when Clara had experienced homesickness for her native country and continued to miss family members she sadly left behind, but she was able to write letters regularly and even call them whenever a family member in Ukraine could arrange access to a phone in their little town. She was enjoying her new life in America and had made many new friends because she worked as a housekeeper for the Wallace family. In grocery stores and other shops, many were beginning to call her by her new American name.

She made good friends at the church where she regularly attended. Honestly interested in her as well as her country, even when she spoke to them in her broken English, her church friends thoughtfully asked about her family and enjoyed learning about her Eastern European background. Invitations to the frequent activities of the church were offered to her, and within months she was accepted as one of them.

Her openness as well as her attempts at conversational English delighted them, and she was encouraged to begin reading the Bible they offered her. In a short time Clara found it easy to ask questions about what she was learning about God in her new Bible, and one man in the congregation who had attended seminary and was extremely knowledgeable with keen insights in the Scriptures welcomed her inquiries and patiently discussed them with her. It was here among these church members she had become a Christian believing Jesus' sacrificial love and death had been for her.

Faintly remembering as a little girl her grandmother telling her about God's love, she recalled the elderly woman holding her on her lap as she read stories from a worn old book. She never had forgotten the songs Grandmother Nikhalaey had sung as she made rye bread, delicious soups, gathered eggs from the hen house and cleaned her home. Too early, when Clara was only eleven years old, this loving woman died. No one ever talked to her again about God until she arrived in America.

Weeks ago on Christmas Eve Caroline Wallace invited Clara to spend the evening with them as they exchanged gifts. On that occasion the family presented her with several gifts. Instead of writing Merry Christmas Clara on her gift cards, Caroline wrote Merry Christmas Galina Nikhalaev. It was her Ukrainian name, and Clara was so touched by that simple gesture that her eyes began to fill with tears. As she saw their faces, she knew they had remembered her in a beautiful way. She could not recall ever being happier in her life than that evening, and she was certain she would do anything for the Wallace family. They had accepted her for who she was.

For a year they had been enjoying some of her Ukrainian dishes, and they often requested them because they were made from lots of garden vegetables. They depended on her to cook their American dishes as well using unfamiliar recipes that were sometimes complicated for her, but Clara learned quickly. She purchased much of the food for their table, kept up with multiple daily chores and especially looked out for Ellie's best interests. Joe and Caroline Wallace trusted her in every way.

She never complained about running errands or doing the routine cleaning chores because she wanted to accomplish these tasks for people who were grateful for her services. The Wallace family had showed their appreciation in ways she never expected and had included her in their lives from the day she entered their home.

———◆———

Throughout the night and early morning hours it had continued to snow, and as Clara stepped onto the untouched whiteness that covered the driveway, she looked around the yard marveling at the clean fluffy blanket draped over every limb and branch. The white stillness around her this morning was beautiful to her with every roof, every bush and yard within sight sparkling under the pale morning light.

Earlier that morning she had stopped to pick up fresh milk, a dozen eggs and a supply of healthy vegetables on her way to their home, and standing still for only a minute holding onto the bag, she was reminded of her childhood when a fresh snowstorm would leave every field, every farm house and all the fences for as far as she could see in a winter wonderland. She closed her eyes for only a moment and took a deep breath of the brisk, cold air. Glancing again at the snow, she was reminded of numerous wintry mornings decades ago when she would dress for school.

In Ukraine it had been normal for a young girl who was born in a humble family to put her school clothes on by the fire in order to keep warm because this was the only area in their homes that was heated. All those wooly sweaters, skirts and thick socks kept her body insulated and well protected as she walked to and from her school. By the time she would reach the central section of her Ukrainian village where her school was located the early winter darkness always seemed to disappear. The sun would almost be visible. The climate of Ukraine was similar to what she was experiencing this morning in Michigan.

As she visualized some of those long ago memories, she felt that familiar wet chill before turning to enter the house. Down the driveway where her tires had traveled, she noticed there were no other tracks and questioned, "Was anyone inside? Was anyone here last night?"

Using the side entrance Clara unlocked the door. Checking to make sure the door had automatically locked when she closed it, she soon walked into the kitchen and was busy placing the food items she had purchased in the refrigerator and elsewhere. Then walking into the laundry room to see what she could place in the washing machine, it was obvious it would not be used. There were no dirty clothes in the basket from either Ellie or Mr. Wallace, but she knew the young girl made a habit of dropping her clothes on the floor as she dressed. She usually left them for her to pick up. A mess would often be found in her bathroom as well, but it was not Clara's place to correct Ellie and tell her to be neater or more considerate.

Concentrating on the silence from the upper level, she listened for a few additional seconds but could not hear any movement. She walked up the stairs to see if Ellie was getting ready for school. If she was not awake, that could be a problem, and she might need to drive Ellie to school so she would not be late for her first class. The teenager could sleep half the morning if she forgot to set her clock.

Sure that Mr. Wallace might have left early for his law office, Clara walked directly toward Ellie's room. "Ellie, you need to hurry and give yourself enough time to walk down the street to catch your ride," Clara said this in a pleasing manner as she opened the bedroom door a crack.

No answer or even a hint of movement came from inside. She knocked, and as she opened the door wider, she looked at the bed and was aware that Ellie had not slept in her bed. There were a few items of clothing on the floor near her bed, but from the appearance of the room, she was sure the girl had not been there through the night or this morning.

She called again as she walked toward the bathroom, "Ellie?" The light was on and the door was open, but she received no answer. Alarmed somewhat she mumbled, "It's not like Ellie to make her bed." The silence and appearance of the room were unusual. Only a pair of jeans partially kicked under the bed, her bookbag lying on top of the bed with papers lying nearby, but Ellie was nowhere. Clara was concerned.

Hurriedly walking down the hallway to the Wallace's bedroom, she peeked in the dark quiet room and saw that there was no evidence Mr. Wallace had spent the night there either. "Strange that neither had spent the night here," she thought.

She left the upper level and hurried down the stairs to get started on her chores as she continued to wonder where they were. As she reached the bottom of the stairs she noticed the unusual eerie stillness throughout the home. At this hour on a weekday morning, there was always noise. Someone would be eating breakfast, Mr. Wallace would be listening to the radio or walking around the house in a hurry to gather things so he could leave for work, and Ellie might be frantically trying to find an item she wanted to wear but was unable to locate.

In the kitchen she would check the phone to see if a message had been left for her. No messages were left.

Yesterday had been Clara's day off, so she thought possibly she was not told that Mr. Wallace and Ellie would be away.

She was sure Caroline was still with her mother in Tennessee and certain she would hear something soon as to why the house was empty. For now she would get busy and catch up on the daily chores until she heard from someone. Sinks always needed a bit of scrubbing, counters were prone to become cluttered if she failed to put things away, and within a day the bathrooms often were in the need of another cleaning. Having yesterday off, she knew there must be rooms for her to straighten and floors to vacuum.

When she awakened that morning, she intended to bake one of the family's favorite dishes because she knew Mr. Wallace often grabbed whatever he could find for Ellie and himself to eat when she was not there to cook for them. With Mrs. Wallace away she wondered what they had eaten last night. His usual habit was to take a casual glance in the refrigerator for something quick to eat or pop in the microwave. Often he would open a can of soup, but it was always something quick and easy.

Clara began preparing the dish for the evening meal while she waited for a call telling her where they were. After gathering the food items to make the dish, she reached for the cutting board near the counter, picked up a large spoon from the utensil holder, located the trusty measuring cup, pulled out the heavy butcher knife and bent over to find a saucepan to begin making a sauce.

She would prepare most of the ingredients for the recipe, store them in the refrigerator, and later they would be ready to take out and combine with a sauce for the casserole dish. Then it could be baked in the oven later in the day. Finding a whole onion in the vegetable bin, she pulled off the outer skin with a smaller knife, laid the knife aside and picked up the larger knife. She began slicing and chopping it on the board. As she considered again where Mr. Wallace and Ellie might be, she heard an unmistakable knock at the side door.

Chapter 20

WITH THE WALLACE'S ADDRESS STORED in his memory, Owen stood at the side entrance of the home. He now had what he needed to change the course of events to his advantage. He made up his mind he would not allow any snobby kid to spoil his plans, nor would he be caught by any law enforcement people. He would never return to jail simply because a young girl had been successful in slipping out of his grasp. He did not plan to hide as a fugitive either. He was confident he would locate and trap that overindulged kid so she would have no possibility whatsoever of ruining him or his business. Absolutely no one would outsmart him, no one, especially that rich little spoiled brat. He might use Ray if he needed him, but he was quite sure he was capable of taking care of matters on his own.

He did not think this Eleanor Wallace had the intelligence to go directly to the police because more than likely she would flee to her home where someone would be. She might even go to a relative's place, but he needed to be cautious because he was determined to find this girl soon wherever she would have gone. Reminding himself of the fact that lawyers and even their kids were not stupid, he had to be on his guard for something unusual. He had to be extra smart if he wanted to finish the job. He mumbled to himself, "She's possibly home now, and I may have her in minutes."

Driving by the address twice to get a good view of the home and yard, he wanted to enter the home easily without much explaining at the door. He had scanned the surroundings and was able to see only one car parked in the driveway. He did not miss the obvious tire tracks with the car leading to the side entrance. Only this older car had entered the driveway since the snow had fallen the night before, but it definitely was not the one he remembered seeing last night.

"So who's home? Mom? Maybe Little Miss Wallace herself?" He was sure he had come to the correct address when he followed the tracks up to the side door. So there would be no possibility of a problem from a nearby nosey neighbor, he would attempt to leave a professional impression to whoever came to the door. After all, he did have on his best clothes.

He knocked and waited as he strained his ear to hear signs of movement inside. His wait was short, and in less than half a minute a middle-aged woman stood before him. Dressed as she was, Owen was certain this could not be Mom and certainly not that teenager he was interested in trapping. He reasoned this woman must be a hired housekeeper. She would be easy to handle, but he would first talk to her and make sure no one else was in the house.

"Good morning, Sir, can I help you," Clara smiled welcoming the visitor with her usual broken English.

For just a moment Owen hesitated before replying, "My name is Norm Forester, and Mr. Wallace sent me over to find some papers he's been working on. He said they would be on his desk. This is unusual, I know, but I simply need to pick up what he needs and get them back to the office for him this morning as soon as possible."

Sensing the request was out of the ordinary, Clara smiled at the man and said, "Possibly I could call Mr. Wallace's office and ask what papers he's requesting." She wanted to be helpful, but, for an unknown reason, she thought it extremely odd that Mr. Wallace had not called her about this. No message had been left, and she had not seen him this morning. Also it seemed highly unlikely his office had not called and asked for the papers. Her employer would consider it rude for her to impede any necessary work that needed to be done, but she would gain a bit more information from this man first before she allowed him to enter the home and rifle through Mr. Wallace's papers.

As she was wondering why Mr. Wallace had not taken a few minutes to call her and let her know he was sending a messenger to his house to pick up needed papers, she noticed how the man's face displayed irritation with the delay. Reluctant to allow him to enter she continued to wonder, "Why hadn't Mr. Wallace spent the night in his bed last night?" Becoming suspicious of the request and the short explanation the man was offering, Clara began to suspect this man could be a possible threat only wanting to enter the home. She became nervous and was conscious of how the man's facial expression was changing.

It was evident to Owen this foreign woman who stood before him was making a judgment about his request. Blocking the doorway she was staring at him as if to say, "I want more information before I'll believe you and let you in."

Clara waited patiently for him to explain more fully his visit, but after an uncomfortable few seconds studying his face and noticing the small tattoo above his shirt collar she said, "I would like to assist you, Sir, so I will call Mr. Wallace's office and talk to my employer. I'll ask him what particular papers he is requesting. Then I'm sure I can locate them for you. Sir, what was your last name again?"

The handsome friendly countenance on Owen's face had been exchanged for an ominous stare that gave Clara an uneasy, dreadful feeling. Stepping back half a step, she moved slightly away from him. Owen was unwilling to give up, and he poked his head inside and looked around. When Clara followed what his eyes were fixed on, he took the opportunity to shove her with his powerful hands. He then struck her with both his powerful fists as hard as he could, which knocked her to the floor with a hard thud. He growled, "I don't have time to play games trying to convince a common maid that I'm an office errand boy."

The tremendous blows rendered Clara almost unconscious, and she did not move. All she could feel were surges of pain coming from her head, her chest, and the leg she had fallen on. Believing she would die, she lay helpless on the wood floor.

Glaring down at her crumpled body, Owen kicked her hard with his foot and then bent over to strike her again with his right fist on the side of her face. Clara's eyes closed completely now as she lay motionless and unable to make a sound. There was no struggle. With her face and front portion of her body turned toward the wall, Owen noticed a slow stream of blood flowing from her limp head as he shoved her to one side with his hands so he could close the door completely.

With a simple click, the door locked. Reaching into his coat pocket, he pulled out a pair of latex gloves and put them on both hands. Glancing at Clara's body lying still and lifeless on the floor, he said with cruelty, "Another foreigner to never worry about." Then stepping around her, he moved toward what he thought must be the home office. Once inside the room, he began a frantic search.

Papers, folders, pens and other items were scattered onto the floor, which made a mess but also a lot of noise.

For a full minute Clara was incapable of knowing what had happened to her. She actually thought she had died, but then she felt pain coming from her jaw, cheek bone, chest and leg. She slowly and partially opened her eyes. Believing she might be better off to appear as though the forceful blows had ended her life, Clara would fake her death until he left. Hopefully he would not end her life when he left.

With her face toward the wall she was unable to see where the man was or what he was doing, but she heard the noises coming from what must be the office. She wondered, "Can I fool this brutal man who is definitely strong enough to kill me if he wants to." But with the incredible pain she felt in her body, she was unsure she could endure more pain without making a sound or moving her leg. She would concentrate on not making a sound.

She lay in the same position, telling herself she was physically no match for this man intent on evil. Absolutely silent and without moving a muscle, she could feel inside her mouth with her tongue. She was sure the salty taste in her mouth must be blood, and she felt a loose tooth. But this was nothing compared to losing her life. She knew even if she could raise her body, he would catch her in seconds and end her life altogether. In desperation and fear, she lay there as lifeless as she could as waves of persistent pain were almost unbearable.

Sure the maid was dead and not concerned about her, Owen took another look at her as he left the office and quickly walked toward the kitchen. Entering he swept the room with his sharp eyes. Then seeing the telephone, he walked toward it where he was sure the family kept their listings of addresses and telephone numbers for easy access.

"Bingo! There it is," he said loudly. The address book he knew he would eventually find was in clear view on the little desk next to the kitchen table. Curling up his lip and grimacing, he opened the book looking at all the family names, addresses, land line phone numbers and cell numbers. Uncles, aunts, cousins, and even friends seemed to be listed. Only one grandparent seemed to be living since some names had been crossed off. Slamming the book shut and placing it in the pocket of his overcoat he swiftly walked toward the side door.

Clara could hear his quick footsteps now as he walked out of the kitchen and into the small hallway close to where she lay. Uncertain about what this beastly invader would do when he reached her, Clara was terrified she would now die. She began praying in earnest and imagined what might be the conclusion of his madness before he left. Holding her breath, she prayed, "Lord Jesus, please allow me to live to tell someone about this madman?"

Unable to see his face she missed the sinister glare, but she did not miss hearing him say, "You'll not outsmart me again, you little brat!" After a boisterous laugh he violently said, "I'll find you Ell-en-or and finish the job."

Looking around covetously at the lovely interior of the home briefly to see where the kid lived, he stood silently for a few seconds. In a hostile manner he spoke in a low raspy tone, "It might take a little more digging and smart work, Missy, but I'll find you." Then he laughed boisterously.

Clara heard everything from her place on the floor, but she was too frightened to even appear like she was able to breathe. The pain was almost unbearable and more than she had ever thought was possible and still be alive, but she thought her best chance was to lie still facing the wall and listen to what was being said while the man was inside the house.

As a little girl with three older brothers who loved to play soldier games, she learned from them how to appear dead. Her brothers and those childhood games had taught her well, and now as a grown woman, she thought like that little girl, "This must work for me. Dear Jesus, don't allow him to kill me."

In terror, she remembered his words directed toward Ellie. She knew he was now standing directly above her because she could hear him clear his throat. Another trickle of blood began to flow from the side of her injured mouth, but she was determined to suffer on the floor, act dead like a slain soldier and concentrate on listening. It might take all her mental capacities and energy to continue lying there without making a single sound or moving a muscle, but she was confident God would give her endurance. Clara prayed again and again for her life to be spared and for the safety of the entire Wallace family.

With the address book filled with names and numbers he wanted, Owen stepped closer to the door to leave. He stood for a second before he reached for the handle to open the door. Taking another brief look around, he stepped back and turned to gaze in the spot where Clara was lying, the same spot where he had left her. Wanting to rush out quickly, he cursed and barked, "Bye, bye, lady, you need to have better manners and not ask so many question of those who come to the door."

After a loud contemptuous laugh he turned on his heel, opened the door, slammed it hard and raced to his car. As he grabbed the car door handle he stopped for a second. Had he left anything behind? Should he go back and follow his footsteps to make sure he had not left any clues behind? He pulled off his gloves and stuffed them in his coat pocket. Certain he had hit the maid hard enough to kill her, he opened the door, jumped inside and started the motor. He placed his car in reverse, backed up onto the street and departed. "I have no time to waste."

Smiling with satisfaction as he thought of what he had in his pocket, he was sure he had exactly what he had come for. Calls could soon be made. Nagging him a bit was whether or not he had left any clues behind. He was sure no fingerprints or items were left in the house because he wore gloves. He would not worry about what he might have left. "Miss Wallace, I'll call you. I'll find you. No one ever messes with me."

"Hurry," he said, "because the police will soon be arriving at the Wallace home to start their investigation. He could not be sure what the police knew after 14 hours, but he was certain they would check everything at the Wallace home. "They'll see the dead woman, and I left a mess in that office, but they'll never know who was there. Never!" He laughed.

Clara heard the door crash shut, but she continued to lie there until she heard a car motor start and then drive away. Taking a slow, deep breath and waiting another full minute she raised her severely injured body as best she could and felt throbbing pain coming from what must be a damaged hip too. When she crashed to the floor, she had fallen on her left leg.

After his cruel kick, she must have been unconscious for a brief moment. But she was fully aware of what he said, and she knew she must call the police because she was certain Ellie's life was in serious danger.

She grabbed the bottom of her blouse and wiped her mouth with it. She looked at the blood only once. In spite of the pain and the fact that she might have problems later,

Clara lifted her body and moved into the kitchen dragging one leg behind her. At the phone, she punched in the numbers to Mr. Wallace's law office and waited for someone to answer.

Clara didn't give the receptionist time to say the usual greeting before blurting out, "The entire Wallace family is in great danger!"

With the only strength she could manage Clara continued, "Minutes ago a man came to the house, forced himself into the Wallace home looking for something in their office. He struck me three times. Please let me talk to Mr. Wallace, or if he's not available, I need to talk directly to another lawyer."

In seconds Clara was speaking to John Payne, a senior partner in Joe's law firm, and was giving him as much information as she knew. He said they would stop everything and take care of the matter. They would also send someone to pick her up and take her to the emergency room of the hospital.

Clara tried straightening her body but was unable, so she leaned against the closest chair and closed her eyes. Another pain shot through her head, her entire body and down her leg. Unable to sit upright, she slumped to the floor. More pain followed, but confident she had done what she needed to do, she would wait for the person who would come to rescue her. In tremendous pain, and now almost unconscious, she began singing a song she had learned while sitting in her grandmother's lap. Tears flowed down both cheeks.

———⊰◈⊱———

Owen drove a mile or so from the Wallace residence and found a place to pull off to the side of the road. No one would be suspicious of someone looking up an address.

Again his thoughts returned to what had taken place at the Wallace home. In his hasty departure had he somehow left even one clue that might connect him to the shootings last night? His fingerprints were on file now since he had been in prison, but he was certain he was safe because he had worn those latex gloves during his entire search.

Owen was sure the maid who gave him trouble was dead. "That woman with her strange, foreign accent didn't have to question my motive, but I knew I'd kill her in spite of what she said or did. She was foolish to suggest calling the lawyer's office to verify my mission to check on whether or not I was a messenger sent from the Wallace's office." Rehashing again what had taken place minutes ago he said with disgust, "Who did she think she was to question me? She probably was told to ask questions . . . or perhaps she was smarter than I thought. She was just a common maid who cleaned up after other people. What a nasty job that's got to be."

His eyes fell first on the listing of George and Virginia Wallace. They lived in Georgia. Audrey and Bruce Seals lived in Maryland. Warren and Megan lived in Idaho. Paula Hill lived in Maine. Ned Wallace seemed to be at Georgia Tech. "Yah, that's probably Edward Wallace, the Wallace's son." Down the list he saw more. Robert and Chelsea-Simmons Collins lived in North Carolina, Ryan and Shelly Ward someplace in England. "That's got to be their daughter."

He paused as he read the next name. Madeline Russell lived in Tennessee. "This family is all over the place."

He would make some phone calls, but he wanted to get to the Wallace girl very soon. Again he asked, "Where would that kid go? Who would she run to? Mom more than likely. I should have gotten that much information from that stupid maid before I struck her. It's too late now."

Turning to the address book's inside cover, Owen could see a woman's name written there. It was scratched and worn from use with an email address and phone number. "Caroline Wallace's cell phone number more than likely. Yes, this has to be Mom." Turning back to the church directory he saw her name there again. "Caroline Wallace, your cell phone number isn't included in the church directory, but it is actually written in your address book as an easy reference for someone like me to find. How easy for me? Now where are you Caroline Wallace? Maybe your brat's with you, and you're both wailing and crying your eyes out for a dead man."

Ten numbers were quickly punched into his phone, and he heard a phone ringing hundreds of miles away. A soft spoken woman at the other end said, "Hello, this is Madeline. You've reached my daughter's telephone, but perhaps I can help you"

Hearing the woman's soft, Southern cultured tone, Owen attempted to reply in an easy manner because he was seeking information, "Miss, could I please speak to Caroline Wallace?"

"Sir, my daughter isn't here. She left four hours ago to return home and forgot her cell phone. She left it plugged into an outlet on my kitchen counter. I should have been more aware of it myself when she left. But possibly, Sir, I can help you?"

Hesitating for only a moment, Owen began speaking trying to get as many of his questions answered as possible, "I'm sorry this happened and that your daughter isn't there. You must be Madeline Russell, Eleanor Wallace's grandmother. Is that correct?" Then giving the woman plenty of time to reply and offer him more information, he waited.

"Yes, I am. Family and friends call me Maddie."

"Thank you for offering your help Maddie. What I need is Eleanor's phone number. That's Caroline's daughter, right?" Owen knew he shouldn't have included his last question, but she didn't seem to notice. He wanted to leave a good impression with this woman, and he might need more assistance from her later. Surely she would be easily fooled.

"Yes, I can give that number to you if you'll hold on for a moment. I need to go to my kitchen where I keep my phone book."

It took Maddie less than a minute to find Ellie's number, and she gave it to Owen and then asked him, "Your name, Sir? I do not believe you gave me your name."

Stopping to think of an interesting name, Owen replied, "My name is Wendell Hollingsworth, and I want to thank you for getting that number for me, Maddie. I hope your daughter will have a pleasant trip on her way back to Michigan. Thank you for all your help, and have a great day. Goodbye."

Owen could not help but chuckle to himself after he said goodbye to the woman. "A person could fool this old lady anytime." Proud of how clever he was and how easily he had obtained the one number he wanted, he now could contact Miss Wallace. "Obtaining her cell number was a snap."

Once Madeline Russell laid Caroline's cell phone down on the kitchen counter, she began running the last few minutes of her conversation with Mr. Wendell Hollingsworth through her mind. "How would he know my daughter lived in Michigan? I didn't mention that to him. Then when I asked for his name, he wasn't very quick to respond to that. I've certainly never heard the man's name mentioned before. That was a weird call. Would Ellie know this man? Strange that he, who sounded like an older man to me, should ask for Ellie's phone number without giving me a reason. There are so many crazy people out there preying on young girls, and this one scares me."

Maddie had a sinking, almost sick feeling about what this man might be up to, because she had given him her granddaughter's private cell number. "I'll call Ellie now since I have her number in front of me," Maddie mumbled to herself as she placed the call. Soon she heard an automated voice telling her to leave a message. She thought, "Surely Ellie will return my call when she looks at her messages." Cell phones were still somewhat confusing to Maddie, but she knew they worked and were convenient.

She left a brief message after hearing the tone telling Ellie that she would like her to call back as soon as she could. It was urgent. She wanted to ask her about this Wendell Hollingsworth, or whatever his name was. She would tell Ellie he had called her mother's cell number, and since he was unable to speak to Caroline, he asked for her number. She would definitely apologize and tell Ellie she foolishly gave this man her number. She wanted also to tell her that her mother had left early that morning to return home.

Maddie would remember to call her granddaughter again in a few minutes. So often she seemed to be talking on her phone with a friend, and perhaps she was talking to one now.

Chapter 21

"MY DAD IS ALIVE!" Ellie cried excitedly. The entire states of both Ohio and Kentucky had been exceptionally difficult when she did not know if her father had pulled through, but she was now thankfully relieved to know he made it. "That's what the policeman told me." It was the best news she could expect to hear as she continued driving south on the main highway that was leading her toward Knoxville.

The long continuous interstate had taken her through several large cities during the night, and traveling on their perimeters in the wee hours of the morning had taken a toll on her nerves. Often while alone, she pretended what she was experiencing was merely a nightmare and that she had been caught up in it. Ellie wanted several times to simply awaken herself. But she could not be a dreamer for long. She knew the terrible dream was actually real. She had wanted her life to remain in its usual pattern and to wake up, climb out of bed and begin getting ready for her classes. Ellie mumbled, "Dad would've been getting ready to leave for work as I dressed. I would be grabbing a quick breakfast and then running to catch my bus."

But the horrible nightmare was a reality, and the dreadful incident in the restaurant had happened. Time and again she relived the harrowing ordeal as she drove those hundreds of uncertain miles.

"That policeman who called was standing beside my dad's bed when he spoke, and although my dad was too weak to talk to me at the time, the man's words were the best proof I have that my dad is alive."

The reminder of the news led to more salty tears, but tears of complete joy, and thankfulness this time. Assured that she would be able to speak to her father as soon as she arrived safely at her grandmother's home, Ellie could relax, confident she had nothing to worry about.

When the policeman had asked her about what took place last night, she was confused after hearing her father had made it and was in the hospital. She did not want to talk to them about what she witnessed or answer their questions until after she spoke to her dad. Once she arrived at her grandmother's and got some sleep, she would call the policemen from there and tell them all they wanted to know. Sleep, wonderful sleep, sounded so appealing to Ellie, but she realized several hours of travel remained. Even extremely exhausted without much energy, she must continue to pay close attention and keep her irritated eyes glued to the road.

Remembering she had her phone with her, but knowing it was extremely low on battery power, she would drive steadily and wait a few hours before using what little power her phone might have left.

In Tennessee the roads had more twists and turns, and there were steeper hills to climb than she had dealt with in Kentucky. Slowing down enough to continue having good control of the car, Ellie thought of the close call she experienced only half an hour ago when a large truck had overturned only hundreds of feet in front of her. Instantly there had been a pile-up. Along with several other cars and trucks, she had to slowly maneuver around the accident to miss the wreck.

She was shaken at the time, partially because she was exhausted, but she did recover within a short time and was pleased she had reacted so well. Now because she was beyond the Blue Grass State of Kentucky and moving into Tennessee, the air felt warmer, and the sun was shining. For her, it was extremely unusual to see sunshine in January. In fact it was late March or early April before the sun would peek through the clouds and remain for any length of time.

Feeling dryness creeping into her throat, Ellie began feeling extremely thirsty and decided to get something to sip on when she reached the outskirts of the next town. Muscles in her neck and shoulders were becoming tight and painfully sore. She needed to stretch all her limbs.

Not knowing when heavy drowsiness might creep up on her again, she thought her next stop would be an excellent place to stretch her legs once she found a convenient place to purchase coffee, something she had learned to enjoy.

It was almost 10 a.m. in Michigan, and she began wondering if she were in the same time zone or had crossed over into the central time zone. As she kept her eyes out for the next exit, she heard her cell phone signaling from the low-volume ring setting.

"I've got a little power left, and this might be Dad," she excitedly said as she grabbed her phone. Expecting to hear her father's voice with effort and a dry, cracked voice she cheerfully said, "Hello."

⸺►◆◄⸺

Owen grinned widely proud of his achievement. Hearing Ellie's energetic voice, he decided to leave the impression with her that he was a professional newsman, "Eleanor Wallace, my name is Norm Forester, and I know you do not know me, but I know your father. I attempted to reach your mother just minutes ago, but it seems she left her cell phone at your grandmother's home by mistake this morning before she left to return home. Your grandmother answered the phone however, and I was able to speak to her. She gave me your phone number so I could ask you a few quick questions."

For a brief moment Ellie did not respond, but in response she said, "Mr. Forester, please call my grandmother again and tell her I slept for several hours, which was longer than I meant to. I had to get a little rest before I continued on my trip to her place. First, I want you to know that my cell phone needs recharging badly, and I don't know when the power will completely quit on me. Tell her also I'm sorry I'll miss seeing my mom at her place. I meant to call her sooner."

Noting the disquietude in the girl's voice, but surprised at Ellie's words of explanation that she was traveling to her grandmother's home, Owen deceptively said, "Oh, yes, Miss Wallace, I'll definitely get back to your grandmother and tell her what you said. But I wanted to call you today to ask you a few questions. What I'm about to say may not be pleasant for you to hear."

Ellie perked up, listening quietly, wanting to know what the man had to tell her, "Yes, Sir."

"Miss Wallace, I'm with the Daily Tribune, and I do want to get some pertinent information that only you can give me since I'm aware you witnessed some of what took place at Mike's Pizza Restaurant last night."

Hearing no sounds coming from his listener, Owen continued because he was anxious to get quick replies and decided to press her with a few questions, but not give her any time to think before she answered. "You were there, Miss Wallace, isn't that correct?"

Ellie thought there was something strange about his direct and insensitive manner of asking her to answer in haste and not give her information about her father's condition. Hesitating because she was alarmed, but with her instincts, she posed a question to him without answering, "Could you tell me what this is about?"

Ellie surprised herself by responding to his question by asking that question. Attempting to answer his question by asking another question was all she could think of at the moment. On several occasions she had heard her father ask questions before answering questions set before him. She thought this might allow her time to think and possibly give her an edge on the conversation.

Being confronted by the girl was not what Owen had expected as he listened to every word she spoke. He did not miss the hesitancy in her speech, and he was determined to find out what he wanted to know as he continued. He rephrased his question and asked in a speedier manner, "Miss Wallace, were you with your father at Mike's Restaurant last night? Like I said, I'm a reporter calling from the Daily Tribune, and I'm inquiring to set the record straight. We hate to publish statements that are untrue." Owen was determined to receive an answer this time. "At dinnertime last night, were you, Miss Wallace, with your father at the restaurant?"

Wary of the man's truthfulness and his intentions because of his demanding tone, Ellie began doubting whether this man was who he claimed to be. Asking her the same question twice and insisting she answer his question was not what she needed right now. Also it seemed this questionable newsman was far too direct. He spoke without any sensitivity about the terrible crime, and this angered her. She began believing he might be a dangerous man, so she made up her mind he would not hear fear in her voice.

It occurred to Ellie that potentially she may have already given this man too much information about where she was headed, and she boldly replied with yet another question, "Sir, why are you asking me this?" This time Ellie was shocked that she had been so direct. In an attempt to be in charge of the conversation and not provide any more vital information she and others might be sorry for later, she came up with the only solution she could think of at the time.

Avoiding conversing any further with the newsman, Ellie decided to terminate the call. She would make him think they were losing their connection and her cell phone was out of power. She simply rubbed her finger nails gently over the phone for several seconds to make it seem like some sort of static or a fadeout was occurring.

Carefully she spoke saying a few additional words, "Mr. Forester . . . ear me?" She again rubbed her nails over the phone. Then interrupting him, Ellie spoke over him as she repeated, "Mr. . . t . . . an . . . hear . . .?" More rubbing of her nails over the phone was done before she slowly punched the off button ending the call altogether.

At that instant, she took a quick look at the number he was calling from and memorized the last four digits. With complete confidence she said with determination, "If this newsman, or whoever the creep is, calls again, I've got his number."

She took a deep breath and replaced the phone on her lap because she would need to call someone about this newsman's call. Who to call, she did not know. Feeling a sickness in her stomach because she had little cell power left, Ellie dropped her phone on the passenger seat and took a brief look at her hands and discovered she was trembling.

Chapter 22

DURING THE CALL FROM OWEN, Ellie had missed her exit, but she would not miss the next one. Questions were surfacing in her mind, Who was this man who claimed to be a newspaper reporter? Was he honestly a newsman? Was he aware of all that had happened last night? How? He did not give her any information, but insisted she tell him whether or not she was there. Did he really know her dad? Did he know her father was alive and in the hospital? Could he possibly be the same man who had been at the restaurant last night and shot her father?

She would take a little rest at the next exit to get some of their strongest coffee with lots of sugar, a beverage she did not enjoy. There she could think and call her grandmother. She continued having questions and asked out loud, "How much more calling can I do on my cell now? It's already extremely low on battery power. I'm beginning to wonder if God loaned me a few extra minutes. Wow! Is it possible? Just maybe I'll be able to get my phone charged at the exit, or I could even borrow someone's phone."

With a hot cup of coffee in her left hand, and using the phone loaned to her by a kind lady at the truck stop, Ellie punched in 10 numbers. Unable to get her phone charged there, she would continue saving as much remaining power she had for the rest of her trip. She was sure she should make one quick call to her grandmother. In two rings Maddie picked up her phone.

"Hello, Grandma, this is Ellie. I'm on my way to your place right now and should arrive in a little more than an hour. I understand Mom left early this morning to return home."

Maddie replied, "How did you know? Yes, dear, your mother left early this morning, but since she was in a hurry to get on the road, she forgot to pick up her cell phone. It was in such a dark corner on the kitchen counter that she didn't see it. She forgot it, and I saw it this morning when I got up. I feel bad about that, but since I have it, I thought I would answer any calls that come for her. She hasn't called and must not have noticed she left it."

Hurrying on Maddie said, "Oh, Ellie, I tried to contact you only a little more than five minutes ago but received a recorded voice message telling me to leave a message for you instead. I wanted to tell you a man called by the name of Mr. Hollingswood. I believe that's what he said his name was. He asked for your mother, but of course she wasn't here, so I spoke to him. The man then asked me for your phone number, and I gave it to him. Do you know this Mr. Hollingswood, Ellie? After I hung up I wondered if it was such a good idea for me to give him your number, and I'm sorry now that I did that."

Ellie was at full attention hearing about the mysterious caller, and without much thought, she had a good idea who Mr. Hollingswood might be. Mr. Forester had leaped into her mind, and she tied the two men together. Strange these two men had called within minutes of each other. Arousing fear again, her conclusion was setting off an unpleasant alarm. What was happening? Suspecting these two men were more than likely one and the same, ominous thoughts were racing through her brain. Those two calls and their timing could not have been a coincidence.

Placing her coffee in the cup holder, she speculated that the strange sequence indicated much more than simply a coincidence. Struck by sudden fear of what this might possibly mean for her grandmother, herself and possibly her entire family, Ellie became anxious and then extremely protective of all of them. Her reasoning could be accurate. These calls were too close together to not be deeply concerned. She might be faced with a much larger problem than merely needing sleep.

Maddie perceived a conspicuous delay in Ellie's quiet manner and asked the question, "Something's wrong. Isn't it? Do you know this man that called and asked for your phone number?"

"Grandma, no! Absolutely not! I've never heard of this man. I'll call you back soon, Grandma, I promise, but you must give me your word that you'll stay inside your house and lock all your doors." The connection ended abruptly possibly due to poor cell tower capabilities in her grandmother's area, and Ellie did not know if her last words were heard.

Ellie bit her lip, thanked the woman for the use of her phone and left for her car. Pulling away from the truck stop, she began mulling over the questions that were asked by the two strange men, or the one man as she had come to suspect.

She was already three miles down the highway when she knew she had to get to a phone soon to make sure her grandmother heard what she had told her. There might be trouble ahead, lots of trouble. Within eight miles there was another exit, and she would take it. Arriving in Knoxville would take much longer than she planned.

Talking as quickly as she could on another borrowed phone, Ellie was able to say, "Grandma, I'm in the northern part of Tennessee and should arrive at your place approximately at noon or maybe later. Hopefully you heard what I said 20 minutes ago. I want you to do exactly as I tell you. Please, please stay in the house and lock all your doors. I don't want to scare you, but we might have a big problem. You and I! I cannot tell you why I'm telling you to play it safe, but I'll explain as much as I know when I arrive. Pray for me, Grandma. Pray for all of us."

Holding back seemed appropriate for the time being, but she wanted to tell more, "I've driven the entire night and have never been so exhausted. Do be careful, Grandma, and don't answer any questions if this man should call back. . . Don't give anyone any information, nothing whatsoever. Mr. Hollingswood, or whatever his name is, has to be a phony, I'm certain. And don't even answer Mom's phone again because this man could be a fraud. My cell phone power has failed, but I'll see you in a few hours. I love you lots, Grandma. Bye, but remember to pray."

Ellie felt sure her grandmother had heard everything she said before she hung up. Asking the friendly truck driver to use his phone had been an excellent idea, and now she was relieved knowing she would soon be seeing signs for Knoxville. "What a fake that guy is, and I believe he's very dangerous. He'll get no more information from me or from Grandma."

———◆———

Checking the gas gauge and seeing that it was less than half full, she whispered as if her father were present in the car with her, "I'm watching the fuel gauge, I promise, Dad. I'll not be caught with too little gas because being low on gas will not be my problem today. I don't need that kind of headache."

Fifteen miles down the highway Ellie pulled onto another exit ramp. A convenience store was connected to the gas station, and Ellie considered it was the best place to get gas and grab a Coke in a hurry. Soft drinks were not a regular habit of hers because they contained too much sugar, but something with caffeine in it was just what she needed to stay awake and concentrate on this supposed newsman who had contacted her. She had to give herself time to think through some ideas. Turning off the motor, she took a deep breath and closed her eyes for only a moment to rest. The car was silent, but she could still hear and feel the motor running on the hard road surface.

She could not waste time here. Time was not on her side. She picked up her handbag and reached inside for a credit card and the last five dollar bill. Dropping them in her coat pocket so they would be easy to locate when she needed to use them, she first filled the gas tank. "It should only take a minute or two to walk into the store, grab a Coke, jump back in the car in a flash and once again be on the road."

No one was working at the cash register as Ellie entered the store, so she walked back to where the cold drinks were lined up to pick up a Coke. As she moved in that direction she noticed a middle-aged man entering the store behind her and following her to the same section of the store where the soft drinks were stored. She was sure this couldn't be the manager. With her nerves on edge from the recent call from the supposed newsman, Ellie turned to look at the man who had stopped and was now standing a short distance away from her staring straight at her. His grin caught her off guard, and she quickened her pace.

Not thinking clearly but with a high degree of fear, Ellie hastily turned on her heel and made a dash for the women's restroom. She knew when she stepped inside that she should have walked around the back aisle and hurried out of the store to the parking lot and to the car, but it was too late now. Locking the solid door securely and turning around with her back to the door, she slid all the way down to the floor.

There she sat trying to soothe her nerves and without crying anymore she said, "I've got to pull myself together, and I've got to take control of the situation." She was almost sure this wasn't the stranger who had called her a short time ago, but she would wait inside this stinky place for a little while until she was sure the smiling man had plenty of time to leave the store. Then possibly the store manager would appear.

After waiting for what seemed to be a full five minutes, she opened the door as silently as possible. Not seeing the strange man, she returned to the cooler where the drinks were kept. The man who previously seemed to be following her once again appeared around a corner and looked at her. Now he was moving toward her, and there was no manager in sight.

"Where is the store manager?" she mumbled angrily under her breath. Opening the refrigerator door she grasped a Coke with one hand and swiftly turned only to meet the man's grinning face peering down at her. Ellie was sure he noticed fear in her face, and not knowing what to do, she shoved the soft drink toward him and said the only greeting she knew in the German language. Taking the can from her and showing surprise on his face because he did not comprehend her words, Ellie quickly snatched another Coke for herself and hastily turned toward the side aisle and almost ran to the cash register. Grabbing the loose $5 bill on her way out, she dropped it on the counter as she all but ran from the store to her dad's car for refuge.

"What a scare!" she said as she turned the key. The man had frightened her and possibly he would not have tried to do any harm to her, but she was not willing to take a chance. Pulling away from the store with panic written in her eyes, she finally gave a sigh of relief and said, "Thank you, Lord, for getting me out of there safely. I know I'm a wreck because of that stranger calling both me and Grandma."

The man walked out of the store behind her and smiled as she drove away. She was certain this was not the same man who had called her on her cell phone. No, but she was not certain of anything at the moment except that she had to get out of there and on the highway. Ellie silently and thankfully prayed, "Thanks again. Now take me safely to Grandma's house."

Miles down the road, Ellie thought about the unusual incident of the man in the store. She came to the conclusion he must have had a mental deficiency because he never said a word. Possibly he was looking for someone to be friendly toward him. In spite of the unfortunate situation, she was finally calmer. Ellie smiled a little thinking of the few words she had spoken to him in her high school German because those words were all that entered her frazzled mind.

Loneliness again was her companion, and she began humming and soon singing a few musical scores she enjoyed in order to stay alert. She mused to the only person with ears to listen, "Who ever heard of anyone falling asleep singing."

Chapter 23

MADELINE'S MIND was quite sharp, but over the phone she had given that stranger her grandchild's cell phone number. It was something she would never do again. Pondering what Ellie had tried to tell her and then had repeated more forcefully on another call, she began remembering specifically the inquiries the man had made. That fact that she had not mentioned the state where Ellie lived, but he had, gave her reason to believe he was a fake and more than likely a scoundrel. Ellie was right, and she would do what Ellie told her to do. "Lock all my doors and stay inside," she repeated Ellie's words.

Adding to the sham, she was troubled that Ellie had driven alone all through the night and was expecting to arrive at her home about noon. She did not understand why Ellie was making the trip by herself, and she could not imagine her mother knew anything about it.

She reasoned that Caroline would have mentioned it before she left even though she did leave in a hurry. Did Joe know? Joe was in the hospital, and he seemed to be avoiding calling her, so she would call him and personally ask him what he knew. She was convinced he should be contacted in any event.

Maddie called Joe's office by mistake, but she was informed that he was not there because he was in the hospital. Panicked that his office had been informed that he was in a hospital, she was careful this time to call Joe's cell phone. After several rings Joe picked up his phone that he had hidden from the nurses. Before Joe could say anything beyond hello, Maddie spoke, "Joe, this is Maddie, only minutes ago, I was talking to Ellie, and she told me she was on her way to my place. She said within the next couple of hours she would arrive."

The incident of the stranger calling her home to get Ellie's cell number was then related to Joe. Instantly he was ready to jump out of his bed, but not having enough strength to even feed himself properly, he tried to calm his mother-in-law, "Yes, Maddie, I did tell Ellie to drive to your home last night because Caroline was there. I heard earlier this morning that she had already left to return home. Something happened last night, and Ellie needed to run . . . It was best for her to go to your place."

Not wanting to reveal all he knew, Joe stopped and began turning over in his mind what this man who had called Maddie to get his daughter's cell number could be up to or what he planned to do.

"I'm fearful Joe that something else could happen because our Ellie told me to lock all my doors and stay inside. What does she know that we don't know? I did not know you were in the hospital either."

Joe wanted to explain the entire situation to Maddie but refrained from disclosing every detail to her of what had happened. So without alarming her he said, "Maddie, last night I was injured, and, because of a difficult situation and also because Caroline was at your place, I told Ellie she must drive to your home."

Madeline was not satisfied with his brief explanation and said, "My insignificant episode of sickness is over, Joe, and I told Caroline to quit fretting over me and return home where she was needed. She left quite early this morning. She missed picking up her cell phone, which was

charging overnight on my kitchen counter. I'm sure
Caroline didn't know Ellie was driving on the highway last
night. She wouldn't have left to return home if she had
known."

Gathering more of what she needed to say, she
strongly said, "Something has gone wrong, terribly wrong,
Joe, and I want you to please tell me what this is all about."

"Maddie, it's difficult to tell you everything . . . but I'll
try, so please sit down because you may find this
explanation frightening."

Joe told Maddie everything he thought she must
know, including the shooting, so she would not be in the
dark before Ellie arrived. He then told her to do exactly as
Ellie had told her, "Please lock every door and stay inside."

"Whew, Joe. This could be a much bigger problem
than we can imagine. I'll do just what Ellie said, but I don't
want to be left out. Hear me, Joe, on this. We'll all get
through this together. Thanks for telling me what
happened, and I'll do all I can to keep Ellie safe when she
arrives. Now you must get your rest because you'll need all
your strength in the days to come. I'm sure Ellie will tell
me what you both went through. By the way, Caroline
should be arriving home by late afternoon. Make sure you
leave a message for her. We'll talk later, and please pray."

⋙◆⋘

Cooped up in his hospital room while his daughter
was trying to ward off a man who was on the loose
possibly attempting to get rid of her was too much for Joe.
He was sure this sinister madman was evil, willing even to
kill if anyone got in his way. He had seen proof of that last
night. He was more convinced of it after listening to what
Maddie had told him. He was dealing with pain, and he
was weak, but that was not what disturbed him or filled

his thoughts. Ellie's safety and the safety of his entire family was what mattered most to him.

In helplessness he bitterly said, "I'm confined to this bed and unable to protect my daughter. She could be in great danger even after reaching Maddie's home. It's time I became involved."

Picking up the card Alvin Underwood had laid near his bed, he made sure a nurse was not spying on him to see if he was resting. He concealed his phone and waited for an answer.

"Inspector Underwood, can I help you." Alvin had been expecting this call from Joe Wallace, and he put aside what he was doing and was immediately engaged.

Getting right to the point Joe said, "Mr. Underwood, my young daughter should be arriving at her grandmother's home in possibly less than two hours. An unfamiliar man has been in touch with both my daughter on her phone and also with my mother-in-law. This caller could be the one who did the shooting last night. He knows for certain Ellie is on the highway on her way to her grandmother's home. The caller must be involved in this crime. He's been able to obtain cell numbers for both my wife and Ellie. How that happened I don't know, but I have to wonder what other information he has about my family. He gave himself some phony identities when he called Ellie and my mother-in-law. We need to act and act promptly on what little we know. Have you received any recent news on the case?"

Alvin walked over to Sam's desk to have him pick up his line and listen in. "Mr. Wallace, minutes ago we received a call from your law firm. A man working there told Sam that your housekeeper was taken to the emergency unit of the hospital. He told us she was assaulted by a man who came to your home. After brutally striking her with his fists and knocking her to the floor, he must have determined he had killed her because she didn't move. This man must have gotten what he wanted from your home because your housekeeper said he left in a hurry."

"Sir, after talking to you now, we know what he wanted. It was addresses and telephone numbers for members of your family. This man was able to get your home address by another means. Would your office ever give out such information?"

"Absolutely not, in our business we cannot give anyone an employee's address or any important personal information."

While discussing the matter, they came to the same conclusion. The danger was real. It was much too real. They had to act.

Other bad news had to be told to Joe, "Now let me give you something else we've gathered. The man at the restaurant who did the shooting was not the man who broke into your home to get addresses and phone numbers. The shooter turned himself in to the police an hour ago, but he gave us the name of the man he was working for. . . I hate to tell you this, Mr. Wallace, but the man he worked for is a felon and an established drug dealer in the city."

The danger had escalated, and Joe began talking rapidly trying to catch his breath at the same time as he firmly said, "We must act on this, Investigator Underwood. This man was able to obtain phone numbers for my entire family because he called my mother-in-law thinking he was reaching my wife's cell phone. He didn't call me because he believes I died last night. He would love to find my daughter because she was there and could identify him. My daughter is an important witness. It's obvious this man is willing to do heaps of damage and even kill trying to reach her. This is an evil man we must stop!

He won't stop until he finds Ellie! Understood, Underwood?"

Feeling a sharp pain from his excitement, Joe spoke in a less agitated tone, "By the way, is Clara being cared for? I want her to receive the best care possible."

"Yes, Sir, Mr. Wallace," Alvin assured Joe. "Clara is in the emergency room as we speak and is doing well, but one bone was broken in her jaw. Her body took a horrible beating. It seems the intruder kicked her after she was on the floor. That was after she was struck down by him. She's one very brave and smart woman." Even as he spoke Alvin knew the case was moving faster than anyone imagined, and he knew they did not have much time to act.

Almost fuming after hearing what the man had done to Clara and what he was capable of, Joe was direct, "You know everything you need to know, more than even I know at this point. I'd say someone needs to get on the next flight out of town and head for Knoxville. He needs to be there to protect my daughter and mother-in-law. Is that possible today? Officer Underwood, do you have the authority to do that? If I could walk, I'd be out of here as soon as I could get my pants on."

As Sam listened intently to their conversation, he spoke to Alvin from his phone, "I can go. I can be ready to leave now."

Speaking directly to Sam, Alvin said, "This might be the best thing we can do, Sam. Mr. Wallace, you have my word, we'll handle this the right way. Call the airlines, Sam, and get the next flight that will get you into the Knoxville airport. No layovers whatsoever. If you cannot find a commercial flight, I'll get you on some private jet going in that direction, but we will get you there as soon as we can."

Then addressing Joe, who had remained on the line, Alvin said, "Mr. Wallace, you can be assured we'll do everything possible to protect your daughter and mother-in-law. We'll pull out all the stops in order to be there. We've already contacted the Knoxville Police Department. If you are aware of any new details, let us know. We'll keep you up-to-date on everything we find out, but we'll need that address of your mother-in-law."

Joe was convinced they would handle it well. He called his law office to talk to his partner and told him about the situation and the latest information. His partner asked to be kept up to date and wanted to know what they could do. Joe said they could use lots of prayer, and he might ask for some help later.

Contacting his daughter was Joe's next priority. Unable to get through because of her low phone battery, he left a short urgent message for her to call him. He had been putting off calling Molly McCoy partly because it would be painfully difficult for both of them to discuss the shooting, but even though he was dreading the call, this was as good a time as any. She was more than likely in tremendous grief over the loss of her husband.

He had to check on Clara's progress as well before she left the emergency room. She was such a faithful person and a great housekeeper, always there to take care of them. Knowing her, she would not allow a violent man into their home if she could in any way avoid it. She really cared for Ellie and overlooked her faults. Caroline depended on her too. Perhaps she might be able to identify this intruder if they could catch the malicious devil. They must catch him before he reached Ellie.

Recalling what Alvin Underwood had just told him about Clara's ordeal that morning in their home, Joe thought to himself, "What a courageous person she was to take such a beating for us. What would we do without Clara?"

His thoughts were moving in every direction. Now they were about his wife and how it might be best to tell her about the possible danger their daughter faced. He would leave a message for her on the home phone and also remember to call often until he reached her. Wishing not to cause any unnecessary anxiety for her, he did want to convince her to come to the hospital. He would tell her about their courageous daughter once she arrived.

He left a message, just enough to get Caroline to come to the hospital. His tangled, troubled thoughts would not allow him to slumber now. If only he was strong enough to get out of his hospital bed and catch a flight to Knoxville to protect his brave Ellie.

Chapter 24

"THAT MAID SHOULDN'T HAVE GONE to work today. It was the biggest mistake she's ever made in her life, but she won't have to think about making mistakes like that anymore. In fact, she won't have to think much about anything again. Her work as a maid is over." Owen jeered and followed it with a raucous laugh revealing his ugly arrogance.

After leaving the Wallace home and heading toward the main street to find a place to get a quick breakfast, he forgot about the woman and allowed his mind to dwell on his unfinished job. But somehow he failed to move the maid out of his thinking process, but as he rubbed a finger over his mouth, he was amused as he thought of all his latest accomplishments in such a short period of time. He was proud of the way in which he handled the situation with the housekeeper, even though he was prepared to break into the Wallace home if no one answered the door.

With a smirk on his face, Owen said, "That contemptible cleaning lady should've been more cooperative, but she didn't choose to be, so she paid the price. She was another stupid loser." He pictured her again lying on the floor and wondered if it was the blow he gave her, the hard kick he delivered or how he delivered the punches. She fell onto the wood floor with such a tremendous thud that he must have actually killed her.

He laughed with scorn, "An absolute loser!" He could still picture the blood flowing from her mouth just before he left.

Eating his breakfast in a secluded section of the little neighborhood café gave him the privacy he desired and the opportunity to begin thumbing through the address book. Within a minute he came across Madeline Russell's address.

Finishing his coffee, he pointed to her name and made the conclusion, "This is the grandma who's living in Knoxville that I called. It's where Little Smartie Mouth is headed."

Not wanting anyone in a nearby table seeing what he was doing, he left. Inside his car he laughed and tauntingly said, "Miss Russell actually introduced herself to me as Maddie and told me Caroline was her daughter. Eleanor's Mommy is heading back home this morning and in haste left her cell phone behind before getting on the road. That old lady was exceedingly helpful!"

Owen had always been pleased with his ability to trick people into giving him information. He then remembered how the young kid had tricked him, and he instantly became angry. "I'll take care of you, Missy. You'll regret your impertinence." Considering how he should get even with the kid, he blurted out, "It's only a matter of time before I find you." He would forget about how easily the girl had tricked him and began looking forward to the pleasure it would give him to make the girl cry for help. "I'll crush you!"

Thumbing through the address book again, he was satisfied he had obtained the names, addresses and telephone numbers of the entire Wallace family without any trouble. It had been so easy once he forced his way into the home, and in a flash the maid again entered his mind. He was annoyed, "She's dead. Move on," Owen.

He planned well the trip he made to the Wallace home and was able to obtain more than he expected. He had to admit it actually felt good placing a few heavy punches on that stubborn maid because she had the nerve to question his explanation and motive. He mocked, "She'll never clean a toilet again," and feeling assured she was dead, he laughed.

While he was in prison the guards seldom saw what the prisoners were doing in their cells. They failed to see him during times when he was being taught a few boxing moves by his cell mate. He laughed, "Practicing those punches regularly while I was in my crummy jail cell gave me confidence in my strength and certainly came in handy this morning." He howled, "With the maid taken care of, I can now take care of other things that need my attention."

It was then Owen decided he would make a brief trip to Knoxville. As he placed the address book on the passenger seat in his car he mumbled vengefully, "I'm not stopping until that spoiled brat is in my grasp. She refused to answer my questions.

"But Grandma, thanks for giving me the telephone number for your Sweet Little Ellie. Yes Ellie's what you called her, and, Granny, did you know your Ellie had the nerve to challenge me by asking questions without bothering to answer mine. Who does she think she is?" His eyes narrowed as he began to inhale and exhale heavily. Then he uttered statements through his teeth no one would ever hear, "Ellie Wallace, I'll track you down. I've got plans for you, and you'll answer to me very soon."

His thoughts switched to Ray, the person he had yet to set straight. Thinking of how he should approach the guy, he decided to play it safe if he was to retrieve his gun. And he wondered what he should eventually do with Ray, who he was sure by this time was trying to avoid him. Since he had not called or made contact, Owen was sure he must be hanging out in his dreary apartment or loafing around somewhere.

It was obvious to Owen Ray was scared of what might happen to him if the police came after him. Was he afraid of ending up in a jail cell? No matter, Ray had his gun, so Owen needed to deal with the man skillfully. But this matter of what to do with Ray would have to wait.

"I don't want Ray to leave town, but if he does decide to run, where could the guy go? Thinking about how much he did know about Ray, he remembered once when he mentioned having some family members living in Canada. But would he go there and drag a family member into his predicament, or would Ray try to disappear by hiding in some other area of the city? Sure, he might do that. Calling him early tomorrow and reasoning with him might be best. All Owen wanted and needed from Ray was that gun.

Tearing off the page in the address book containing Madeline Russell's address, he was already beginning to plan what he intended to do once he arrived in Knoxville. It was settled. He would make a little visit to Granny's house and greet the ladies.

Chapter 25

IT WAS TIME to make another visit to the hospital. Possibly Joe Wallace would be able to talk. Alvin wanted to know exactly what Kurt had said to him about the drug peddling. Information had been coming in little by little from police records, but just how involved the employee had been at Kurt's station must come out in order for them to put more of the pieces together in the case.

Seated at his desk, Sam was busy on the phone making a plane reservation for the trip to Knoxville, and Alvin interrupted him before Sam could finish writing down the information he needed, "Sam, I'm leaving to talk to the lawyer again, but I can take you to the airport and drop you off first if you need a ride."

Sam replied, "I'm ready now and can drive myself to the airport. I'll leave a police car there for a day or so. We can keep in touch by phone. Tell Wallace I should arrive in Knoxville by mid afternoon." In two steps he grabbed his notes, coat and headed out.

Joe was sitting up in bed when Alvin entered his hospital room. With a smile, Joe greeted the officer, "Hello, have we heard anything from Ellie? I tried to reach her, but failed twice. I think her phone needs recharging. She's low on battery power, I'm sure. She probably was able to use someone's phone to talk to her grandmother and warn her to lock all her doors and stay inside."

Turning his head to look out the window, Joe continued, "Alvin, talking to my wife about Ellie will be difficult because when I tell her I don't know where she is, the news will frighten the daylights out of her."

Standing at the foot of the bed Alvin listened without saying a word as Joe continued to talk, "The nurse took my cell phone from me, so I wouldn't be tempted to stay awake and make more calls. I was able to talk to my mother-in-law and my law office before they stowed it away out there at the desk, but I will need to make a few calls soon. Begging certainly didn't work, but if you were to talk a nurse into giving the phone to you, she might loan it to you for the time you're here. They're convinced I should get lots of rest in this sterile room. It's impossible to rest with all the traffic coming and going as they check my pulse and my vitals constantly. I need that phone in case Ellie or my wife tries to contact me?" Joe looked straight at Alvin as if to add the word please.

Alvin tried being patient with Joe's great concern about his daughter and his wife and replied, "Yes I'll try to get someone to bring your phone to me, and if we can get you anything else, we'll be happy to do that. And, no, to answer the first and foremost question that's on your mind. We haven't received any word from your daughter in over an hour."

Walking closer to Joe's bedside Alvin spoke with candor, "Mr. Wallace, I want to say that you are more than lucky to be alive. Last night the gunman who entered Mike's Place was ordered to shoot everyone in the place. You shouldn't be here talking to me now. But I'm glad you survived and that your daughter was able to escape. You have my word we will do everything in our power to protect your daughter, and when we hear from her, we'll be in touch with you without any delay. You'll be the first to know where she is and what's happening."

More quietly Alvin said, "I returned here today because I need to ask you a few more questions about what you witnessed last night. I'm sure you understand why we are asking these questions. You seem to be up to it."

Wallace glanced around his room for a few seconds thinking about his 17-year old daughter making an arduous journey through several states as he lay in bed unable to reach her by phone or keep her safe. Trying to clear his thoughts, he turned, "Yes, I wish what little I know will be enough to help you solve this crime. Excuse me, but my sole concern now is the safety of my daughter."

Agitated and impatient that he was lying in bed with a needle stuck in his arm and was only able to answer questions, he blurted out, "I want you to know that Kurt was an outstanding man who lost his life last night because he was willing to speak out against illegal drugs that are distributed so easily and openly in this city. Clara was terribly injured in an attempt to save my Ellie."

With more energy Joe added, "Kurt was convinced drugs were being sold to customers coming to his gas station. He could have turned his head and allowed that selling to continue and claim he didn't know anything about it if it was brought to his attention. But he was courageous when he wanted the dealing to stop. He faced his employee with difficult questions and then decided to ask for advice from an attorney before he called the police. By the way, he was going to go to the police after our meeting. I told him he must do that. He didn't know how lethal exposing drug peddling could be to his life. Has anyone in the police department visited his wife?"

Alvin answered, "Yes, she was visited late last night after Kurt's identity was known. She was also checked on this morning. Mrs. McCoy said she wanted to be with her children at this time, and they are with her now. She was cooperative in every way, but surprisingly, it seems her husband didn't share any of his suspicions that a possible drug trafficker might be working at the station. That fact stunned her, but she said Kurt was always protective of her. It's understandable with all the problems in our city."

Pulling up a chair beside Joe, Alvin lowered his voice to make sure no one could hear, "I want you to tell me every detail you remember about the incident last night since you're wide awake now and able to give us better information, but before you talk about it, I want to reassure you my partner is now in the air on his way to Knoxville. He'll protect Ellie and your mother-in-law."

Clearing his throat, Alvin took a deep breath as he prepared to listen to Joe recount the facts that were fresh in his memory. He asked him to give explicit details of everything from the time Kurt McCoy contacted him to the time when he called 911. He told Joe even a seemingly small unimportant detail could help in catching the man who was responsible for the crime because they wanted to find the source and people hiding behind this particular crime.

Alvin attempted to convince Joe of the importance of solving the crime, "Getting the details of this case could expose many drug dealers and those who are behind many of this city's criminal element, those who have no regard for the welfare of our law abiding citizens. You and your daughter just happened to be caught in the middle of these abusive crimes."

⟫◆⟪

Joe went through every particular detail he remembered offering descriptions and attempting to utter the very words he recalled hearing Kurt and Ray use. Hearing the details in an orderly format and concentrating while writing down factual bits of information, Alvin was

now convinced there were other sleazy individuals
working behind the scenes as suppliers of the drugs. He
also knew these suppliers were connected to other
criminals. Some details that had been puzzling were now
becoming clearer, and Alvin knew from experience this
was a solvable crime. It might take hard work on their part
to get to the bottom of these crimes because the police
didn't know how involved or how far reaching they were.

New questions were emerging. How dangerous was
this guy who had beaten the housekeeper? Who was the
guy's supplier? Was there another contact person out
there who was a threat to members of the Wallace family
or anyone who might have knowledge about the drug
trafficking at Kurt's station? It was a hideous, but true
fact, that criminals dealing in illegal drugs protected their
businesses at any cost, often with unscrupulous, crude
methods. No crimes were considered too perverse or
corrupt to protect the business.

Details he was hearing led Alvin to believe Ellie, the
runaway witness, was definitely in imminent danger. This
man they were investigating could be after her today. He
might be making plans to silence her. Alvin was convinced
Wallace would never have told his daughter to run for her
life and to take such a trip unless he sensed an urgent
threat to her existence. Trying not to arouse unnecessary
fear for Joe or his wife, this brilliant investigator assured
Joe the police force would make every effort to guard
Ellie's life from any potential killer.

As Alvin was about to leave he received a phone
message from the police station. Excusing himself he
stepped out into the hallway to talk. The message was
about Clara, the Wallace's maid, and Alvin listened to
every word. He was informed that Clara was able and
willing to identify the man who had forced his way into
the Wallace's home early that morning. Clara said the

intruder claimed to be an office messenger from Wallace's workplace and claimed he was sent to pick up some papers from Joe Wallace's home office. Since she had serious doubts about what he was telling her and would not allow him to enter, he struck her knocking her to the floor. She said she noticed a tattoo located low on his neck. Although she was unable to make it out because his collar covered a large portion of it, what she did see were parts of a large symbol. She said it was when her eyes fell on that tattoo that he struck her. With several broken facial bones and other major injuries, the woman is in constant pain, but her mind is clear.

Returning to Joe, Alvin shared the additional information and again tried to give this father assurance that his child was now their greatest concern. They both knew they had more to worry about than the shooter. A maniacal, unrestrained criminal was loose out there willing to strike or kill anyone in his path to protect his drug turf and get what he was after.

Joe's breathing became heavier when he heard the news about Clara, and in rage he blurted out, "My teenage daughter is in great danger because a madman is bent on finding her and wants to shut her up as soon as possible. It seems he'll stop at nothing to harm her and probably wishes to kill her. It's obvious to me Clara tried to stay alive as best she could during that ordeal in order to let us know of this foul and vicious man."

Desperate to find the man, Joe reached for his call button for the nurse to come. He felt useless lying in bed waiting for others to do what he wanted to do. Running his fingers frantically through his hair with his good hand, he asked, "Where's the nurse? Nurse! Nurse! There she is. Officer, would you ask her to come to my room? And, Officer, you know I'm trying to be reasonable, but I must get out of this bed and find my daughter."

The nurse hurriedly stepped in to restrain Joe from getting out of bed and firmly warned, "Mr. Wallace, you've lost a great deal of your strength, and you're weaker than you could ever imagine. No, you cannot leave for at least six more days."

Understanding the situation Alvin calmly said, "Sir, she's absolutely correct, but we must do more. We'll call the Knoxville PD again and alert them. We'll ask them to loan us a couple superior officers to protect both women. They have sent officers to be on the lookout for your daughter as she arrives in Knoxville."

With his emotions out of control, Joe raised his voice addressing the nurse and Alvin, "My daughter needs all the protection we can give her and all the protection the Knoxville police can give her. Ellie has never driven more than 15 miles from our home, let alone more than 500 miles by herself during the wee hours of the morning through a blizzard!"

Joe turned his body and reached for the needle in his arm. As the attending nurse restrained him, Alvin could only look on and imagine how Joe felt. The nurse firmly pleaded with Joe to stay in bed, and as reality brought him to his senses, he knew he could do absolutely nothing. He was entirely useless, and never in his entire life had he felt so utterly helpless.

Chapter 26

AGAIN ELLIE PULLED OUT THE MAP her father kept in his car to reassure herself she needed to continue on Interstate 75 to reach Knoxville. Then she would take the Interstate 40 East exit. Her assumption was correct, and the exit should be within several miles. "Almost there," Ellie sighed with relief, sure she soon would finish the lengthy, arduous journey. "It should be less than an hour before I pull into Grandma's driveway. Thank you, Lord, for keeping me safe."

Never in her life had Ellie endured such a grueling trip. Relief would come to her aching back, neck and shoulders. Every muscle above her waist had been tense for hours longing for exercise. Her legs were begging to be stretched, and her brain had gone far beyond mere tiredness. She reminded herself it was because her dad wanted her to be safe from any exposure to harm, and because he was wise regarding impending danger, that he told her to make this physically draining trip.

What Ellie wanted more than anything was to talk to her father, and be reassured he was safe and in good hands. Out of habit she found herself checking her cell phone only to see a blank screen. She would need to wait until she reached her grandmother's home to try calling him. She wondered where her mother was and if it was possible she had passed her somewhere heading north as she drove south on the same highway.

Ellie smiled as each mile was bringing her closer to her destination. She now was truly eager to see the grandmother she had known all her life. She was there to welcome her at birth, cared for her several times when she was ill, read Bible and other stories to her as a child and introduced her to the woods and streams near her home. This elderly woman now in her late 60s had been there to encourage her throughout all her years.

Then as her mind wandered, Ellie began considering what she should tell her grandmother when she arrived. "How much should I tell her about the horrible scene I witnessed last night? Sparing unpleasant details might be best since I'm unsure how those details might affect her."

With a little giggle Ellie said, "But Granny will suspect that she's not hearing it all. She's smart and will want to know absolutely everything."

Now with her thoughts traveling back in time, Ellie had many great memories that were shared with her grandparents and with other members of her extended family. Many happy events took place at her grandparents' home. Large family dinners included aunts, uncles and a house full of cousins. Those times would always remain with her as happy and significant memories. They were vivid memories of experiences she could never forget.

As recently as two years ago, 26 people had gathered for dinner to celebrate her grandmother's 68tth birthday. She also recalled how as a little girl she played at her grandparents' home and dressed up in what she considered ancient clothing. Then running and playing tag among the vegetable and flower gardens in the big backyard and beyond to the old barn with her siblings and three cousins was a highlight of one early summer.

That huge gnarled walnut tree with branches reaching high into the sky that Ned and Shelly would coax her to climb popped into her memory. She would sit up there with them as they tried to hide from their parents. There they could see several pastures nearby where cows were feeding. It was a wonderfully wild adventure for a small child perched up there with her big sister and brother. The last time she saw the walnut tree, it somehow did not seem as tall to her as it had to her as a young child.

Then there were those hiding places near the spooky, deserted barn that made playing hide and seek so much fun for them. Even her parents would join in and play on warm summer evenings, and she would squeal when Dad and Mom found her. Those times she thought her parents must be peeking to know where she was, but now she knew they had played the identical game in their youth and were experts at locating a bunch of kids. Her thoughts wandered as she recalled other pleasant memories.

Those special homemade cookies, freshly baked and warm from the oven, would never be forgotten. Grandma's delicious pies and cakes had a special taste. Then there was the high bed she would more than likely sleep in when she arrived. It stood in that second-floor tiny bedroom in the far corner of the house. As a child she had loved that bed. Early in the mornings chirping birds would usually awaken her, and she loved playing with Charger, their little dog who died recently at the ripe old age of 16. Grandpa was still alive four years ago, and shortly before he died, he purchased a new dog to replace Charger. Poppy was her name, and she would probably be there to greet her.

Grandad had been nine years older than Grandma when they married, which to some people was considered too many years separating them. But they had a great marriage. He was sent off to the war in Korea, and upon his return, he was honored for his bravery and sacrifice as a soldier. He received medals. Ellie remembered seeing those medals tucked away in a desk drawer in her grandparents' bedroom. As a child she thought they looked like old relics.

She could not relate to another place in the world or a previous time in history because the events took place before she was born. Ned was interested in the medals when he was a kid and would pick them up asking questions about them. After Grandma would say a few things, she would hold them in her hands for a while. She would tell Ned about events that had long been forgotten by many. Those medals and memories were precious to Grandma, and she would carefully place them back into the desk drawer.

Now Ellie was remembering those medals and what they meant to her grandmother who regarded them as keepsakes. They represented to her a man who willingly would give his life for his country. The brief lessons Ellie studied in school about the Korean War had seemed so unreal when she read them in the textbook. During this visit she would like to see those old treasured medals again and somehow stretch her understanding of why Grandpa was sent to war.

As her thoughts continued to drift, Ellie began remembering times when her mom and dad had spent precious time with her. During her early grades they encouraged her to study and do well in school and appreciate her teachers even if they seemed unreasonable. They did not side with her if she complained about them or used a wacky reason for not liking a particular teacher. On Sunday mornings they would all get up early enough to eat a small breakfast together before attending church.

She had always been assured that her parents loved her and would only do what was best for her. Belief in

God, learning, working hard, kindness toward those in need, practicing family values and preparing for her adult life were of utmost importance to them. They were great parents, and she knew that. No kid could ask for a better mom or dad, and God had given these two exceptionally priceless gifts to her.

When Grandma had picked up the flu earlier in the month, her mother had driven to Knoxville to care for her. And last night her father, after working for 10 hours at his office, traveled out of his way on a wretched, bitter cold night to help a friend who needed help with some legal advice. Now her dad was in a hospital fighting for his life. Overcome with these thoughts Ellie prayed, "God, thank you for both Mom and Dad. They are great, and please give the doctors and nurses the ability they'll need to care for my dad."

She was eager to talk to her parents, and since the outskirts of Knoxville were only minutes away, she was excited to call and tell them she was safe. Right now, she would love to tell them she was about to approach her grandmother's home, and she would definitely remember to tell them they were the best parents a girl could have and how thankful she was for them.

Ellie exclaimed, "I might even promise them I'll study chemistry harder. Someday I might want be that dentist I told everyone I was determined to be when I was little."

Squeezing her useless phone, she became upset with the one item she used constantly and depended on every hour during every day. Absolutely no signal was visible now. Without any battery power, she would not be able to contact anyone, but she was confident she could follow her nose to reach her grandma's home.

For the first time on the trip she felt enormously hungry and could not force herself to think beyond the emptiness of her stomach. Exasperated she said, "Why now?" Somehow she desperately needed something to eat, but she was determined she must finish the few miles that remained. The only time Ellie could remember feeling so hungry was when she and her friends had decided to go on a strict diet they had concocted.

She remembered persevering for almost a week with that nonsense, but when her parents noticed her picking at her food during dinner for several evenings, they set her down and reasoned with her. They warned her of the physical dangers she could face if she starved herself. Seeing the concern in their eyes and how they gently presented the facts to her, she came to her senses and was convinced they were right.

Today though neither weariness nor hunger would be excuses for her to neglect her need to be alert as she drove the remaining few miles. She felt pampered and spoiled in a wonderful way as she moved down the road. "I'm such a lucky kid."

Chapter 27

DEPARTURE AND ARRIVAL TIMES from Detroit to Knoxville had only taken Sam minutes to check with the airlines. A reservation for the flight was made for 12:05 pm, and he was on his way to the airport with nothing more than one small duffle bag. He was less than an hour early to catch his ride, and he should arrive in Knoxville at 3:15, which was in about three hours.

Having never been given an assignment like this before, Sam was energized with the opportunity to be sent on this important mission. He felt his phone vibrating, so he snatched it from its holder and held it to his ear, "Sam here."

Alvin had additional information he wanted to give, "Another little insignificant twist in the case with the Wallace girl. Another man came to the police station to say he was the person who shot the three men last night at Mike's Place. He confessed to the shootings, but we had to dismiss him because we think he's a want-a-be-killer. He couldn't give us any additional facts beyond that. His story didn't convince anyone. We believe we already have the real killer in custody, and we don't have any reason to believe he'd intentionally be lying to us.

We're in the process of checking out the gun he gave us. A couple of bullets were left in the gun so we should have the results soon. The first man was a wreck emotionally, and for now we'll stick with this guy who confessed to the crime and was able to give us additional information we did not have. I'll let you know about any further developments in this. Have a good trip. And, Sam, get this creep!"

Sam was taking in every word and replied, "Hey Alvin, do you want me to forget this trip to Knoxville for any reason?"

After several seconds Alvin answered, "No, I believe you should go. There's definitely more people involved in this case than the shooter we have in custody. From what we've learned and what he told us, he was intoxicated and ran into the pizza parlor shooting these men and then left because he was told to kill everyone present in the restaurant. Like I said, we're now checking to see who the owner of the gun might be and who purchased it in the first place."

Alvin continued after a few seconds delay, "This guy who seems to definitely be the shooter was getting those drugs he was selling from somebody, possibly this Wolf guy he mentioned. This is something we have to follow through on. Drugs are truly a dirty, expanding business in our state and throughout the country. Yes Sam, you know the details in this case better than anyone, and I want you to make contact with the police department in Knoxville immediately and protect those women. As soon as you arrive, call me."

Sam was looking forward to getting out of Detroit for even one day. He parked his car in a distant parking slot and hurried toward the airport terminal. Anticipating Knoxville would be a lot warmer at this time of the year, he was hoping he might see some sunshine for a few hours.

Sam shivered as he lifted his collar and walked in the icy air heading for the warm building when something occurred to him. What if this guy already has been able to find out where Ellie is going and able to get a flight to surprise her? He would have had to do some accurate guessing, but if he did find the information from the Wallace home, he could already be on his way. He began speaking out loud, "Both Alvin and I know this man is one noxious, determined devil. If I had any reason to believe Ellie might not arrive at her grandmother's before this criminal did . . ." Sam began walking faster and soon was running to the check-in counter.

———◈◆◈———

Caroline was cheerful as she turned into her driveway, relieved from her long drive. She was tired from sitting in her car and she mumbled, "Oh, it's so good to be home."

As usual she used the side entrance of the house. Unlocking and opening the door, she took one step inside and instantly gasped. Seeing wet blood on the floor in front of her she yelled, "Oh! What happened here?" She screamed, "Clara? . . . Clara? CLARA?"

Walking hurriedly into the kitchen, she saw some papers and folders scattered and tossed aside. Then spinning around she walked into the home office and saw the desktop and carpet littered with papers that had been tossed in every direction. "What a total mess!" she exclaimed as she ran up the stairs to the bedrooms. "CLARA?"

Her bedroom was in good order, but Ellie's bedroom was not as she usually left it before she left for school. The bed was made and most of her clothes were orderly, not thrown and scrambled as she often left them wherever they dropped.

"CLARA? Are you here? What could have happened?" Caroline shouted as she flew down the stairs to call Joe at his office. Returning to the kitchen to pick up the phone, she saw a pile of vegetable peelings lying in the sink. Extremely uneasy about what she saw, she suspected something terrible had taken place.

Joe's secretary seemed guarded not wanting to add distress to the situation when she only told Caroline to call the hospital to talk to her husband. The receptionist at the hospital connected her to Room 506. Impatiently Caroline fidgeted as she waited for Joe to answer. Once he picked up, she was talking before he had a chance to say hello, "Joe is everything OK?"

Joe wanted Caroline to be calm so he first told her about how Clara had refused to help a man who came to their door, and he knocked her to the floor in order to enter. Then he told her Clara was in the hospital and that the intruder was looking for some information that was in his office.

"Caroline, I want you to come to the hospital. I'm in Room 506. Don't be overly anxious and please, drive carefully. We can talk here, and I can explain fully what happened."

Caroline was back in her car and pulling out of the drive in less than two minutes. She wanted to know why Joe was in the hospital and why someone had broken into their home. She would pray all the way. "Had all this happened after Ellie went to school today, and was she on her way home from school now? I'll call her from the hospital. Oh, why did I forget my phone?"

Parking and rushing into the main entrance of the hospital, Caroline noticed how busy it was at this time of the day. On the way up the elevator to the fifth floor she asked a nurse who was getting off at that floor, "Please tell me in which direction I will find Room 506."

Joe could hear Caroline coming down the hall. It would not be easy to start from the beginning and tell his wife everything that happened in the past 21 hours, but he knew she deserved to know the truth.

Shocked at her husband's pale appearance with huge bandages on his arm and chest Caroline asked, "What happened to you?" She was not expecting to see him with a drip needle in his arm. "I couldn't imagine why you were here, but I did try to prepare myself. Was there an accident, and where's Ellie?"

Not wanting to cause him further discomfort, Caroline approached as close as possible and tenderly placed her arm around Joe's neck. Kissing his cheek she sat down on the side of his bed and cried a little as Joe tried to calm her.

In an attempt to make it easier on her, Joe began at the beginning telling her why he chose to go to Mike's for a bite. "Love, now I'll tell you something you'll find hard to believe." Joe told Caroline the rest of the story. He didn't hold back on anything as tears ran down her cheeks. He covered every detail. Caroline took Joe's right hand, and they prayed together. They asked God to watch over Ellie and Maddie, to give them courage and wisdom to know what to do, and to keep them safe. They wanted to be present in Knoxville to protect Ellie and Maddie, but they knew that was impossible.

Caroline needed to stay with her husband now. More than ten hours ago she left her mother's home, the home where Ellie should be arriving within a short time. They were about to call Maddie's home to contact their daughter when Joe's phone rang.

Reaching for the phone Caroline said, "Hello, this is Caroline Wallace. Can I help you?"

"Mrs. Wallace, this is Sergeant Alvin Underwood. Could I speak with your husband?"

Handing the phone to Joe, Caroline closed her eyes hoping her husband would receive only good news.

The voice Joe was beginning to recognize said, "Mr. Wallace, my partner, Sam Reynolds, is in the air and on his way to Knoxville. He should be arriving shortly. He and I want you to know that we are doing whatever it takes to protect your daughter and Mrs. Russell. We have a man in custody who's admitted to the shootings. And, yes, he was dealing in drugs just as Mr. McCoy suspected . . ."

Taking a deep breath Alvin finished, "That other man who was the supplier of the drugs seems to be the guy who ordered the shootings. We're in the process of finding him. I'm sorry, but that's all we know at present. I'll call to let you know when Sam arrives at your mother-in-law's home and pass on any additional information we're able to obtain."

Pleased that Alvin had kept his word about keeping him in the loop about the progress of the case, Joe was sure the police under Alvin's supervision would go to great limits to protect the two women from harm. Gratefully he responded, "Thank you, Officer Underwood, for calling and giving me this update. My wife has arrived, and she's sitting here with me now. We've both prayed for God's intervention in this, and I believe we have already received indications that God has been with our daughter and continues to be with her."

Joe had one additional question, "Sir, do you know who this other man could be?"

Replying truthfully and wanting to give Ellie's parents hope Alvin said, "Yes, we know his name; we've been given his name by the man who did the shooting. We know he was in prison for five years. A crew of officers is working on finding him. My partner, Sam, is an excellent officer, and you can count on him to use everything in his power to protect your daughter. You can also be assured that our police department is moving as quickly as possible on this case because we know every minute counts."

Chapter 28

AFTER THE SHORT TIME TALKING to Joe on the phone, it was evident to Maddie that Ellie might be reaching Knoxville within the hour. Making the necessary preparations for her arrival was capturing her every thought. The earlier call from Ellie had aroused her, and with trepidation she wondered what happened last night that she did not tell her. Ellie had said to lock all her doors and stay inside, and Joe had agreed that she should follow that advice. Maddie's curiosity accelerated and caused her to want to know more about why she must confine herself to the interior of her four walls.

Speaking regretfully she said, "Without the slightest hesitation I gave Ellie's cell number to that phony stranger who was intent on evil. His was a strange, troubling call from the beginning, but I gave the number to him. Such a good liar he was, . . . but he is a complete fraud! Oh why did I give Ellie's number to him? That thoughtless incident without doubt might be the information he needed to potentially do her great harm. I was downright stupid."

Desperate and in a frenzy at first she knew she must find a way to protect Ellie when she arrived. The disturbing details about what took place the previous night gave her a sinking feeling, but no longer frantic, she was resolute and firmly said, "I must maintain control of this situation if it takes every ounce of energy I have."

Too many unknowns continued to disrupt Maddie's ability to think clearly. This was an enormous problem that could result in great harm to Ellie, but it was obvious none of them knew the possible dangers. Maddie would do as she was instructed, and if a sinister monster was lurking out there intending injury toward her grandchild, she would take on the job and do whatever was in her power to protect Ellie and provide a safe haven for her when she arrived.

Knowing that since both she and Ellie could be in grave danger, she must forget the foolish mistake she made in giving her grandchild's number to the deceptive man and make a plan. Thinking how she could protect the two of them if the man came to her home, she began thinking, and she would begin by preparing the corner bedroom upstairs for Ellie as she gave herself time to think of a few solutions. Ellie would need rest when she arrived, and although she did not have time to prepare one of her granddauthter's favorite dishes, Maddie vowed she would keep Ellie safe.

Rushing up the stairs with a sense of urgency, Maddie was compelled to be as efficient as possible in every movement she made as she formulated plans at the same time.

As she rushed around busying herself on the second floor, the disturbing news of Ellie's flight to find refuge in her home convinced her she must conjure up a solid plan as quickly as possible. The man's easy manner and convincing way of asking her for a phone number constantly raced through her mind. "That devil's up to no good, but he was certainly good at deception!"

As she pulled out fresh linens from the closet and checked on the adjoining bathroom, she vowed again she would protect Ellie at any cost. Various possible solutions were beginning to take shape. One pleasant idea to her was

to capture the fake. Aware this corrupt liar would sooner
or later come to a bitter end and that God surely would
deliver justice in His time she prayed, "I would be grateful
if some of the man's bitter end would take place sooner
rather than later." She was certain the slimy snake was set
on evil and possibly plotting destruction, but she was
convinced there was no reason she must wait for God to
deal with him.

Capturing the man alone without help seemed out of
the question. Wounding him and applying an adequate
amount of pain would be her first choice. Indignantly
Maddie announced, "He might only receive a short
sentence if he's taken to a jail. Some crooked, conniving
lawyer could arrange for his freedom. No! Absolutely not!
It'll only satisfy me if he can be rendered physically
helpless. If that wretched, despicable monster is
attempting to harm my grandchild, he'll not receive an
ounce of compassion or sympathy from me! He's willfully
choosing evil, and I won't tolerate an attack on Ellie while
it's in my power to avoid it. Forgive me, Jesus, for what I'm
thinking."

Imagining once again the possibility of capturing the
man Maddie asked, "What if I actually could seize him,
apply pain and cause him to be defenseless at the same
time?" Confused about how she could accomplish all that,
she was convinced she must settle on something soon.
Ideas of how she might trap him at her home were either
retained or rejected as she wasted no time preparing for
Ellie's arrival.

One incomplete idea had been bouncing around in
her head. Then in a flash, her eyes lit up and widened as an
earlier unfinished idea sprang up and began taking shape.
With a little tweaking on her part, it would become a solid
solution for everyone. She was certain that if her plan was
to succeed, she needed to think through every detail and be

ready for an unpredictable incident to occur. Now she would begin working on an alternate plan.

———◦•◦———

From every indication flight 276 would be leaving the Detroit Airport on time. They already had cleared the larger runways of icy snow that accumulated throughout the early morning hours. Arrival time for Knoxville was scheduled for 3:45 p.m. and was leaving on time. Passengers who would board the flight were sitting patiently in the holding area waiting for their flight number to be announced.

Appearing as any other traveler, Sam Reynolds had been glancing briefly for more than ten minutes at each person waiting for the Knoxville flight.

Sam remembered Alvin complimenting him a month ago when he said, "I recognize an innate ability of discernment and common sense in you Sam." Alvin had then taken time to patiently teach him how to sharpen those natural skills and insights. In Sam's studies of criminology he was taught how to analyze people. Now he was practicing what he had learned as he watched how people dressed. He listened to their speech and noticed their actions. Today that natural ability to be observant was being practiced and tested. He was using his perceptive talent and applying the knowledge he studied in the classroom along with all Alvin taught him.

He was keenly aware of every passenger as they entered the area as well as those already seated around him He was discreet as he observed each traveler, but would not reveal or leave the slightest hint to anyone what his occupation was. So far it was working. He was reminded of his mission. Then, his eyes moved from one passenger to another. He questioned, "Although the person responsible for last night's shooting may not be leaving town, there is that slim possibility the man we're now learning about will go to any length to trap the kid. Is there someone in this large room sitting or standing who was considering a means of ridding himself of the one witness who had the power to send him back to a dreary cell? Could that malicious person be interested in endangering the young girl's life by boarding this particular aircraft? On this bitter cold afternoon would we possibly be flying together?"

Doubting several times the necessity for the hurried trip and questioning whether he would be able to spot an unrestrained, persistent criminal, Sam attempted to relax and not reflect those doubts for the rest of the trip. At stake today was the protection of Miss Ellie Wallace and Grandma Russell, and that task remained uppermost in his mind as he remained alert.

Eliminating most travelers without the slightest hint of anyone knowing his identity, Sam became interested in the behavior of three men. He knew a person of interest would not be nodding his head from sleep deprivation. An ominous, potential pursuer of a kid would not be reading a novel or passing his time engrossed in a crossword puzzle. He might however be hiding his face behind a newspaper or magazine.

Someone who might be fidgety or standing at the window looking out onto the runway was a possibility. Conduct of a passenger which indicated impatience could be a determining clue for Sam. A person who appeared to be anticipating future actions would be suspect to him, and he was especially wary of anyone who displayed intensive concentration. He did not hesitate to spy occasionally on persons who exhibited suspicious body language. Some behaviors would alert him, and he would keep a close watchful eye on those persons for the entire flight.

As Sam observed travelers who were ready to board the flight, he continued reminding himself the trip might be a miscalculation by both Alvin and himself. Perhaps the deviant who'd attempted to obtain information from the girl was hiding somewhere in the Detroit metro area and wasn't interested in pursuing Ellie. Perhaps he had no intention of endangering her life to protect himself or his drug business. And more than likely he would not be aboard this Knoxville flight traveling to Grandmother's house.

This felon might not reach this far from his home base to harm the girl, but prevention of a crime of this magnitude and the protection of an innocent teenager was of utmost importance. Sam believed if the man wanted to strike, he'd strike soon.

Finding another seat at a considerable distance from the crowd that was now gathering at the door, Sam made a quick call to his wife to let her know he was about to board a flight to Knoxville. He explained it was a last-minute assignment for him and that he might be staying there for at least a day or two. Offering a condensed explanation of the reason for the trip, he was answered with, "Take care Honey and hurry back home. I love you."

Placing another call to his partner, Sam left a quick message for Alvin to return his call when he could. He added he would call once he arrived at the police station in Knoxville to be briefed on any new results that came from the crime lab during his absence and to hear about any recent developments that might have surfaced. After finishing the message, he packed away his cell phone. Now it was imperative for him to keep his eyes open and observe three men.

Less than three minutes before the flight attendant began calling out the rows for the seating of the aircraft, a well dressed man stepped into the holding area, and without making eye contact with anyone, he casually walked to where the line would soon form for departure.

Sam took notice of him and momentarily stood. Reaching for his small duffle bag, he slowly walked in that direction to observe the newcomer more closely. Without even giving the appearance of being aware of the man or watching him, Sam caught glimpses of his face several times from a short distance. Now he would need to observe four men when they stepped aboard Flight 276.

Chapter 29

THE ROADSIDE SIGN read "Welcome to Knoxville," and Ellie didn't miss it. She estimated it would take approximately 20 minutes to reach her grandmother's home. Just ahead she would pass the main road en route to the mall where she had roamed so often in recent years with the intention of always acquiring another article.

Those shops with their smart, enticing ways of displaying their merchandise had made it difficult for her to say no when it was time to make a decision to either purchase the item or leave the store forgetting it. Even when she was completely unsatisfied with what was available, she never seemed to tire of shopping in those bright well stocked, state-of-the-art stores. Today none of those beautiful items that were displayed in the familiar shops could interest her.

This trip had given her plenty of time to evaluate her values. Seventeen now, it was time for her to acknowledge she needed to grow up and not give in to the clever marketing tactics or to every whim. For years Ellie was aware her parents had enough money to indulge her, and for years she had taken advantage of their ample provisions, but during this trip she was beginning to question how she dealt with their generosity. Her ability at persuasion was innate, and she liberally applied her talent of manipulation as she pleaded and even begged occasionally. It had served her well whenever she wanted something. Greedy traits had established themselves deeply into her mind and had become a permanent pattern in her life.

Yes, she was charmed and often held captive by all the latest beautiful fashions in clothing, shoes, trinkets, makeup, accessories and gadgets. What young girl wouldn't find them appealing, but her obsession for acquiring those items had become her main passion. She desired those precious things above other things. They were beautiful, usually costly, and having them had become her life and identity in recent years. During the night's lengthy drive she had examined herself and had considered what was truly important.

Constantly obtaining more stuff had never satisfied her. New items certainly did not make her happier or content.

She was spoiled in so many ways, but she had also allowed herself to be weak and often would easily give in to her intense desire to be noticed as the coolest dressed kid in school. Irritated with herself, she whimpered with the little energy she had left as she realized she actually had believed having more great stuff was what was important. In many ways, her cravings had been identical to that of most of her friends.

The silly comparisons they frequently made had brought on envy, bragging and often brief spats between them. What this friend had, what that girl owned and what someone else was about to purchase had become unhealthy and trite competitive sessions which eventually led to numerous new attempts to out-do and out-purchase someone the following weekend. Ellie began recalling incidents how friendships were frequently based on nothing more than petty rivalry among themselves. At times it even resulted in ugly resentments and hurt.

Ellie began considering what her mother had been trying to explain to her, and some of the actual words spoken by her were recalled, "Mom told me needing something new every weekend to show off at school could eventually ruin my estimation of myself and determine my sense of what was of value.

After thinking about that thought, Ellie said, "Mom tried talking to me about my insatiable appetite of continually wanting to acquire something else. It was vanity, nothing less, and always wanting to possess another item that looked good on me has grown into a powerful uncontrollable dragon that lives within me. Never content with what was already in my closet, I constantly asked for more.

"On one occasion Mom and Dad complimented me on how attractive I'd become, and they attempted to make me aware that the knowledge of my beauty and the clothing I wore could encourage haughtiness in the way I perceive myself if I didn't deal with it appropriately. It wasn't easy for Mom to tell me that."

As Ellie drove up the ramp onto Interstate 40, she considered how she had reacted to her parents' expressions of concern for her. They always offered her their love, and she was often so blasé. Exasperated with how she had reacted toward them, she was sad as she thought of how they both in their own way attempted to help her understand that although she was pretty, excessive pride in her appearance would be detrimental. She often had been indifferent then as she dismissed their advice. Sadly she mumbled, "I must change my attitude about myself."

She never had accepted her parent's counsel with a genuine thankful attitude either. During the wee hours of the morning Ellie was given opportunities to think about her father and mother's love for her. So often they voluntarily sacrificed their time and energy for her benefit.

Alone and speaking to God during the night, she had gained an appreciation for their constant, unconditional concern for what she might become and what values she should hold onto for the rest of her life.

Regretting the surly attitude she often displayed when she couldn't get what she wanted, Ellie now recognized her selfishness and believed her parents were right when they said true happiness never came in having something new to wear. Angry, resentful words spoken to her by one of her best friend's last week after becoming exasperated with her sped through her mind, "You're spoiled rotten, Ellie. You're a miserable, selfish brat and have one gigantic problem! Yourself!"

Ellie shamefully admitted she had become thoughtless toward her friends and disrespectful to her parents. Thinking first of herself and mostly herself, Ellie said a short prayer with her eyes open while she drove down the highway. A confession was offered to God that she was sorry she was overly concerned with herself primarily without regard for others. She pleaded for Him to forgive her for the excessively high opinion she had of herself.

Sorrowfully she confessed her addiction to shopping. Ellie finished the prayer just as she entered the Knoxville mid-day city traffic. "Mom and Dad, I don't want to be a material girl." Then recognizing the area she knew, she said with excitement, "Hey I'm almost there!"

Although she was sure she would receive rest when she reached her grandmother's home, a few tiny tears flowed from her sleepy, strained eyes. The happy, yet soul searching, tears were swiftly wiped away.

She was happy as she said, "Maybe taking this lonely, difficult trip gave me time and the opportunity to examine myself and discover how determined I've always been to please myself. What would I ever do if I lost either of my parents?"

Now as she turned onto the street that would eventually take her to the country road that finally led to Madeline Russell's house, she was glad she spent the time to acknowledge the unrelenting pride that had been for too long inside her. She was determined to face her problem and would listen gratefully to her parents in order to make positive steps as she left childhood and moved in the direction of becoming a daughter who was ready to take on responsibilities. She whispered to herself, "I'll do what's necessary to become the woman Mom and Dad encourage me to be."

⋙•◦•⋘

A dirty, mud splattered, well traveled Chrysler pulled into Madeline Russell's gravel driveway, and hearing Joe's car pull up to the side of the house, an eager woman sprang from her kitchen in anticipation of greeting her youngest grandchild. Anxious, but cautious, she squinted as she briefly pulled back the curtain at her front door to peer through the little window to reassure herself that Ellie was the driver. At once she was out her front door just as the motor was turned off. She rushed to welcome the weary traveler.

Ellie sat with her head down for a moment thankful she ultimately completed the exhausting journey and had safely reached her destination even though she was hoping to arrive hours earlier. Feeling extremely fatigued, she stepped from the car almost stumbling onto the stone walkway. Then with a large smile on her face and taking a few deep breaths as she stretched her legs and straightened her back, she smiled too and gratefully said, "I'm here, Grandma. I made it."

With her arms outstretched, Maddie eagerly reached for Ellie and hugged her. Aware they should move inside without making more noise, she held Ellie's hand as she whispered in her ear, "Dear, we must quickly go inside the house to talk."

Maddie locked the front door securely once they entered and walked directly into her cheerfully decorated kitchen as she held onto Ellie's hand.

"Grandma, it is sooo . . . good to finally be here. I need to call Dad right away to let him know I've arrived safely. I know he'll be glad to hear from me, and I want to briefly talk to him. I want to hear his voice and know how he's doing."

A glass of cold water was already being placed in Ellie's hand, "I'll dial your father's hospital telephone number for you."

After a surprised but understanding glance toward Maddie, Ellie was certain her grandmother knew about her father's situation and possibly more than she did.

Dropping her fashionable handbag and soiled, not-so-new jacket on a kitchen chair she took the phone. Ellie stretched her weary body raising her one free arm and reached as high as she could. Standing on her tip toes, she waited impatiently for her father to speak on the other end of the line. She stopped reaching higher after the second ring when she heard her mother's familiar voice.

Eager to soon hear her father's voice, Ellie was somewhat surprised when her mother answered. "Hi, Mom, I'm glad you're both there. How's Dad?" It was all out before her mother had a chance to say anything.

Not waiting for an answer, Ellie said gleefully, "I made it, Mom. If Dad's there, tell him too that I made it. I'm so happy you're in his hospital room. The policeman told me that Dad couldn't talk to me this morning, but he did tell me he was expected to make it. You cannot imagine how thankful I am that he's alive after being shot by that horrible madman last night. I love you, Mom. Can I talk to Dad? I want to hear his voice."

Two parents had been waiting for that call, and both were expressing to Ellie how incredibly thankful they were that she arrived safely and was in good hands. Caroline was so grateful to hear Ellie's voice that she began to shed tears of joy. Joe used the corner of his hospital gown to wipe away a couple of stray tears as he grabbed the phone to talk to his daughter. "Ellie, we're so thankful you were able to escape last night and not experience any harm. And you also were able to make that long trip safely. You did drive through the night all the way to Knoxville."

"Yes, Dad, I did. God was with me all the way."

Emotionally drained and wishing she could be in the room with her parents, Ellie was crying with her mom and dad as she spoke, "I love you Mom. I love you Dad," and then she repeated the same words more slowly and with more emotion.

Hearing from her father that the single bullet that had entered his left shoulder and then into his arm had been removed and that he was on the mend, Ellie was able to say, "Dad, I know Mom will see that you receive only the best of care, and, Dad, I want you to know that last night you gave me the courage to finish that wild, tedious trip."

Everyone cried for several minutes, and Ellie said, "Although I've never been so exhausted in my life, you have no reason to worry about me now. I'll get back with you after I get some rest, but I want you both to know you're the best parents a girl could ever have. Dad, I prayed for you during the entire trip. I really did. Mom will make sure the hospital staff takes excellent care of you, and hopefully I'll see you both soon. I want to tell you everything, but I'm so tired now that I can hardly stand up. We'll talk later. Love ya both. Bye."

When the phone was placed back in its cradle, Ellie collapsed in one of the kitchen chairs as she felt extreme weariness engulf her. The trip had taken its toll on her more than she thought and had left her somewhat dizzy, unable to put her thoughts together well.

Looking on and watching her grandchild closely, Maddie said, "Ellie, take a few bites of this muffin I made earlier this morning. Then we need to get you upstairs for a quick shower and a long restful nap."

In minutes after drinking a small glass of milk along with the muffin, Maddie compassionately put her arm around Ellie's waist and squeezed her. "Up you go, girl. We'll have time to talk after you get some well-deserved rest."

Kissing Ellie gently on the cheek, Maddie walked Ellie up the stairs to the corner bedroom, the same room she slept in many times throughout the years. Placing a fresh fluffy towel and washcloth on the bed, Maddie touched her arm and said, "I'm so thankful God brought you safely here. Now rest completely."

Relieved Ellie had finished the long trip without encountering any more trouble from the ruthless pursuer, Maddie stepped out of the room as she thanked God for taking care of her grandchild, "Now that she's safe, I must again consider my plan to mete out justice to that merciless imposter." This was the same plan that had remained in her mind for hours.

Looking around at the familiar bedroom, Ellie was grateful she was there at last after such a grueling trip. Stepping into the bathroom, she decided not to look in the mirror until after she showered, but accidently glanced in that direction and saw her face. She could only laugh at herself as she picked up the little pill her grandmother had left her. A little note read, "This is a mild sleeping pill that should help you sleep. I'll wake you in four hours." Popping the tiny pill into her mouth, she drank plenty of water to wash it down.

Ten minutes later after the invigorating hot water with sweet smelling soap was applied to her frazzled body and shampoo was generously used on her hair, Ellie was able to stretch her body as she began drying off. After rubbing herself with the thick fluffy towel, she slipped into the long soft cotton nighie laid out for her at the foot of the bed. Ellie crawled between the crisp cotton muslin sheets and pulled the warm comforter over her. In minutes, the sleeping pill worked as it was designed to work. Sweet sleep overcame her without any delay.

Chapter 30

SUNSHINE AND FRESH AIR AWAITED passengers arriving at the Knoxville Airport. This was quite a contrast to Michigan's climate at this time of year. Smiles and happy attitudes were evident as arrivals gathered their unchecked belongings and left the aircraft with the gloom of winter behind. The Tennessee air had a nippy chill, but the continual cold blasts would be forgotten for awhile by those who were entering the city.

Attentive throughout the flight, Sam continued observing the four men he had chosen to keep his eyes on. They were seated in the cabin closer to the front so it was easy. A choice of whether someone used a carryon or luggage could be a clue to the reason they made this trip, and three of them were using a medium-sized carryon, but one man had nothing. This man captured his full attention. Sam reached for his duffle once the jet motor of the plane was turned off. As passengers were allowed to disembark, he along with other travelers walked hurriedly into the building. Sam would no longer be able to watch them once they scattered in various directions.

Sam had been able to partially profile each man during the flight without being obvious in any way. Now within minutes every passenger would be out of sight, so he would need to pay close attention as the four men engaged in moving toward their destination. One of the men he was concerned about caused the airline flight attendant too much trouble to remain on his list, and that man was escorted off the plane upon arrival. Chances were slight that someone with criminal intent would make such a scene on a flight only hours prior to enacting a violent crime. This man was erased from Sam's list, and now there were only three remaining.

Another of the original four men was met by a woman near the baggage claim section. She kissed him, and this ruled him out as the potential predator. The other two men were quickly swallowed up in the crowd because they did not have checked baggage. Now Sam had only his training and memory to rely on, and he knew all too well that memories of a face could fade quickly. But he would remember particulars of the two men he continued to consider with suspicion.

He again considered the likelihood that this man passing himself off as a friend to Ellie's mother may have decided to remain in Michigan. In his mind there was also the possibility that the man he was chasing would send someone else to find Ellie. That was not a pleasant thought.

⊰◦⊱

Sergeant James Cranston was waiting in an unmarked car parked at the curb when Sam walked through the baggage claim area and out of the airport. Glad to see the tall, lanky man waiting for him, he walked in his direction. After introducing themselves, Sam thanked the sergeant for picking him up at the airport and being willing to help him on the case. He tossed his duffle in the back seat, and within seconds James and Sam were heading toward the police station. The two men were close in age, and after a brief exchange of their reasons for joining a law enforcement agency, Sam began discussing in more detail the reason for his visit.

James also was a recent graduate of the police academy, and he listened to Sam's explanation of why their help was so urgently needed. Observing his interest and obvious willingness to help, Sam was sure James was eager to lend a hand and follow his lead. James understood why it would be necessary to use a few experienced policemen who could adapt quickly.

Pulling his phone from its case, Sam turned his head and said to James, "In a couple of minutes I'll fill you in on more of this assignment, but excuse me while I contact my partner to find out if there are any new facts that might have come in since the flight."

After hearing the first buzz, Alvin snatched his phone. He coughed and cleared his throat before beginning, "Sam, we definitely have additional information on Owen Wolf. The results I'm giving you are from the latest search we were able to make on the guy Ray passed on to us earlier. Our man Ray is asleep, locked up in the city jail. He's been extremely helpful, and we'll definitely take this into account, but he was such a louse to follow through on that shooting last night."

"I'll read now from a last-minute fax that was sent to me only minutes ago." Again Alvin cleared his throat, "Wolf was incarcerated for five years in a Michigan state prison for theft at a grocery store. He was not a seriously problematic prisoner and kept to himself; he only had a few friends. Several times he was beaten by a few rough prison gangs because he displayed too much pride in his intellect. He gave the impression to his fellow prisoners of being above them, and therefore was shunned. At times a fight would break out with other inmates because of his superior attitude. Often he showed signs of wanting revenge for the verbal insults and beatings other prisoners gave him, but because of their number and strength, he was unable to retaliate. Anger was his trademark."

Alvin stopped for a moment before he continued, "Obvious hatred toward fellow inmates was evident, but he seemed to be biding his time until he was released. He was only 19 when he arrived at the prison." Alvin inserted, "Today he would be about 28, since he's been out for four years." Then he continued reading the fax, "He weighted 167 lbs. during his time at the State Penitentiary. He stood 5'11" in his shoes. He had dark brown hair and brown eyes. He had a tattoo placed low on his neck along with other inmates during his prison time. There seem to be no prior arrests on his record before the robbery that took him to prison. He has not been arrested since his release."

Remembering the man who caught his attention inside the airport just before departure made Sam yank his pen from his shirt pocket as Alvin read the physical description of the prisoner. He was concentrating while he listened to the transmitted listing of the man and was writing down all he could as Alvin spoke. His mind was now fixed on that one man he was highly suspicious of who stepped into the line during the last few minutes before the flight. As information from the fax was read, the image of the man leaped into his thoughts.

Sam would linger over each fact and every detail of the man's description, but he would not be hasty and jump to any conclusion until he had a photo. He was sure the prison would be accurate in their description of each prisoner and therefore in the physical description they sent to Alvin. There would be no discrepancies in their appraisal of a prisoner's attitudes and conduct. If only he could obtain a photo, he would have a better way of matching it with the man now penetrating his memory.

"Could you fax a photo of Wolf to the Knoxville Police Station? I can pick it up there within ten minutes or so, and I'll keep in touch with you throughout the evening. I can be contacted at Madeline Russell's home once I leave the station. I know you've written down her address and phone number in your notebook." Sam waited for Alvin's positive response and finished with his usual statement, "I'll be in touch."

As he snapped his phone shut, Sam continued to consider what he was given. He pictured that same well dressed man he had seen before stepping onto the plane. He stood less than two meters away from him, and even then had surmised him to be Wolf at the time, but was unable to act. As the memory of the man filled his thoughts, Sam was agitated that he had not been given that lengthy description before he boarded the plane.

"Only six feet away!" Sam said emphatically as James turned wondering why the words were so energetically spoken.

The distance between them had been nothing then, but Sam knew miles were separating them now. He began to wonder if he had a tattoo on his neck. It would not have been visible since he was wearing a turtle neck shirt under his luxurious overcoat. Perhaps that was the reason he wore that turtle neck. Once again Sam reminded himself to be cautious because he would not settle on just anyone who fit the description and in the end allow a treacherous criminal to slither through his fingers.

When Sam finished writing his notes, he turned to James and began explaining that he needed a loan of at least two men for backup during the evening and also they would need to stay on duty for 24 hours. He expressed how he greatly appreciated their desire to cooperate with him and thanked James for their help at such short notice as they sped into the city.

In the next ten minutes Sam gave James a condensed version of the crime that was committed, what actions had already been taken and what needed to be done to protect the girl. He emphasized that Ellie Wallace did see the shooter's face.

⊰⊱

A modern structure had recently been built for the Knoxville Police Department to handle the city's law enforcement work. Crimes of all sorts were multiplying along Interstate 40 as in many large cities located along the Nation's highways. With the population growth of the city in recent years, along with the tremendous appetite among the criminally minded on grabbing what they could from whoever was out there to enrich their lives, the police were adding recruits regularly. Among the population there was always a small percentage that had few scruples and absolutely no ethical principles whatsoever. Corruption was undermining basic laws slowly, and citizens were contaminated with these constant threats to the stability of their communities.

From the moment they entered the police building Sam could see it was a busy place, and James began introducing him to his coworkers on the ground level. In the elevator Sam was taken to an office where detectives were engaged in the business of the day.

Meeting the Chief of Police and explaining briefly the reason Alvin Underwood, his senior partner, had sent him to Knoxville went smoothly. After more introductions, immediate action was taken to line up another well-trained officer to work alongside James. Wendell Sanders, an older, more seasoned officer was chosen by the Chief along with an officer who would step in if needed during the night.

James and Wendell were assigned to work with Sam for the remainder of the day, throughout the night and throughout most of the following day. This would be a long shift for all of them.

In one corner of an available office Sam sat down with the two officers, and he covered the facts of the case going over necessary details and the task he was assigning each of them. Once they arrived at Madeline's home and were able to meet Madeline Russell, they could look over the area. They would be given more specific instructions then. Both officers had been attentive as Sam presented the case, and each displayed a healthy vitality and ability to be quick on his feet. Sam believed energy and skill were necessary to catch this tenacious, clever predator.

Chapter 31

TRAVELING IN A BEAT-UP, RUSTY OLD TRUCK were three men. They appeared to other motorists on the highway to be out to do a bit of fishing, but they were on their way to the Russell residence. Upon arrival they were graciously greeted by Maddie who met them at the front door and welcomed them into her home. Leading them into her kitchen, she offered each of them a cup of fresh coffee and a generous helping of the leftover apple cobbler she made the day before. Pointing upstairs she told them her granddaughter had arrived only an hour ago and was sound asleep in the corner bedroom after spending the entire night and the better part of the day driving.

She cautioned them to step quietly throughout the house so Ellie would be allowed to rest for another hour. Walking from one room to another on the first floor, Maddie gave them a tour of her modest but tidy home. With the layout of the rooms on the main floor firmly in their minds, she took them upstairs to the second floor to view the bedrooms. She merely pointed out the room where her granddaughter was sleeping.

Walking silently back down the stairs and into the kitchen Sam spoke for himself and the men, "Thanks for allowing us to use your home on such short notice, Mrs. Russell. When I called an hour ago to let you know I'd flown from Detroit to guard both you and Ellie tonight, you'd made it clear you wanted to stay here for the night instead of going to a hotel nearby. I suggested you stay in a hotel, and the two of us would go with you. One of us could stay here to guard your place. Do I understand you want to stay here, or have you at this point changed your mind?"

"Officer, we have no proof that anyone will force their way into my home to find Ellie, and hopefully this man we're concerned about will not come. I definitely want to make sure he's found, and found soon because my granddaughter will not be safe anywhere if he's allowed to be on the loose roaming the country searching for her. I believe it's best for us to stay here, but we must take every precaution and be smart, much smarter than he is. I'm sure he's extremely evil and has absolutely no respect for human life."

Noting that the woman was unafraid and considered herself completely in control of the situation, Sam simply said in reply, "I agree Mrs. Russell. This man is definitely evil. But if he's the man we think he is and we can see his face, we can catch him. We might be able to wrap this case up soon."

Since he now had everyone's attention, Sam continued, "The plan is for all of us to be on duty here throughout the night and tomorrow if necessary. Then if this man we suspect does not appear, we suggest you, Mrs. Russell, along with your granddaughter should go to a family or friend's home for a week or so."

Then remembering the cobbler they all enjoyed, Sam said with a big smile, "Mrs. Russell, thanks for sharing that great cobbler with us, but please don't worry about any food for us because we purchased several cold sandwiches, Coke Colas and plenty of chocolate candy bars on our way out here.

We'll each have our own station in and around the house where we'll be able to watch over both of you. Don't worry if you don't see us, Mrs. Russell. We'll be here. If at any time you want us to take you and Ellie somewhere else where you'd feel safer, let me know."

➤◆➥

The three men and Maddie left through the front door and walked around to the backyard and stood near the vegetable garden. At this location Maddie was able to point out the closest neighboring homes, their garages, outbuildings, barns and fields. Maddie's barn was approximately 100 yards from the back of her home. Heads turned in every direction to scan the structures nearby. The trees, bushes, equipment and other large objects were taken in as they studied the landscape. Visually and mentally they noted anything capable of concealing a person.

James stayed behind to guard Ellie as Maddie took Sam and Wendell for a short walk to her barn. Examining it inside, they headed back to the house. Sam and Wendell were able to point out a number of places where a person could easily keep out of sight without being detected from the back of the house, and the empty cornfields in the distance would need to be watched. Upon the approach of darkness they knew there would be a lack of visibility, and nightfall would impede their ability to clearly observe the presence of an unwanted visitor.

Returning to the garden Maddie stopped and spoke in a soft tone as she pointed to the back porch, "I wish to mention that my back door is locked and will remain locked until I have a section of my porch floor repaired. It was scheduled to be fixed two weeks ago, but I'm still waiting for my friend to come and take care of it when he has extra time. With my limited budget along with the fact that I'm so tight fisted, I'll often wait to have repairs done. Let me show you what needs to be done and why no one should use the door."

They walked up the four steps to stand on her simple but brightly painted porch that was surrounded by plant containers and three cushioned chairs. Two broad windows had recently been installed in one corner that she used as a sitting area. Near a specific spot only a yard from the door, Maddie stretched out her arm and cautioned them to stop. She knelt down and picked up the end of a light-weight rug that she had placed over a large rotting handmade wooden lid.

"You can see it's not safe to stand here because this well lid simply will not hold any adult. So please don't even consider using this door as an entrance to the house. When I was a girl this was my parents' home, and it was a much smaller house then. My husband and I bought the place when my mother and father were elderly, and they then moved to a small apartment. It was then we built a large extension onto the back of the house in order to have a larger kitchen."

Tapping her toe on the edge of the lid she continued, "There was a well in this very spot, and it began to dry up. We're standing now where the beginning of the backyard was 42 years ago, and this is where our well was."

With care Maddie replaced the rug over the old cover as she continued to explain, "The county was bringing city water into this part of town in the late 50s, and since we wanted the city water instead of depending on the questionable amount of water the well could supply, we signed up to receive the city water. It still is not full, but we placed at least a truckload of available dirt, rocks, tin cans and old timber into this deep well because we would no longer use it. My husband made this cover from wood scraps he'd kept and placed it over the top of the old well."

"Over the years it has decayed, and now it cannot be trusted to hold much weight at all. I'm hoping my handyman will be able to replace it next week because the county recently inspected it and gave me three months to have this worn out old top replaced, so it will not be a danger to anyone. Hopefully I'll not have to have my entire porch floor replaced to take care of the problem. I'm tired of stepping over it when my phone rings and I'm out here in the backyard. It's annoying. I've learned to step over it onto a secure spot before entering into the kitchen, but please remember you cannot use my back door and especially not when it's dark. It's locked and bolted for everyone's safety."

Chapter 32

WAKING UP AT 5:30 in the evening was unusual for Ellie, and as her eyes opened and gradually moved around the bedroom, she remembered where she was and why she was there. Although even the mild air in this familiar room irritated her swollen eyes, her mind began to unravel the frantic events of the previous night. The intense terror she experienced in Mike's Restaurant sent a renewed cold shiver through her body.

Once her head had touched the pillow hours ago, she did not move a muscle. After her three-hour nap her normally energetic body needed to move. The dull ache that had taken charge of her head earlier was gone, and she began running her fingers gently through her hair. Relieved the throbbing pain had left, she felt hungry, very hungry. Food would help.

As she lifted her stiff limbs and crawled out of bed, she was reminded of the hundreds of miles she had spent sitting tensely in one position. Slowly rising on her toes, Ellie held that position for as long as she could as she inhaled and exhaled huge amounts of fresh air. She slowly counted to ten.

Feeling revived Ellie stretched her limbs and then relaxed them as she began breathing evenly. She pulled the gown up and over her head and began dressing in a hurry. On a chair beside the bed her grandmother had placed the tee shirt and sweat pants she left behind the last time she visited. Even though she felt the chilly January air, Ellie decided not to put them on but wrapped the light blanket at the foot of the bed around her shoulders and stepped out into the hallway.

Standing at the bottom of the stairs and smiling up at her, Maddie quietly whispered to her, "You should put on some clothes before you come down the stairs."

Ellie jumped back into the bedroom realizing someone must be in the house besides her grandmother. As she wondered who it might be, she slipped silently into the underwear she had worn the entire trip along with the shirt and pants before leaving the room.

She was not expecting to see someone she had never seen before as she walked down the stairs and into the living room, but a tall man with a serious look on his face was standing leaning against the archway between the living and dining room.

Peering at the stranger and then taking a quick glance in the direction of her grandmother, she noticed the grave expressions marked on their faces. Suddenly she was conscious of the black metal gun secured in the man's holster, and startled for a moment. Regaining her composure, Ellie reasoned he must be the policeman her father had referred to earlier.

As Ellie continued to stare at the man Maddie began explaining, "Ellie, this man is Sergeant Reynolds from the Birmingham Police Department, and he's here tonight to protect both of us from anyone who might try to harm us. Your father spoke to him earlier today and wanted him to be here for us."

Understanding Ellie's reaction at seeing him, Sam said, "I was able to visit your father in the hospital, Miss Wallace, and I'm sure you're glad he's alive and recovering from his gunshot wound. You've shown a great deal of courage after experiencing a very unpleasant incident, but he was concerned about you and your grandmother. That's why I'm here."

Waiting for Ellie to acknowledge his reason for coming, Sam continued, "We're all relieved you've finished that long and difficult trip. As your grandmother said, I was sent here to protect both of you. Also, I'm not here to rush you in any way, but I will need to obtain information and some details from you soon. We need information we don't have, but you may know."

Attempting to concentrate and process what the policeman would need from her, Ellie turned to Maddie who then said, "We must give Ellie a little time to eat something, Mr. Reynolds. Then we can talk, and she can answer those necessary questions. A little food in her empty tummy is sure to help. What kind of food sounds good to you, dear?"

"I'm famished Grandma, but I can eat just a small amount now because my stomach is a little queasy. I've only had junk food for the entire trip. Maybe a glass of juice, some crunchy salty crackers and that yummy sharp cheese you keep in your frig sound good right now." As they headed for the kitchen, Ellie sheepishly smiled at Maddie and asked, "And do you have a few large green olives, Grandma?"

Following behind the women, Sam walked over to the back door window to stand. Parting the curtain to look out, he turned saying, "I'm here whenever you're ready to talk, Miss Wallace. We know you're worn out from the trip."

"Sergeant Reynolds, if you want I can tell you some things I remember while I eat. You must know I was dazed and really frightened when I first heard those gun shots, and I didn't know for sure they were from a gun. I finally got enough nerve to leave where I was in the women's room to find out what happened. After seeing my dad and Mr. McCoy lying on the floor and then realizing my dad might bleed to death, I placed his cell phone in his hand. I was uncertain whether I should leave him alone, but he made it clear to me I should scram out of the place and make this trip to Grandma's."

Ellie's voice was shaky as she recalled the scene and spoke about what she'd seen. She sat down in a kitchen chair and began eating a few bites. Then nervously she began twisting her left hand fingers with her right hand. Looking up squarely at Sam she continued, "I didn't know what I should do, but my dad told me to take his wallet, his keys and get out of there. He told me to drive to Grandma's because he was afraid the shooter might return while I was still there. He would see me and then shoot me too. I don't remember every word my dad said because I was terribly confused and really scared, but I do remember him clearly telling me about a dangerous man out there. When I left I never saw anyone. There was so much snow out there."

When Ellie stopped for a moment, her face revealed she was in a state of detachment as her thoughts visualized the horrendous scene. Bowing her head, she yielded to a few tears and said, "But God was so good to me. He watched over me every mile I drove. I know that, and he took care of my dad, didn't he? God kept him alive."

With the utmost concern to not cause Ellie any unnecessary additional anxiety Sam agreed, "Yes, Miss Wallace, God took care of you and your dad. I assure you, your dad is getting the best care possible in the hospital. He was shot in a region of the chest that could have been very serious, but he's doing well. Because you hid in that room, and were with him when he needed you, and then were able to hand him his phone, he's alive today."

"Your leaving the scene of the crime was the right thing to do, Miss, so don't even think for a moment you were wrong to leave him. He was concerned about your welfare and wanted to keep you safe and out of reach of the killer. He told my partner and me he wanted to be here himself to protect you, but he knew he couldn't come. That's why I'm here."

Stinging tears began filling Ellie's sore eyes, and Madeline bent over placing several tissues in her lap and putting her arm firmly around Ellie's shoulders. "If this becomes too much for her, Mr. Reynolds, you'll stop and not question her further. Ellie has been through so much."

Understanding the importance of providing the police with details they needed to catch the criminal Ellie said, "I'm sure, Grandma, I can tell this policeman some details, maybe a few things he needs to know."

Swallowing the rest of the orange juice her grandmother gave her, Ellie continued telling Sam all she knew that happened during and after the shooting. She included in the details the cell call she received from a phony newsman, how another unfamiliar man minutes earlier had called her grandmother giving her another name, and the unsettling questions he asked.

Listening intently to these new facts about a caller contacting Ellie and her grandmother during her trip, Sam's face showed surprise. Sam was instantly curious as to when the man had called and exactly what he asked.

Stopping to think, Ellie said, "It was shortly after nine or maybe ten this morning I think. First of all, Sir, I'm sure he was not a newsman at all because he didn't know that my father was alive. The man said his name was Norm Forester."

With obvious distaste toward the phony newsman Ellie added, "Just minutes before he called me, Grandma was called and asked what my cell number was. The man who called Grandma said his name was Hollingsworth, Hollingswood, or something like that. Right, Grandma? I believe these two men are one and the same. Neither of us is familiar with someone named Hollingsworth. Oh, yeh, I remember the last four numbers of his phone. We'll probably never hear from those creeps again."

Sam's deft mind was active, and he was concentrating on the new information Ellie had given him. He asked her to repeat as accurately as possible all that the supposed newsman said. As she gave him the words she could remember, he wrote them down along with some brief questions that had popped into his head. He had a few more comments now to give to Alvin when he called. Sam would also run these by him.

"Miss Wallace, I believe the man you've mentioned is a man behind the shooter, not the shooter himself. We have the man who shot your father in custody. I'm referring to a man who told the shooter to go to Mike's last night. This man is more than likely the person who gave the gun to the shooter. We're learning more about Mr. Hollingswood, or whatever his name is, all the time. The man who walked into the restaurant to shoot everyone has told us about a drug dealer who he'd been working for. The drug dealer works silently behind the scenes with those who do the peddling for him. We've reason to be concerned about his intentions and, sorry to say, his capabilities." Sam said this as he watched Ellie and Maddie's reactions. "By the way, Miss, you were smart to remember his number when he called."

Trying to console them and deciding to discontinue revealing anything else that might frighten them, Sam told them not to worry. He knew the time would come to fill them in on additional facts. Sam finished by saying, "Ladies, two well-trained Knoxville policemen are hidden outside in close proximity to the house, and they'll be there through the night guarding the premises. You're both safe, but let me warn both of you not to leave the house. Neither of you are to venture outside. Understood?"

Showing her surprise Ellie stood up and ran to the window to see where they might be, but Sam cautioned them not to look out any windows or even to walk by one. Maddie began wondering where those two policemen she met earlier were hiding. She guessed they were out in the cold evening air and placed where Officer Reynolds wanted them to be on watch for a clever individual.

As Ellie was questioned by Sam, Maddie had taken in every word. She concluded from the questions Sam asked Ellie, and what he said about why the policemen were outside, that there was a skillful criminal trailing behind Ellie who was determined to find her. It seemed Sam was greatly concerned with this criminal and the tricks he was using to obtain Ellie's phone number as well as her address. This man seemed to be able to find whatever he wanted. Maddie became highly suspicious that this sharp witted individual was evil to the core and capable of devising hideous plans. He possibly might be planning to trap them both so there would be absolutely no witnesses to his criminal actions.

Assuring the women once again they were safe, Sam said, "This might be a good time for both of you to get some rest." He stopped short of what was on his mind. He finished by stating, "Ladies, nighttime will come soon enough, and when darkness comes, it's possible our industrious newsman may want to make a visit here. Hopefully not, but don't be alarmed because we've made plans to stop him in his tracks. We want everything to look normal here. Nothing must signal we're around or that we expect him."

He wouldn't frighten them by saying more. But just as the women trailed off to walk upstairs, Sam concluded with the warning, "And remember what I said. Stay inside. Neither of you is to venture outside, and do not go near any windows. Remember, you are both safe."

After Sam warned them about staying inside, Ellie had snatched a quick glance at Mattie and saw her eyes open wider and a delicate biting of her lower lip indicating that the wheel in her grandmother's brain was beginning to turn.

For hours a scheme had been developing in Maddie's head, and Ellie had read the signs. Years ago she had become accustomed to recognizing her grandmother's facial expressions when she was deep in thought. Ellie wondered what was going on in her noggin? Ellie decided to approach the subject in a hushed tone once they left Sam. She followed her grandmother to the upper level, and they both entered the same bedroom.

After the door was closed Ellie asked, "Okay, Grandma, what's going on in your head? The policeman said something down there that lit up your curious eyes. You can't fool me."

Considering whether she should confide in Ellie, Maddie took a moment before she answered, "I think you and I could do something together to ward off this sinister creature if he should show up at my door, but we must be extremely wary and not do anything foolish. We must remember that these policemen are here to keep us safe. What do you think? Do you think that criminal would attempt to come here?"

Stifling a little chuckle, Maddie lowered her chin and glanced over her glasses at her granddaughter. Amused that she hadn't fooled Ellie at all, she whispered, "We need to talk, you and I."

A half hour later Ellie was stretched out on the sofa. She had picked up the latest publication of Southern Living, her grandmother's favorite magazine. Maddie stayed in her room, and Sam walked into the dining room to examine what was outside the windows there. After checking each window wanting to know what could be seen inside the house from each, he exited through the front door and walked slowly around the house glancing into each window from the outside. Pacing and measuring every step, Sam was testing the speed with which someone could cover each side of the house. He did not hear Ellie as she left the sofa and ascended the staircase to go to her grandmother's bedroom again.

Chapter 33

OBTAINING A MEDIUM-SIZED VAN had been accomplished in minutes by Owen, since the car rental agency was only a short distance outside the airport. In twenty minutes he was on his way down the highway and moving into the Knoxville city traffic. He needed to locate a uniform supplier. Those few hours on the flight had given him plenty of time to consider a disguise. Determined to capture the Wallace girl and rid himself of her, he thought of how he might accomplish the task.

Dressing in a standard uniform appearing as an electrician was his choice for an appropriate disguise that would allow him easy entrance into Maddie Russell's home. He did not decide on the type of disguise he would use until he saw a picture of an electrician in the airline magazine. After settling on how he might go about fooling the old lady, attacking Ellie and finishing the job that he came so far to accomplish, he needed to find a business quickly that carried various types of uniforms.

Owen curled up the side of his mouth as he savagely said, "You outsmarted me once, but now it's my turn. You're in big trouble now. Leaving my turf with my expanding business unattended was a huge imposition on me. You'll regret putting me through the trouble, Miss Know It All. I intend to find you, and I don't care who gets in my way or what I have to do to reach you. But trust me,

I know where you're headed, and I'll find you. You can be sure of that!'

Seething with anger he growled, "You'll be sorry for your bold, belligerent attitude toward me. I plan to keep you alive just long enough to hear you say you're sorry and beg for mercy. No one, absolutely no one, ignores or belittles me. No one gets away with talking to me like you did. You're nothing but a spoiled, obnoxious rich kid. You little runt!"

Ranting and cursing, he began calling Ellie every crude thing he could think of as he drove toward the center of the city. He assured himself he would take care of the business he had come to do. He would give himself the entire evening to finish the job. Early in the morning he could then take a return flight back to his enterprising drug business. In the process of catching the girl, he would be careful not to leave a single traceable clue, and no one would be able to trace his movements or come to the conclusion that Owen Wolf had ever been in Knoxville.

Keeping his eyes open for a large hardware store where he might find a few items for his handiwork, he looked at the hills in the distance that surrounded the busy city and wondered who was in charge of the drug business in this area.

After driving a couple of miles on the main highway toward town, he finally decided to stop somewhere to ask for help in locating a uniform and also a hardware store. It was not an option for him to pack everything he might need before leaving since he knew the tight security personnel at the airport would undoubtedly check his bag, and he would be asked to explain his need for the tools he had in his bag. He was thinking a crowbar and a few screwdrivers would be enough to do the job. He could not purchase a gun on such short notice.

Stopping at the next convenient gas station, he asked where he might find the nearest hardware store. "Only a mile or so down the road on the left" he was told.

"That was easy," he mumbled to himself. He then asked to use their telephone book which they happily handed to him. In an attempt to be of service to a visitor to his fair city, one attendant mentioned he would be glad to help him in any way he could. "This was going smooth," he thought. Two uniform suppliers were listed, and he questioned the attendant in what part of the city would he locate the supplier who had the largest inventory of uniforms.

Without hesitation Owen was given a name and directions to the address. The uniform supplier was located the better part of an hour away, and although he was disappointed, he was sure he had the time to get there before it was too dark. He reasoned it was definitely his best shot as he wrote down the name of the business and the roads. He was careful to include every turn he would need to take since he wanted to give himself plenty of time in case he missed a street.

With the availability of the telephone book, and without their awareness, he cunningly looked up the address for Madeline Russell and wrote her address on a piece of paper they gladly handed him. Slipping it in his pocket with the other address, he hurriedly asked for directions to Maddie's road as he returned the telephone book to the attendant. After getting all the information he needed, he thanked the attendant for his assistance, and as Owen was about to leave, a basic map was placed in his hand.

As Owen jumped into the van, he looked at his Rolex watch, something he definitely would remove before making his trip to Grandma's house. It was almost 4:00 pm, and he should arrive at the uniform supplier before 5.

With moderate traffic, he would certainly be able to accomplish what he had in mind by dusk. To stay ahead of the game, he would call the uniform supplier and ask what type of uniforms they had in stock. Hopefully, they would not consider this an unusual question. His call was answered with a friendly hello.

Considering a fake identification Owen introduced himself to the listener, "This is Hank Porter, and I've recently been placed in charge of a crew of men that do odd jobs. Since I'll be supervising and working alongside them, I need to get a uniform for myself. I'm sure I'll need several more in the near future, and I'm also sure we'll be giving you more business soon. I was wondering what kind of uniforms you might have on hand that I could look at and purchase today. Of course it does not need to be new, but it must in good condition and in my size. I was hoping to pick one up within the hour. Would that work for you?"

"Mr. Porter, we have several uniforms in either navy or gray which you could choose from. Let me remind you that we do close at five. If you can be here by then, I'll have several for you to look at. We take cash or check only. No cards of any kind," the manager replied.

Attempting sincerity Owen said, "I wear a medium to large size, and I should be there within the hour if traffic moves well, and cash is fine with me. Thanks for your help, and I'm pleased we could do business on such short notice." He dropped his phone in his coat pocket and took it off.

"Everyone has been so accommodating," Owen mused and then chuckled as he jumped back into the van and sped down the road. He mocked as he laughed, "So, Mommy left her cell phone at Granny's. How convenient, and Granny said the kid was on her way there. What a break for me! Everything is going great . . . If for some reason the kid doesn't show up, the old lady will end up getting an unexpected surprise from a friendly electrician. Stupid, Granny! You are so stupid. Your grandkid is smarter than you, but she's not as smart as she thinks. You're both in for a big surprise."

⟫━◆━⟪

Owen hurried out of the friendly hardware store with his purchases. Back in the van and moving down the highway, he thought of his purchases. He deposited the leather tool belt on the floor. Also placed in a plastic bag was a crowbar along with three different sizes of screwdrivers and a small container of dark oil. As he glanced at the bag, he laughed scornfully, "No previous training as an electrician, but I can do some interesting work. These items will prove that I'm able to finish a job well."

Pleased with such a clever idea, he uttered, "These are sure to do the damage, and Miss Wallace, you'll never be able to ignore or override anyone's questions again."

He was beginning to enjoy the way his plan was working. Proud of himself, he smiled in a contemptuous manner, "A little dark grease rubbed onto the tool belt and a little more under my fingernails should give the impression to the ladies that I'm an electrician. My presence outside or inside the house will not raise any questions. I'm sure my appearance will fool them, and I'm sure it'll be easy to get into the house. I can be finished in an hour."

He arrived at the uniform supplier 12 minutes before closing time and found the man he spoke to standing at a counter ready to serve him. Six different uniforms were displayed for him to examine. Owen recalled from the picture he saw in the airflight magazine that the electrician was dressed in a blue uniform. He settled on a medium sized uniform since it fit him perfectly. A simple hat was quickly chosen to finish his disguise. He paid for the uniform and hat with cash and was out the door before the five o'clock closing time.

Back in the van, he was aware that he would need a business name of some sort written on the side of the van that would be an identification of the type of work he did. If he could find large letters, he would be in business. Sighting a large home improvement store close by, he pulled into the parking lot and found what he wanted within minutes. "Letters along with a telephone number containing several zeros, and no one would be the wiser this late in the evening."

Taking a hurried look out the window, Owen could see that the January sun had already fallen behind the rolling hills surrounding the city, and he was certain darkness would be his friend tonight.

"Now I need to find a safe place to pull off the road and place these letters on the van," Owen mumbled as he visualized how he would place the name and phone number. Pulling into the back of a vacant lot, he placed his new business name on each side of the van. Stepping back in the pale light he checked the placement of the words, Dan's Electrical Service. "These oversized letters and the uniform will be certain to succeed. Who at this hour would doubt a handy electrician going about his work?"

At a large truck stop on his way toward Maddie's home, Owen entered the men's room. He dressed in his new uniform. After carefully folding the clothes he'd taken off and placing them in the plastic cover that had been used to protect the purchased uniform, he stood looking at his reflection in the mirror. Satisfied with his new appearance, he grinned with amusement.

He took the small can of dark oil he purchased at the hardware store and rubbed a tiny amount around his fingernails. A more generous amount was spread on the front and sides of his tool belt. He dabbed drops on the rim of his cap working the oil into the cloth. Hating to ruin his new Cole dress shoes, but knowing it was necessary, he wiped each shoe with a huge amount of oil. Then running his oiled fingers through his hair and wiping the remainder onto the trousers, he stepped back to admire the complete disguise.

He snarled and gruffly said, "Now let's get to work, Dan."

Chapter 34

SITTING ON THE FLOOR in a corner of the dining room with a view of many of the windows on the first floor, Sam was able to move his head forward enough to see a fraction of the moon through the small front door window. In the opposite direction he could see bright early stars through one of the larger windows in the kitchen. Uncomfortable as it was, he chose this spot because it allowed him the best view of the windows and doors.

Grasping his phone Sam contacted James, "Stay alert and let me know if you notice any unusual motorists moving down the road. The wind has picked up and rain could be on the way. We must count on it becoming colder within the hour. Although this is the South, I'm told January nights in these mountains can be unpredictable and quite chilly. I keep reconsidering our present plan. Perhaps we should have taken the women to a nearby hotel, but since they're napping, I'll go along with their desires. Hopefully this case will be wrapped up by morning, and we can all go home. Have you been in touch with Sanders?"

James answered, "I called Sanders minutes ago. Perched high in the hayloft of the lady's old barn, he said he has an eagle's eye view of the backyard and rear entrance of the house. In the other direction, he can see open fields and a couple of distant homes with his field glasses. He mentioned that he feels like a tramp who found a dry place to sleep for the night in a hayloft." He laughed a little. "I assure you Sanders is one of our best scouts and will remain at his post for the entire night, or for as long as you need him. There is one other thing he mentioned. He's a bit cold up there, and he needs a warm blanket. Neither of us was prepared for this."

Considering for a moment where he might obtain a few warm blankets, Sam told James to call Sanders and let him know he would make certain something warm was sent his way hopefully before it was completely dark.

Darkness was descending as the night hours approached, and a light drizzle of rain began to dampen the air. Sam needed to get blankets to the barn and across the road soon because a little trick like that might alert a person who intended to victimize his prey. He would talk to Maddie soon. A trap set for a dangerous man would be ruined if he didn't hurry. This wasn't the usual way to catch a drug dealer, but Maddie had been game for the plan, and now they were forced to go ahead with it. Nothing would give Sam more satisfaction than to catch this cunning criminal tonight.

Everything at this point had to be handled discreetly without offering the vaguest impression that any law enforcement personnel were present. That's why Joe Wallace's Chrysler had been moved hours earlier to the inside of the barn.

James had parked the damaged, old rusty truck they used to drive to the house across the road in a field with weeds hiding a large portion of it. Parked in such a way that nothing would seem unusual, the tail end gave the impression that the truck had been there for years. Crouched low in the seat of the truck holding onto his night binoculars, James was keeping watch over occasional vehicles that drove by on the country road. James was instructed not to use a light of any kind.

Total darkness was only an hour away, but it seemed to Sam they were prepared except for those promised blankets. Climbing the stairs and softly knocking on the bedroom door, Maddie silently walked to the door as Ellie ducked into a bathroom out of sight. Taking a moment before answering, Maddie said, "Just a minute."

The women had been talking in low tones about what their roles were in the capture of the devious man who entered their lives abruptly without invitation. They both had reason to not allow the criminal to run free and were determined to make sure he would be punished and face justice equitable to his crime.

Their soft whispers were not heard by Sam as Maddie opened the door. Maddie appeared to be wrapping a warmer sweater around her shoulders when she opened her door, "Oh, Officer, how's everything going with the men?"

"I'm sorry to trouble you, Mrs. Russell, and I know you've been resting, but we need three warm blankets. Since we'll be outside, we need two for the men outside, and I'll need one. No need for your better blankets, but anything warm you can spare. From what I can see, it's best all three of us remain outside," Sam said without looking around her room.

The request for the blankets was acknowledged with a quick wink but without another word. Within minutes three fluffy warm blankets were stacked in the hallway, and Sam carried them as they both crept down the stairs and into the dimly lit kitchen.

Two large, heavy-duty black plastic bags were pulled out of a kitchen drawer and given to Sam to haul the blankets out to Sanders and James. Stuffing them in the bags and fastening them as if trash was being disposed of,

Sam took one of the bags across the street and threw it within feet of the old truck. The other bag was taken to the barn and dropped just inside the door. "Trash" was simply spoken as a signal to the hayloft occupier. No one would suspect garbage bags being hauled out of someone's home.

———◆———

Total darkness had arrived as the light rain stopped. Several new bright stars could be seen in the sky as Sam retraced his steps from the barn back to the house. Under a dim light outside the kitchen door Sam was almost certain he could barely make out Maddie's form. She seemed to be on her hands and knees and moving a large solid object. By the time he reached the garden area though, Maddie was already inside the house.

Unobserved he walked around the house and entered the front door. Seeing that Maddie was busy emptying her dishwasher and putting dishes away, he dismissed the thought that was lingering in his mind, but casually asked Maddie if he could help her in any way. She said sweetly, "Thank you, I cannot think of a thing, but could I get you anything?"

Chapter 35

A BARELY PERCEPTIBLE AMOUNT of daylight could be seen on the roads when Owen finished with his disguise and returned to the van. Total darkness would ensure that he would appear to anyone in the area as a professional worker dedicated to keeping electrical power in the area maintained. He sneered and then laughed fully, "I'm enabling citizens to use their many appliances without worry. Electricians are people who make sure homes are heated, offices are kept warm and working environments are comfortable. My motto tonight is, 'We can be trusted.'"

Dan's Electrical Service could be seen on both sides of the van with the telephone number 865-6500 listed below. With a wide grin, he was proud of what he'd been able to accomplish and was especially satisfied with his ingenious disguise. Night time was about to arrive, and he was anticipating great success.

Following directions given to him by the two individuals at the gas station, he should show up at Madeline's door within 20 minutes. He had been discreet in his inquiry by not using her name, only the street name. No one seemed to be suspicious in any way. If anyone were to trace his moves or what he intended, it would only be conjecture on their part. Only someone attempting to solve this crime and who was willing to spend a great amount of time and effort would be able to put any of the pieces together. That would take months, but he would be long gone from the area. With his twisted, perverted mind, he laughed to himself about how utterly inventive he was and how lacking in brains the police were.

It was evident the light drizzle would not continue much longer. Through the few fine drops of rain hitting the windshield Owen had no trouble seeing the road ahead and viewing the street signs. With the headlights beaming brightly and following the map he was offered, he was assured he was going in the right direction and would soon reach Grandma Russell's street. Finally the last turn could be seen ahead. He became excited as he turned onto the street. His keen eyesight began concentrating on the addresses of each mailbox. He was certain the home he would visit was nearby. He thought of how everything was going according to his plan. The road ahead was dark, and that was what he needed.

As he approached the general location where the home should be, he slowed his vehicle and focused on each house, barn and field. He was also searching for a black car with a Michigan license plate parked in a driveway. That would be sound proof the kid had reached her granny. He said, "It's always possible she hasn't arrived yet."

Continuing to concentrate, he thought, Would the kid have been frightened after the questions he had asked and decide to hide the car in a garage or someplace else? Skeptical and uncertain, a few doubts began entering his mind. But shaking his head, Owen tenaciously reminded himself that a little uncertainty would never hinder his efforts tonight. He would find the kid who was the only witness to the shooting, and he was determined to capture her. "I'll force Little Miss Smarty to answer my questions. If for any reason the kid hasn't arrived, Grandma will be mine, and I'll take care of her without anyone knowing

what happened. Out here on this lonely road it will be
delightful!"

Set back more than 200 feet from the road, a neat
modest two-story country home with shutters at each
window and a small friendly front porch came into his
view. With the correct address on the mailbox, he almost
shouted, "Bingo! That's it, but where's the car?"

The misty rain had stopped, and without many stars
visible in the sky or any street lights in the vicinity, it was
now pitch black except for faint moonlight and a few lights
in the house. No cars were parked outside. He noticed the
old truck across the road, but turned his head becoming
interested in checking again the number on the mailbox as
he muttered, "Here we are ladies."

Owen wondered if possibly the car he had seen the
night before could have been moved to the barn he was
seeing that was located hundreds of feet to the rear of the
house. Through the windows on the main floor he was
sure someone must be inside. At least one light was
illuminated in what must be the living room, and a
dimmer light could be seen flowing through a room on the
second floor. It was an attractive home that appeared to be
set apart from the other homes in the area.

With pleasure he observed how the neighboring
homes were far enough away to be beyond earshot.
Nothing would be heard with their windows closed. It was
too chilly to have windows open tonight. Owen instantly
noticed the many bushes and trees that lined the property,
and he was happy because sounds would be also muffled
by the foliage of these full bushes that had a healthy supply
of thick leaves. He would use the cover of these bushes to
protect himself from anyone who might happen by. They
would be excellent hiding places if for any reason it would
be necessary for him to flee.

Inhaling the night air he was confident his disguise would fool those inside. He was certain he could walk up to Grandma's front door and be inside within seconds. She was an easy mark when he spoke to her earlier that morning, and she fully trusted him then.

But he would not take careless chances as he skillfully surveyed the fields surrounding nearby homes and the outbuildings on the woman's property again to assure himself there was nothing unusual happening. With his sharp eyes the examination was accomplished quickly. Nothing was seen that would hinder him from his ruthless task. He grinned with pleasure as he made his final plan.

Pulling the van slowly up the gravel driveway and parking close enough for the words, Dan's Electrical Service, to be seen with the light coming from the front porch, but not too close for it to be easily examined, Owen stepped out of the van and reached inside for his tool belt. Standing outside the van and strapping it around his waist loosely, he continued to scour the area with his eyes as he placed the screwdrivers and the small crowbar in the loops. He made the short hike to the house and up the front porch steps. He was sure he would pass any close examination with flying colors.

He knocked on the front door fully confident his identity was concealed by the uniform he was wearing. As he waited for an answer, he looked around attempting to appear naturally interested in the immediate surroundings. Owen turned from side to side taking in as much of the yard as possible to be assured he was alone except for those inside the house. With his skillful scrutiny nothing was missed. The porch light was turned on and then a much brighter light spread over the porch and part of the front yard. He was not expecting the extra brilliant light.

He heard the door being unlocked. Grandma Russell was opening the front door, but only a crack because the heavy chain lock attached to the framework around the door was preventing the door from opening all the way. She was holding onto a phone obviously talking to someone. She was showing surprise to see an electrician standing at her door at that hour.

———⊱◦⊰———

Maddie smiled and pleasantly greeted him. "Hello, may I help you?"

With a fake Southern accent Owen said, "Good eve'nin', Ma'am, I do hate to bother you at this hour, but we're experiencin' some electrical power problems in this part of the county. It's inconvenient, I know, but we need to do some quick checkin' at your power box. If you could show me the box, I can do my work and be out of here in no time at all. This should only be a preventative measure for you, but we're trying to prevent a power outage for this area of the county. I'm sure you don't want to wake up in the morning with no heat in your house and no way to cook your breakfast."

"Sir, you'll need to go around to the back of my house to reach my box. I'll be off the phone in a bit, but I can go around to my back door in a minute to let you in." Maddie held the phone as she hastily closed and relocked the door.

Across the street, James had been watching the scene through his binoculars as the van pulled up and a man walked up to the house. Uneasy about the situation at this hour and not willing to take any chances even though both the van and the man appeared genuine, he grabbed his cell phone. Contacting Sam he said, "James here. Some electric company van pulled into the driveway. The man looks legit, but the lady actually opened her front door slightly and actually is speaking to him. Oh, hey, now she seems to have sent him around to the back of the house, and he'll be out of my sight because he's moving now in your direction."

After Sam placed his phone back in its holder, he stooped silently into a perfect hiding spot he found earlier inside one of the larger bushes along the backyard border of Maddie's home. In seconds Sam knew he would see the dark shadow of a man coming into view.

Bundled up in his blanket, Sam had been protected from the chill of the wind for over an hour. He allowed the blanket to drop silently to the ground behind him. He was sure the bush was an ideal spot to detect foul play from an unwanted intruder coming to the rear of the property where most break-ins usually occurred. The man was now headed toward him.

Receiving the message from James, Sam was astonished but perturbed that Maddie had so quickly failed to obey his orders and allowed a total stranger to walk around to the back of her house. He had warned her not to fall for any kind of trick that might be used to enter her home, and he had also given Joe Wallace his word that he would protect both of them. Thinking about what he had not expected he thought, I'll need to track every move this man makes as he walks toward the back of the house. It's the darkest area around the house. I can't lose him.

Chapter 36

NOW SAM WOULD NEED TO USE those hunting skills he was taught as a child. During his youth his dad had taken him out to open fields to pursue and capture wild animals. Now he might need to capture a shrewd and calculating criminal. Sam's concentration intensified as he thought, If the man's legit, fine. If there's any doubt of his intentions, his actions will give him away. He commanded all his mental powers to be totally responsive and vigilant whatever the outcome.

The uniformed man seemed to know exactly where he was going as he began walking down the side of the house. Slowly but with self-confidence, Owen moved toward the back of the house where the elderly woman had told him to go. The deepening darkness at the side of the house did not cause him to slacken his pace or to halt any of his movements.

Sam heard the footfalls as the man stepped on small twigs and dry leaves, but since it was so dark, he was unable to see his frame clearly. Every step was bringing the man closer to the large dense bush where he was hiding. Sam's plan was to observe every movement the man made and hopefully catch a glimpse of his face before he made any move toward the back entrance of the house. Within seconds he realized it was much too dark to see the man's face.

Finally seeing the full figure of the man, who now appeared in every way to be trustworthy as he made his way to the rear of the house, Sam's perceptive skills were completely engaged. As the man turned toward the porch and the back door, Sam thought, He appears to be an authentic electrician after all just doing his job.

Owen approached the steps to the porch, and then for some reason stopped, turned his head and looked in the direction of the barn and the vacant field beyond. In total darkness he scanned the trees and bushes lining the sides of the house for a full three seconds, but he could only make out larger objects that were in close proximity.

Directing his full attention on what Sam believed was odd for an electrician to do and focusing on the motionless figure, Sam waited silently in the bush thinking it was also strange the man stopped short of climbing the few stairs that would take him up to the back door. The man seemed to be wary as he observed his surroundings. And now he seemed to be straining his ability to listen as well.

Once again, but cautiously this time, the man placed one foot on the stairs. A small amount of illumination coming from the inner kitchen lit the man's face, but Sam was unable to see it. Then the man stopped again stretching his neck and looking behind him.

I still can't make out his face, Sam thought. That was a long wait though, and what is he doing? He reasoned it was an unusual action for an electrician out on call, and he reached for his gun. In another second he might need to act.

Standing there for another short moment, the observed man turned his head forward again in the direction of the back door. He raised his head as high as he could and seemed to be listening to any sounds or movements nearby. Then relaxing his neck because he could not detect anything that alarmed him, he straightened his body and took another step up the stairs.

Sam was now almost positive from the manner in which this man reacted that he was the dirty drug dealer who was behind the shootings. He would not take any chances with the two women inside unaware of the danger. He would not wait to act in order to protect them.

At that moment Owen heard Maddie at the back door as she turned a deadbolt. Seeing her pull back the curtain and peek out at him, he was convinced he was alone with the woman at last.

She turned on the porch light and he surmised, I can easily seize this old lady. She's making it so easy for me. I can carry out my deed on this unsuspecting old lady tonight, and I'll trap that miserable brat later.

Hearing the turn of the deadbolt and click of a lock, and seeing the door move a crack, Owen was elated. With a sneer on his face, he quickened his pace and leaped up the remaining stairs and toward the door. Anticipating spending the next few minutes with two female victims, he grinned expressing to himself silently, No one will hear their piercing screams in this quiet country setting.

<hr />

From the hayloft watchtower, Sanders had been observing all Owen's movements with his trusty binoculars. Signaling James across the street to be on guard earlier when he had first seen the van turn into the drive, he was not sure Sam saw the man as he walked toward the back of the house, and he decided he must contact him.

When Sam's phone buzzed at the lowest level possible, Owen stopped dead in his tracks with his feet at the top of the steps conscious of the sound of an electronic signaling device coming from the direction of the bushes.

Two options were available to him, and he had to make a decision fast. He could jump off the porch and run back to the van or leap for the back door in front of him. Certain the house was the closest and safest, his choice was obvious. It had been unlocked, and Owen decided to reach for the door.

Sanders and Sam were running toward the electrician as Owen took one final giant leap and reached out with his hand for the doorknob. In that split second he disappeared, and a loud, bellowing screech was heard. Springing onto the porch where the man had suddenly disappeared, Sam looked down into a deep, black hole. Both James and Sanders rushed close behind him, and James had to be grabbed before he also fell into the hole.

Maddie, amused at the thought that she had actually caught the villain, began to laugh gleefully and almost cried as she stood safe inside her kitchen holding onto the frame of her back door. Both she and Ellie carefully stepped out and around to join the men.

Gazing down 12 feet or more into the old well, all five soon caught sight of a traumatized man glaring up at them. Three policemen tried to control their laughter. With a flashlight in her hand, Maddie was able to see what she had trapped. She handed the light to Sam, and they all could see clearly a mud-soaked, intensely enraged man gawking up at them. With Owen's eyes riveted on Maddie, he began to curse her. Then turning his malicious eyes on Ellie, he swore loudly and offensively at her. He verbally attacked her, calling her numerous crude, vile names.

No one had ever expressed their rage and vengeful attitude using such indecent words before toward Maddie, and she was angered this morally wicked man was speaking to Ellie in such an arrogant, crude, loose-tongued manner. She cupped the sides of her mouth with her hands as she hollered down at him, "Mind your words you brute, you devil, you who intended to harm my grandchild. A deep dark slimy hole is where you belong, and I hope you get everything you deserve when they come for you."

For the next few minutes, they all stood looking down as they watched Owen slip and slide on the wet, muddy sides of the old well as he desperately attempted to climb up the side. Maddie told them the circle of rusty metal close to the bottom was barbed wire she had been storing in the barn for years.

"My husband wrapped it into a huge wreath like shape and hung it on a hook just inside the large barn door. I'd seen it every time I went to the barn but never found any use for it until this afternoon when I went to get it.

"When I was preparing for Ellie's arrival earlier, I thought of my old well that was about to be filled, and later realizing I'd been keeping that barbed wire for some good use, it popped into my mind to place the whole thing into the well just in case this evil person came to my house while Ellie was here."

All except Owen had a good laugh as they continued watching Owen try to climb out of the well without falling back onto the barbed wire. When he first fell into the well, his feet hit the sides of the wire with such force that the barbs were driven deeper into the well. He screamed because one rusty point had dug into an ankle. Now with each attempt he made to find his way out of the hole, the wire was forced further into the bottom of the well.

With an unholy anger on his face from all the painful jabs he was receiving, Owen finally found a spot where he could stand upright without feeling the cold metal touch his body. With the buckets of water that Maddie had also poured into the well that afternoon, his shoes were sinking each time he took a step into the red clay.

James wanted to leave Owen in the deep well for the rest of the night because of his intense display of haughtiness and words expressed of revengeful hatred.

One by one Owen began hurling up the tools he had purchased. First the crowbar came especially aimed at Sam who was standing near the edge of the well. Then the screwdrivers were each thrown as he tried to hit anyone in his audience. Missing each time, he would swear at them with contempt. He was now acting like a victim as he complained that Maddie had definitely broken one of his legs and probably caused damage to his other leg in the fall.

Unbearably cold and shivering from the wet dirt and unable to move because of the sharp barbs, he continued cursing again and again even as his voice became hoarse and began to fail. Humiliation along with his discomfort caused him again to feverishly attempt climbing out of the hole.

In an hour he quit his bellowing and hunched down beside the wall of the cold muddy well. With all his wild jumping, at least a foot of mud thickened water was now standing in the bottom as it sucked at the lower part of his trousers. Loose sand and clay continued to fall back into the well from his clawing as he grabbed the sides with his free hands. After another half an hour he finally came to the conclusion that his attempts to escape were futile. Giving up completely, he sat down and began to sob. He begged them to take him out of the dark, wet cold hole.

Owen Wolf had told himself he would never grovel, but now he knew he was defeated as he cried, "Please, please get me out. I feel like a rat down here." Miserable but without thinking of what he had said, Owen was instantly reminded of the words he had heard so often in prison from inmates when they didn't trust him. The word "rat" was out of his mouth without thinking.

Forgetting any dignity, he begged to be brought out of the well, but he told himself even then he would not give up even after all this if he had one single chance to escape from his captors. He would lie, make a promise or say whatever was necessary so he never would end up in a jail cell again.

———◆———

Ellie had been included in Maddie's plan to trap the person responsible for shooting her dad and killing Kurt McCoy and the waiter. At first Maddie did not want Ellie to be part of the plan, but she had been grateful for having someone who was truly interested in her plan. When her granddaughter giggled at the prospect of catching the man and was confident the plan could work, Maddie was encouraged to go through with it.

From the upstairs bedroom both women had heard the van turn from the road and drive up the side of the house. Maddie had slipped down the stairs, grabbed her phone and was ready when she heard the man's knock on her door. Cautiously Ellie had waited upstairs until she heard the man leave the front porch and make the trip around the house toward the back. She was sure the man never saw her. Before that she was instructed to wait until the flood light was turned on before looking out the upstairs window. That was the signal. The brighter flood light was to allow Ellie to get a good look at the kind of vehicle pulling into the driveway.

Maddie had seen the van pull into the driveway and had been able to see a man dressed as an electrician step out and close his door. Earlier she had reminded herself how easily she had been tricked and how foolish she was when she gave an absolute stranger Ellie's cell number. Because the man probably had obtained her address along with other members of the family, she believed it was certainly possible he might brazenly try to fool her once again.

Sure enough the phony came. In the darkness he was passing himself off as an electrician. She knew what electricians wore, and that wasn't it. Before she went to the door, she peeked through her sheer curtains in the living room and saw the man turn his head and look across the street toward the fields nearby. She prayed then that he would not spot any of the men. Before that Ellie and she had been on duty upstairs for hours listening to vehicles as they drove by.

She paid close attention to him and examined his every move as he walked toward her front door. When he knocked she went to answer the door. When she turned on the bright light, she got a great look at him. She had been extra cautious to unlock only the main one and open the door only a crack. As he spoke, his accent did not fool a woman who had lived in that area her entire life. His speech and the sound of his voice reminded her of the man she spoke to earlier that day.

Then she noticed the shoes he wore once she switched on the flood light. She knew they didn't belong to a man who made his living as an electrician. She also knew electricians were careful to wear rubber soles to guard themselves from faulty electrical circuits. His seemed to be expensive and smeared with some dark oily substance.

From under his hat, she had managed to see his hair. It had been cut meticulously in a style she rarely saw. She had seen all that in seconds and was highly suspicious of him, but still she did not assume he must be the man the police were interested in capturing.

When she told him to go to her back door, she had a couple terrible last-minute thoughts enter her mind. What if he wasn't counterfeit after all? He might be what he claimed to be. He might truly be an electrician sent out by the county to check her meter, but the nagging unwillingness to place Ellie or herself in the hands of a man who would definitely harm them remained. She decided to hold her phone to her ear in order to offer an excuse. She could instruct him to go around to the back of the house. Even then she thought she might be in a heap of trouble if she sent a good man to the spot on her porch where the empty well was waiting under only a lightweight rug and where the barbed wire could tear his flesh.

Once inside the kitchen, Ellie met her in the kitchen and hid. As they stood in a dark corner breathlessly waiting as the man made his way toward the back door, they intended to warn him of the open twelve foot well if they were unsure of their assessment. The women could barely see his face, but were aware of how he turned around suspiciously several times when he reached the steps.

As he stepped onto the first stair step, they were able in the pale light to partially view his facial expression and the gleeful look in his eyes. For another second they wondered if he possibly was afraid of the dark. No, they decided, he was not genuine. He was not a true electrician. They were certain this man was a genuine fake.

Chapter 37

THE PREDAWN AIR was thick with moisture as handcuffs were tossed down the well to Owen. This had been his second night without rest, and after standing in the icy water that had covered his pricey shoes and socks for hours, his legs were frozen. Wherever he stood his feet, every toe and both ankles were numb. Shivering, he sat down with his arms wrapped around his body. The women had gone inside where it was warm and dry.

Looking up at the man standing at the top of the hole with both his large hands firmly resting on his hips, Owen considered his options for a few silent moments. He surmised the man looking down at him must be the one in charge, and somehow his face looked familiar. Owen lowered his head trying to remember where he had seen that face. It came in a flash. It was before the flight, but who would have known he was a policeman and tracking him. "You were sent to bring me back to Michigan."

Owen's body was stiff from the freezing water and the cold night air. Hardly able to move a finger and unable to fight his way out, he doubted he could ever outrun these men. He could not manage to reach the barn, and would never be able to lose them in the field beyond?

Given the choice of either spending the rest of the night in the dank, dark hole or taking a chance on a possible escape, he did not consider his options long. The decision had to be made now before he was left forgotten to freeze to death. His uniform was filthy and soaked with icy water, and now his entire body was shivering uncontrollably.

His imagination took over, and he began to fear what the granny might want to do with him. She might cover him with the heavy red clay and leave him there forever. Who knew, out here in this part of the country, with the old lady ready to bury him alive to rid herself of him, he might not see another sunrise. He had a dismal vision of the two women reaching for shovels and pitching dirt. He would not endure another hour in this clammy pit or spend time considering how his end might come.

The man in charge stepped back out of sight, and Owen concluded his only chance for freedom might be walking away. Calling to Sam, the mud encrusted man shouted, "Hey, whoever you are, I'll go peacefully and save everyone a lot of trouble."

Hearing those words, Sam walked back with a frown on his face. "Hey, I was beginning to enjoy watching you down there. Are you sure you don't want to stay there for a few more hours, maybe until daylight?"

A flashlight lit Owen's face, and Sam could see the captured man was placing the handcuffs on his wrists. The knotted end of a rope was then tossed down the well for him to grab.

Gripping it tightly with his frozen, dirty hands, Owen was drawn up without any trouble. Thick red mud covered him, and he began frantically spitting out gritty dirt that had found its way into his eyes, mouth and nose on his trip up the well. He began rubbing his eyes from the irritable specks of dirt that had lodged there.

As soon as he was out, his feet were grabbed and deposited on the old wooden well cover. With his eyes closed and without warning, Owen sputtered and spit out more dirt as Sam and James each took hold of one of his ankles and spun him around causing him to lose his balance. Almost falling, Sanders caught him. Startled Owen reached again for his irritated eyes with his knuckles and rubbed them. For a split second he was able to see his feet firmly planted on a large piece of wood. Now the police were actually nailing his shoes onto the wood. Missing his toes by less than a centimeter, he wailed, "Hey, what the . . ." He was unable to see his new expensive shoes as they were each pierced with two nails on each side pinning him to the heavy wood cover. Unable to lift either foot, his hope of escape had shrunk to zero.

Resigning himself to the pitiful situation, he breathed heavily, dropping his shoulders. Arrogant no longer, he stood shivering from the winter air as it whipped around him. Looking through the remaining dirt in his eyes at the three men who seemed satisfied with their work, Owen began to cry as they placed a fuzzy warm blanket over his shoulders. Sam, James and Sanders picked Owen up, took him down the stairs and placed him in the backyard. They walked over to the side and waited until Owen was calm.

A bright light was turned on in the kitchen, and Maddie appeared at the doorway. She asked Sam if she could have a few words with Owen, this man who had caused Ellie and her so much anguish. Dragging Owen on his platform and placing him ten feet from her, she was able to safely speak to the man. For a brief moment she looked at him, but then said, "My handyman will be out first thing tomorrow to finish the job of filling my well and sealing it securely. No one has ever fallen into my well before, but the timing for your fall was beautiful. I'd planned to have the well fixed weeks ago, but the job was put off. Only God knew I'd need to wait until my friend could fix it.

"Mr. Hollingsworth, or is it Norm Forester, or whatever your real name is, you've caused my family a great deal of agony. And Galina Nikhalaev, the housekeeper who faithfully has worked for the Wallace family for years, is possibly the best Christian woman I've ever known. This afternoon when I should have been resting, I called the hospital. I wanted to know how she was doing after you left her for dead.

"She performed quite a courageous stunt. You remember her, don't you? She's the woman you cruelly struck down yesterday. She didn't die, thank God, but was terribly maimed by you. She fooled you. In tremendous pain, she crawled to the phone and called Joe's office. Then she called an ambulance for herself. She gave the police a description of your face, your hair color, your height and approximate weight. When you appeared at my door, I was certain you were that man. Ellie and I set a trap for you, and you grabbed it hook, line and sinker.

"Joe Wallace is also one of the best persons I've ever known. You wanted him to die, you snake, but you failed. He was supposed to die so you wouldn't lose any of that crummy drug business you run. That was not enough, and you came for my 17-year-old granddaughter. You went too far then. Our Ellie was running for her life. She is the bravest young girl I may ever know. She defied you and was able to alert all of us that a pernicious, cunning demon was on the prowl."

Sam cautioned Maddie to keep her distance as she spoke. "Your only hope is that you will seek God when you go to prison. It will be the best thing you can do. Prison Fellowship would be a good place for you to start. We can all pray that you'll attend their meetings and listen to their good advice."

Knowing Maddie had said enough to both chide and humiliate the man, Sam told her she had said enough.

Owen was reminded of his Aunt Martha as the woman spoke to him. Aunt Martha had been the only Christian in his family, and he was struck by Maddie's sincere recommendation for him. His aunt was the only one who had ever written to him when he was in prison and had died a year before his release, but she told him before she died that she was praying for him. She tried to be involved in his life while he was growing up, and on a few occasions she had attempted to offer him good direction, but he rejected her partly because his mother had interfered.

Owen was picked up with his shoes still nailed to the well cover. James and Sanders left soon after two uniformed officers arrived to pick up Owen and lead him to the paddy wagon. Securing him to the bench inside, they closed the rear doors and drove down the road.

Sam thanked Maddie for her ingenuity and told Ellie she was courageous to outsmart such a dangerous man. He smiled as he shook their hands. For a short time they spoke about the unusual way the capture had taken place before Sam left for the police station.

Ellie and Madeline walked back to the house at 4:30 a.m., just minutes before a pale light began appearing over a lofty mountain in the distance. It would be a bright new day.

CPSIA information can be obtained
at www.ICGtesting.com
Printed in the USA
BVHW030222230821
615006BV00005B/103